RANGER

The Bugging Out Series: Book Five

NOAH MANN

ISBN-10: 1532950233
ISBN-13: 978-1532950230

I know not what course
Others may take,
But as for me,
Give me liberty, or give me death!

Patrick Henry

Part One

Returns

One

I woke in the middle of a road with drops of cold rain pecking softly at my cheeks.

I'm outside...

That was the first thought that stuttered up from within as my eyes opened. Cracked asphalt stretched out before me. Barren trees to either side of the road. A whisper of wind in the grey daylight.

What happened?

What did happen? How was it that I was outside, lying on a two lane road? I wasn't dreaming. Not now. This felt too real. The chill on my skin. A stinging ache on the backside of my right arm.

An accident...

Yes. That. I was in an accident. But what kind of an accident? I rolled slowly until I could gaze down the road in the opposite direction, the weathered strip of narrow blacktop disappearing beyond ranks of dead woods as it curved through the once lush forest in the distance. If it was an accident that had left me here, stunned and hurting, then where was the vehicle? There was no wreckage to be seen. Not on the road or in the adjacent knots of pine and fir.

"Ahhhh..."

I exhaled and moaned at the same time as I slowly pushed myself up until I was sitting on the hard, pitted surface. That unseen pain on the backside of my arm was matched, if not exceeded, by a shallow soreness that spread across my chest as I moved, muscles there seeming to resist even the minor exertion I was attempting. Damp air filled my lungs as I breathed deeply. The air tasted...stale. Then I realized it was not the air lacking in freshness and flavor—it was my mouth. My tongue. All those parts that sampled taste. I struggled to produce a bit of saliva then spit it out toward the muddy shoulder of the road.

The staleness decreased. I spit some more between breaths until that flat sensation in my mouth was gone. But what had caused it?

What had caused everything?

I struggled to my knees, and then to my feet, steadying myself as I stood at the center of the road. The urge to call out surged, but I forced it down. Who was I going to call out to? And for what? Help? I didn't seem to be hurt, just sore in places that made no sense. No, before I sought assistance I needed to take stock of myself and try to get my mind clear.

"I'm Eric Fletcher," I said.

I knew that. At the very least I was certain of who I was. But there was more to me than just my name. More to my existence. To my place in the world.

What was the last thing I remembered? I focused on that. Some morsel of memory was certain to pop up. That's what I told myself. What I waited for.

But none did.

I did remember some things, however. The blight. That I recalled, and could see its effects in the grey woods bordering the road. I hadn't dreamed that. The slow motion apocalypse which had decimated the planet had been real.

As had other things.

I lifted my left hand and saw the ring on its third finger. A wedding band. Simple and perfect all at once.

"Elaine..."

I spoke her name just to hear it in the space outside my thoughts. We'd been married. Hardly a month after Martin and Angela had wed. The ring on my finger that symbolized our union had been crafted by Hanna Morse in Bandon. Elaine had commissioned the gifted woman to make it for our big day. For that wonderful day.

That wonderful day that I remembered.

But I didn't have any recollection of what had brought me to this place. This strange, unfamiliar place.

The sputtering rain turned to a steady fall of cold water from the sky. I was not dressed for the weather. My feet were bare, and what I did wear was hardly adequate to beat back any chill, much less a soaking one. Just sweats and a tee shirt. The same attire I would wear when going to...

...bed.

Tase him!

I actually shuddered as the memory burst up from somewhere unknown. A voice. A harsh voice. One that I'd heard.

In a bedroom. Not our bedroom, but *a* bedroom. That was where that phrase, that *command*, had been spoken. Had been given.

Tase him...

I looked down to my chest and lifted my damp shirt, high enough so that the pair of circular bruises were visible just below my sternum, small, scabbed puncture wounds plain at the center of each.

Tase him...

"A Taser," I said.

Eric!

Elaine had shouted my name. Then she'd shouted no more. I'd flailed against hands reaching out of the darkness. Trying to get to her. To protect her.

From what, or who, I had no idea.

I walked to the side of the road and planted my hand against the stout, dried trunk of a towering fir, my head hanging, eyes closed, trying furiously to dredge full recall from the fog of my thoughts.

It wasn't at the house we called home in Bandon. It was another house. One down the coast a few miles. A getaway we'd decided to take shortly after being married. The closest thing to a honeymoon that we could manage in the world as it was.

"What happened?"

I posed the question to myself, or to any power that might bring that knowing to me.

"We went to that cottage," I reminded myself aloud, slipping pieces of my fragmented memories into place, bit by bit. "We drove there. It was in one of the Humvees that came in on the *Rushmore*."

The Navy supply ship had made a second visit after bringing its initial load of promised supplies for Bandon, along with the garrison to secure the settlement. Four of the aging and ubiquitous military vehicles had been provided for the town's use, along with more capable trucks. The town's diesel plant was back up and operating after the return from Alaska, so fueling the transport was little issue. I'd simply requested permission from the mayor and Schiavo to use one of the Humvees for a couple days, and the okay had been given without hesitation.

"We drove there," I repeated, thinking back, not only seeing that short trip in my mind's eye, but feeling it. "We."

Elaine had been at my side. On the way there. And at the small cottage nestled close to the shore that had been previously scouted and found to be safe. We weren't the first from Bandon who'd journeyed there. A reservation book for the location actually existed at the town office building on the coast highway. Schiavo had set the garrison's headquarters in the same facility, taking over what had been the offices of the police department. We'd signed the reservation book for the dates we'd desired and that was that.

"But something happened," I said.

I shivered, both the penetrating chill and fear of the unknown I'd just expressed mixing to send a sharp spasm through me. Yes, something had happened. Something that was very clearly not good. Ending up in a strange place, alone, with no idea where Elaine, where my love, was, could be nothing but worrisome at the very least.

At the very worst...I didn't want to imagine.

The desperation to know, to understand what had transpired was fierce. But amidst that overpowering need a reality forced itself to the forefront of my thoughts.

I had to get home.

But where was home in relation to my present location?

I looked to the sky. Or, to be more precise, to the clouds that masked the bright blue day above. A flat, ashen brightness spread from a point roughly twenty degrees from dead above. Had the clouds been gone, or simply parted, the sun would be right there, hanging above the earth that was trying to heal. But was I looking at a rising sun heading toward noon, or settling toward the day's end?

I needed to know which it was. Were I to guess, and begin trudging along the road or through the dead woods without that knowledge, it might be hours of walking before I knew if I was heading in the right direction. A direction that would take me home. Or at least closer to that place than I was right now.

West. Unless I'd been picked up and spirited off across the Pacific Ocean to Japan or the Asian continent, Bandon would lie in that general direction from my current position.

I was wet, and I was cold. I needed to find shelter, and, if possible, make a fire, though how realistic the latter was I didn't know. And I couldn't know. Not until I moved from the spot to scour for resources along the path I would choose that would take me home.

But shelter, and the possibly impossible fire, would have to wait. I needed to stay put, in this spot, and watch the sky, tracking the vague center of brightness filtered through the clouds until I was certain of the way I must travel.

I stood close to a tree just off the road, accepting the scant shelter its bare limbs and dead trunk could provide. My eyes stayed fixed on the storm above, the highest point of a towering fir the marker against which I would judge the movement of the shrouded sun in the southern sky. If it tracked directly toward the tree, climbing higher into the sky, then west would be to my left. If it tracked away, to the right would be the direction I would travel. Away from me, or toward me, would give me similar indications as to the correct path to take.

All I had to do was wait and watch.

Time ticked by as I studied the movement. As I estimated the drift of that bright blot upon the clouds. Five minutes it might've been. Ten minutes. Probably closer to the latter, I thought. But by that time I had my answer.

West was to the right, almost arrow straight along the road. I would have to maintain that bearing beneath the clouded skies. Doing so, keeping the vague point of the sun's position just above my left cheek, would require focus. Focus that would be increasingly difficult to manage as the soaking cold chilled me with each step.

I began to walk down the center of the road with two purposes in mind. Get home, and, before that, get out of the weather and get warm so that I might live to see my friends, and my love, again.

Two

I counted steps. As much to keep my mind off the penetrating cold as to guesstimate the distance I had covered.

Two miles. Then three. By some good fortune the road did not stray from a true westerly direction by much. The few curves that it took through the woods corrected around the terrain, making unnecessary any overland travel on my part.

Two thousand two hundred steps. Another mile. Four.

That number again, which I had thought multiplied by my stride would roughly equate to distance of a mile, passed.

Five miles. The sun sank lower ahead and to my left. It was the middle of spring, or had been when Elaine and I had set out on our getaway. Assuming that no more than a day or two had passed, I could tell by the position of the setting sun that I had maybe three hours of daylight left. Night would follow.

And with that, cold.

As I pressed on I looked to either side of the road. Through the trees into the thinned-out woods. There was the occasional limb that had fallen from the dead canopy, but not enough in total to be useful in constructing some makeshift protection from the elements. And without some sort of tool, a knife or an axe, or even some piece of metal to be wielded as a cutting instrument, I had little chance of chopping and breaking what I would need to fashion a shelter.

Another mile I walked. And another nine hundred and eighty steps past that before I stopped, shivering, and stood at the center of the road looking off to my left. At what had caused me to pause.

A narrow but plain path was worn between the stands of fir and pine trees. Not wide enough for a vehicle, it was nonetheless a way that had been traveled before. By someone. Going somewhere.

Since before the blight, I thought. There was evidence of lower limbs having been chopped away, possibly for firewood. Or, it appeared, to make a clearer way through the once lush woods.

I was looking at a trail.

To take it, and head south by doing so, was one half of a choice to be made. To continue west with the daylight that remained was the other. The way through the forest might lead to shelter. An old cabin. Or an abandoned hunting camp.

Or it might be nothing more than a hiking path meandering through the grey wilderness for tens of miles.

I was cold. The constant rain had beaten a chill deep into my bones. Walking was growing more difficult by the minute. In another mile my bare feet and wobbly legs might be able to carry me no more.

My mind was not far behind. Every thought was a struggle. Moments of clarity were few and far between. A quarter mile up the road my senses might be dulled enough that I wouldn't see something similar to the path off to my left. I might miss my best chance at staying alive.

I took a few steps toward the path, pausing where it began at the shoulder of the road. It might lead to nothing. And it might lead to everything.

There's always hope...

My friend's words, spoken first to me even before the blight ravaged the land where I now stood, both buoyed and stung me. His simple encouragement had become a mantra of sorts, spurring me on when faced with difficulties. When faced with uncertainties like what lay before me.

But his abrupt departure, under the most inexplicable circumstances, hurt every single time I married that desire to persevere with his memory. I didn't want to forget him. No. That wouldn't erase the pain of what he'd done. What I wanted was to understand the why and the what of his leaving.

"You'd take the path," I said aloud, referencing what I knew my friend would do.

And what I would, as well.

I left the road and walked along the soggy trail, mud caking my feet and legs up to the ankles, soaking and staining the loose cuffs of my sweatpants. I didn't count steps here—I just walked. Moving forward. Up a gentle incline the path crossed, and then down into a hollow beyond, bare trees and small boulders filling the natural depression, the tangle of features thinning out as a clearing opened up, something at its southern boundary.

A building.

It was a cabin. Not a shack. A true stone chimney rose from the wall nearest me, and as I moved quickly toward it I saw a window, intact, set into the western wall of the small structure. Its walls were made of aged logs, stacked decades ago, I guessed, and the low roof, simply shingled with split wood, bore spots of wear where the elements and neglect had taken their toll.

My pace quickened, bringing me nearer to the old getaway. Someone had spent time here. Using it as a base for hunting and fishing excursions, I imagined. A place of solitude off the beaten path. It was a place where someone had enjoyed life before the blight.

And it was a place where that someone had died after the apocalypse had raged its way across the globe.

I stopped near the back corner of the cabin and stared at the body beneath a dead pine. The parts of the body, I corrected myself. Beneath a noose that had been suspended from a high limb the remains of a man lay, head in one spot, body from which it was severed in another a few feet away. For a moment I was confused by the sight. Then I was not, the images of what had happened tumbling into my head like a disjointed film playing at some advanced speed.

The man, the unfortunate soul, had retreated here, to his getaway, after the blight struck with full force, much as I had retreated to my property in the north of Montana. He'd hung on here, wherever here was, until doing so was no longer an option. Some fear of going on, of starving, of wasting away had cemented his decision, and he'd looped a hangman's noose over a limb close to both his cabin and the meadow. Maybe last spring, I thought. That was when he'd stepped onto the fat log positioned beneath the rope and stared out at the open space, imagining it as it had been when the world was green and fresh and alive.

Then he did the deed. Took control of his fate, on his terms.

And from that moment a year or so ago, nature took over. Nature and decay. At some point, as his body decomposed, tissue and muscle and bone was no longer stout enough to maintain the integrity of the human form. A separation occurred at the neck, body dropping one way, and head another, leaving what I was witness to.

He was gone. Dead. But I was alive. And I planned to stay that way. What the man, a good man, I told myself without any knowledge of the truthfulness of my estimation, had left behind would be my salvation. I believed that until I came around the front of the cabin and saw what had happened to the structure.

The entire front wall was gone, logs snapped and blown outward, as was half of the west wall, leaving the interior open to the elements. Above that devastation the roof on the front half of the cabin was shredded, rain pouring in, soaking the interior. I peered in and, with daylight fading, took stock of what remained.

Bits of metal were embedded in the remaining log walls, evidence of some explosion within. A propane heater, perhaps. Or one running on kerosene. The man might have left it running as he ventured out in search of supplies, or other people, returning to find that some malfunction had resulted in a gas-fueled blast. Maybe that had led to his decision to end his life.

Maybe...

All I was doing was giving time to maybes. To possibilities. I needed to deal with the certainty that at that moment I had to get out of the rain, and get dry, and, somehow, warm.

I stepped into the weakened shelter of the cabin, just that move stopping the drumbeat of cold rain upon me. I looked around the simple one room building, but found little of use. No clothes, nor bedding had survived the explosion which had torn through the place. Cut logs that had been stacked by the fireplace were scattered about along with the rest of the contents.

Something, though, had not been shredded or tossed from its place. Atop the thick and sturdy mantle jutting from the fireplace's stone structure was a small box. It rested there, tipped on its side, but even in that position I knew what it contained.

"Matches," I said.

I hurried to the fireplace and took the box in hand, my excitement ebbing almost immediately. What I felt in my hand bore almost no weight. I shook the box and heard just a small rattle of matchsticks. Opening it I saw three of the wooden sticks, their tips a bright red.

Three matches.

All around me the wood, which included no kindling, was damp. Soaked, even. The old, dead wood that the man had cut down on the verge of falling apart. It would burn, I knew, but not with what heat a single match would produce. Or two. Or three.

Then something I'd seen but hadn't noticed struck me.

The logs he'd gathered for burning were not chopped. They were cut. I went to one and examined the ends.

"Chainsaw," I said.

The thick branches and lengths of tree trunk hadn't been processed with a saw or an axe, but with the ripping blade of a chainsaw. A motorized tool that should still be here. Or near. And though I had almost no hope that such a tool would still work after being exposed to the elements for as long as it must have been, there might be something more than useful I could extract from it.

Gas.

I scanned the battered interior of the cabin quickly, then moved outside, circling the structure until I was near the man's body. The coat he'd worn, soaked and shredded now, was useless to me, but it had been tossed back on one side, exposing his belt and a sheath attached there, the bone black handle of a Buck knife protruding. I approached and crouched, gingerly retrieving the blade, its steel marked with signs of rust, but a slow draw of my thumb along its edge confirmed that it had held its sharpness.

Standing again, I looked into the woods across the clearing, an oddity immediately catching my eye. A shape that should not have existed in any area of natural growth.

A straight line.

Holding the knife, I jogged across the narrow meadow, rain soaking me once again. At the far side I stopped and looked upon a row of wood that had been processed for burning, stacked and laid end to end, with precision and care. The man who'd done this had been meticulous.

Except with his chainsaw. It sat in the open behind one of the low piles of wood, a quarter of it submerged in the soggy muck. Part of me mused as to why a man so ordered had let his tool remain exposed to the elements. Perhaps he'd been where I stood when the explosion rocked his cabin. That event might have been what pushed him to the decision he made. Lacking in food, his shelter suddenly compromised, he'd reached his limit.

Physically, I was not at mine, but I could see it on the horizon. Hypothermia would drag me down to a sleep I would never wake from. I had to get warm, and dry.

I had to make fire.

I went to the chainsaw and crouched next to it, twisting the gas cap counter clockwise, the dry, wispy vapor that hissed from the tank as I uncapped it telling me what I'd found before I even looked.

Nothing.

It was empty. There was no gas. I lifted the impressively light tool a few inches out of the mud and rocked it gently back and forth, confirming my suspicion. There was no gas. If there had been any when the man last set the chainsaw down to rest, it had evaporated.

On a last hope I checked the reservoir which held the lubricating chain oil, but it, too, held nothing.

Panic didn't set in. Not yet. But it became very clear that I needed a plan B. And fast.

Frustrated, I shook the chainsaw lightly, a brief admiration of the tool's lack of heft slipping through the grim seriousness wrapping me.

Light...

The thought didn't come from nowhere. It came mated to a memory. A recollection from my old life. My years as a business owner. A contractor. I'd witnessed dozens of accidents on jobsites in that time. Maybe hundreds. From the impossible to foresee to the bonehead moves of workers not paying attention to their environment. Cuts. Falls.

Broken bones. Toppled equipment. Snapped beams. I'd seen it all.

Including fire.

One in particular seized my thoughts as I held the surprisingly light chainsaw in one hand. A subcontractor's pickup had burst into flame. The reason why, I didn't recall. But I did very clearly remember the fat rear tires of the dualie popping, their rubber feeding the blaze, turning the bed of the truck into an inferno before the firefighters arrived.

And I remember sparks. Erupting from the bed like a shower of silvery fireworks going off. It was only after the red engines rolled up with lights spinning and sirens blaring did I learn from the battalion chief aboard that what I was seeing was magnesium igniting in the hellishly hot fire. Probably, he suspected, from a chainsaw, whose frames were often made from the material, or an alloy containing it. Used because of its lightness.

I looked to the tool in my hand and set it back down into the mud, kneeling in the soggy dirt as I used the knife I'd taken to pry away the synthetic body that concealed the guts of the device. When I'd finally exposed the dull metal frame I ran a finger across it. The lack of heft, of density, was almost discernible to the touch.

"It might work," I said to myself.

Might being the operative word here. If I could use the knife to shave off a good pile of the magnesium, hopefully pure enough, it would take a flame easily. And if one of the three matches would strike. And, of course, if I could process some of the wood remaining in the cabin into kindling that would dry and catch fire. All those variables needed to align so that I could, without any drama, live. So that I could find my way home.

I gripped the chainsaw in my free hand, knife in the other, ready to stand. That was when I glimpsed the man through a narrow space between the stacked logs.

Three

He stood across the clearing, just outside the cabin, peering past one of the remaining walls to the dim space within. He held a rifle low, but ready. It was no modern weapon, but a throwback. Lever action, walnut stock, topped with a scope. Were it not for the blighted world all around he would have looked like a deer hunter out to bring home a buck.

But that world no longer existed, and seeing the man, the stranger, in proximity to me did not give me the relief it might. I didn't jump up and call out to him in hopes that he would help me. That very natural instinct was suppressed by the reality of my situation, what I knew about it, and, more importantly, what I did not know.

So I stayed low, hidden by the stacked logs, watching the unexpected visitor. Appraising him. Beyond the weapon he carried, and a pistol he wore on his hip, a somewhat large backpack was cinched tight to his frame. His head was topped by a simple cowboy hat, its brim and crown softened by time and the elements. It was a Cattleman style, I knew, my life in Montana ingraining in me that bit of seemingly useless knowledge. Not a Gambler, a Gus, or a Tom Mix. A Cattleman. Rain ran down its brim and spilled near the dead man's severed head as the stranger turned his attention from the cabin and looked to the mangled body lying on the ground beneath the noose.

Who are you?

I wondered silently about the man. Could he have been one of those who'd taken me? And left me out in the elements to fend for myself? Possibly. But...

But why let me go and then track me? Because tracking was precisely what this man was doing. I knew this as he crouched near the body and studied the muddy earth near it, reaching with a free hand to trace indentations in the saturated soil. It was unlikely, I believed, that he would note any indication of my passage through the area. The weather was almost immediately erasing any hint of footprints in the soaked earth.

Still, that he was looking at all meant that he wasn't just wandering aimlessly. And I feared that one of my first estimations of the stranger, incongruous as it was in this new world, might be more correct than I'd allowed.

He very well could be hunting. And the only prey that remained walked on two feet. Like me.

I didn't move a muscle as the man stood and let his gaze play over the meadow that lay between us. He didn't seem to focus on any one spot, the woodpile holding his attention just for a few seconds before he looked to the grey woods that surrounded the clearing. Then, without word or fanfare, he turned and made his way past the cabin, heading back up the trail that had brought him, and me, to this place.

For several minutes I waited. Not moving. My own gaze playing over the woods beyond the meadow, scanning for any movement. If the man had suspected a presence near the cabin it would be logical for him to approach through the forested land surrounding it and take up a position to surveil the area unseen.

But I saw no movement. Heard no sloppy footsteps through the mud. When I was certain I was alone, I stayed put. Watching more. Listening more intently. Even as the soaking cold bit deeper into my body. Through skin and flesh down to bone.

Finally, I had to move. Had to make an attempt to get out of the weather. As quietly as I could, I rose, the chainsaw and knife in my hands, and walked across the meadow toward the cabin. With every step I expected to hear a voice order me to stop. Or, worse, a rifle safety clicking off. If I was to be shot, I'd never hear the bullet fired. I'd be dead before the crack of the shot reached me.

There was no voice that called out. And no shot. I reached the cabin and moved into the meager shelter it provided.

Drenched without rain washing over me, the chill hardened upon my body. I had to work quickly, but with my coordination dulled by the creeping effects of hypothermia, every action was doubly difficult. I placed the chainsaw on the dry stone edge of the hearth and began working the knife along a length of its magnesium frame, working back and forth with the dull blade, a pile of shiny shavings building beneath it. Slowly. My fingers began to ache and then tingle, feeling leaving them. I pressed on, ignoring the sensations and focusing on what I was thinking about. On who I was thinking about.

Elaine.

I had to get back to her. Back to Bandon to make sure she was all right. That she hadn't been spirited off from our getaway as I had.

I shaved the frame. More. Harder. The mound of magnesium grew. And grew. I imagined I would need as much as possible, thinking that what I was dealing with would not be as pure as the magnesium firestarters most outdoorsmen were familiar with. I would have to make up for insufficient quality with abundant quantity.

Finally, when my hands were nearing a point of uselessness, I stopped, satisfied with what I'd managed to shave from the old saw's frame. I gathered logs that had been tossed about the cabin and arranged them around the pile of magnesium in the hearth. They were thick, as beefy as my forearms and larger, and would not be easily lit just by a brief flaring of intense heat that I hoped to generate. No, I needed actual kindling.

Just above my head I found it.

Jutting from the structure of the stone fireplace was a length of thick, seasoned lumber that functioned as a mantle. The rustic beam predated the blight by decades and, most importantly, was dry as a bone.

I stood and worked the knife along its lower edge, the dulled blade carving long slivers of the rich wood with difficulty. My fumbling hands did nothing to ease the effort, but my determination to live would not allow me to stop. I'd been soaked and cold now for hours. The temperature had to be hovering in the mid-forties. After sundown it would creep into the upper thirties. The hunk of wood I was attempting to slice and dice might be the only thing that would allow me to make it through the night.

Piece by piece I cut slender lengths of kindling, gouging the once lovely mantle. Once again, when my hands and fingers and arms were left trembling and weak, I stopped, awkwardly gathering the strips of old wood and arranging it above the pile of magnesium shavings.

For a moment I cupped my hands in front of my mouth and exhaled, warming my fingers as best I could so that some dexterity would return to them. I would need that ability to hold and manipulate something small. If I could not manage that, then my time would run out.

I looked to the box of matches on the mantle, stretching my fingers as I continued to breathe upon them. They moved without excessive tremoring, and they did what I wanted them to do. It was time.

This had to work.

I took the box and slid it open, removing one match as I crouched near the makings of a fire I'd collected and made. Behind me, rain hammered the world outside, small streams penetrating the roof overhead, nearby but not close enough to threaten what I was about to attempt. Darkness spilled into the damaged cabin, night coming fast. The cold was building by the second, it seemed. My mind and body craved warmth.

"Come on," I said to myself and I dragged the match head along the abrasive strip on the side of the box.

A lovely yellow flame bloomed at the end of the match. For a moment I did nothing with it. I didn't put it to the magnesium shavings. Didn't move it an inch. I just stared at it.

Then, I eased it toward my kindling and the accelerant I'd scavenged from the chainsaw. The tiny flame licked close to the silvery shavings. Closer. Closer. The precious fire was almost in contact when a sudden gust of damp wind ripped through the open front of the cabin, snuffing the match out and scattering the pile of magnesium.

"Damn..."

My hands trembled, iced to the bone now, knuckle joints almost locked by the penetrating cold. I used my left hand to brush the magnesium back into a pile beneath the kindling and shifted my body to better protect the makings of my fire. Then, I struck another match.

I felt the wind rushing over my hunched back as I hovered over the tiny flame I held. The almost comically small bolt of hot yellow danced as the gust swirled past and into the hearth, but it held. It had to. Still one more remained, but I seriously doubted if I would retain any dexterity to manage a proper strike to ignite it.

This one had to take.

I guided it gently toward the low scoop of shavings, bringing the flame to the bits of magnesium. In contact with them. A few glowed. A few more sparked. Would there be enough purity in the likely mixture of metals in the alloy to allow a full and satisfying burst of heat and fire?

"Yes..."

I breathed the word as the pile began to blaze, a slow-motion inferno building. A blinding pulse of hot white erupted, spreading to the kindling. Bits of wood from the mantle blackened, then began to burn.

I had a fire. I had made a fire.

For the next ten minutes I nurtured it, feeding small lengths of kindling and scavenged wood into the growing fire until the larger logs I'd arranged began to smolder. Then burn.

I spent no time warming myself further right then. Instead I did what any outdoorsman would do—gathered more wood. More than I thought I would need. When I had a stack half as tall as me I let myself huddle close to the hearth, stripping my clothes off and hanging them from a jagged bit of wood on the mantle. They dried as the chill was slowly driven from my body.

Lightning struck outside. Thunder followed. Rain poured. I listened to the storm and curled up on the stone extension of the hearth, bathing in the wonderful warmth. Giving thanks that I was alive. And that I might stay alive.

Great flames leapt into the chimney. Smoke would be jetting from its outlet above. There was a chance I would give my presence away to the stranger I'd seen, but I thought it a small chance. The downpour would smother and prevent the spread of the scent beyond a few dozen meters. If he was closer than that, then he already knew exactly where I was.

"Who is he?"

I asked myself the question as I tried to stay awake long enough so that I could put my clothes on again when they had dried. Whoever he was, was it possible that he was unrelated to the situation I now faced? Could he not have been involved in my abduction?

"It doesn't make sense," I said to the fire.

And, I realized, at the moment, it didn't matter. And if it did, if *he* did, what mattered more was making it through the night and finding my way back to Elaine and my friends in the light of a new day.

I took my now dry clothes from where they'd hung and slipped into the meager protection they provided from the elements. Outside, the storm built. Rain sprayed at a severe angle into the cabin, drenching the floor just a foot from where I'd found refuge close to the hearth. I hugged my body and pressed against the warming stone surrounding the fire, feeding fresh logs into it as the night took hold.

"You'll make it," I told myself. "You'll make it back to her."

The words were both encouragement and promise. Sleep began to summon me. My eyes grew heavy. I was cold, but not in danger of succumbing to the elements anymore.

You're going to wake up in the morning...

That further assurance came without spoken word. Existing in my thoughts. Precisely where other musings raged.

What happened? Is Elaine all right? Who did this? Who was the stranger?

I fell deep asleep with my mind screaming dark thoughts and fears.

Four

Sometime just after dawn my eyes opened, snatched from a dream abruptly. So quickly that what had lived as I slept seemed to exist in my waking world for a moment.

Ranger... Ranger... Ranger...

I had been dreaming about Neil.

Ranger... Ranger... Ranger...

The words repeated in my head as I lay there, shivering, the fire reduced to small licks on the glowing remains of the logs. I pulled myself into a ball and slid as close to the shrinking fire as I could without being burned.

Black is white. White is black.

More words from my friend. He'd said that to my face in the moments before he'd been spirited away in a stealthy chopper with Grace and Krista at his side.

You can't trust anyone.

That, too, he'd emphasized. The entire exchange between us, our last in person, maybe forever, had been a very clear warning from my friend to me.

But a warning about what?

He'd urged me to get out. To find a hole somewhere and hide.

"Bandon," I said, the word drowsy and dry.

My body trembled as I thought on that. On the place I'd come to believe was home after some initial, fleeting doubts. Thinking that it was somehow the focus of Neil's warning and worry, and that my friend, my lifelong friend, was somehow privy to knowledge of a danger facing it, both troubled and vexed me.

More questions. That's what I was left with. After what he had done. And after what had happened to me in the past forty-eight hours. Questions whose answers would have to wait as something else drew my attention.

A noise. Tickling my ears through the softly falling rain. A sound from beyond the cabin walls, faint, rumbling in the distance, low and rhythmic.

It was real. Not some phantom sound spiking up from my nearly hypothermic brain. It was there. It was faint. And it was familiar.

"A diesel," I said.

I pushed myself up. Next to me the fire was crackling down, the last of the dry wood fueling it almost consumed. But out there, through the weather, beyond the grey woods...

"A truck," I said.

A burst of energy powered me as I came to me feet and stumbled through the space where the blasted wall had once stood. The throaty growl grew louder, out on the road somewhere to my front. I pushed myself and began to walk down the dirt path that had brought me to the ramshackle cabin. Then I began to run. And stumble. Three times I fell into the mud before I came within sight of the road. And within sight of the most wondrous thing I could imagine.

Vehicles. A large military truck following a smaller Humvee, both of which I recognized. Each left by the *Rushmore*. Each from the place I now knew as home.

"Hey!"

I shouted as I scrambled up the path, my voice weak and raspy, drawing no notice. The vehicles lumbered on. In each I could make out silhouettes. People. Drivers and passengers. There was no definition to them. No features that gave me any clue as to who they were. And for an instant I wondered if, along with what had happened to me, the town itself had suffered some attack. And with that musing rose the fear that the people in the vehicles might not be those I wanted desperately to see.

Then, I heard my name.

"Fletch!"

It was the nick Neil had given me so long ago, when we were just goofy kids. Now it was being called out by one of those I'd come to know, and respect, from our adopted hometown.

"Martin!"

I screamed his name as I lost my footing on the rutted shoulder of the road, the pair of vehicles a hundred feet past my position now. They weren't stopping. My hands grabbed at the edge of the asphalt and pushed off, lifting my body so that I stood now, unsteadily, waving my arms as I shouted again through the rain falling lightly.

"Help!"

Brake lights bloomed suddenly red, both vehicles slowing. Then stopping.

"Hey!"

I began to stagger toward them as the passenger doors of both opened, Martin emerging from the Humvee and Sergeant Lorenzen from the truck, each geared up and armed as they jogged toward me.

"Fletch!"

Martin shouted my name and I stopped, relieved, the strength I'd managed to summon draining instantly away. I fell slowly to my knees on the harsh surface of the road.

"Are you okay?" Martin asked as he reached me and crouched to support me.

I nodded and looked past him, Private Quincy stepping from behind the wheel of the Humvee and Nick Withers, one of the town's three mechanics, leaving the same position in the truck to join those already surrounding me.

"Just cold," I said.

"Let's get him in the Humvee," Martin said.

He and Lorenzen took my arms and eased me off the ground.

"Send a signal, private," Lorenzen said.

Quincy jogged ahead to the truck and retrieved a stubby grenade launcher from the cab, loading it with a short, fat shell before bringing it to her shoulder and taking aim at a point in the sky roughly northwest of our position. She squeezed the trigger and the weapon bucked with a solid *POP*. A few seconds later, lost somewhere in the cloud cover, a rattling explosion rippled, sounding like a thousand loud firecrackers going off in quick succession. The military grade noisemaker, meant to be used to disorient and discourage unruly crowds, sent a series of sharp cracks echoing across the landscape in every direction. In this weather the signal might carry only a few miles, or twenty, depending on the terrain. But without having to be told, I knew what message it was meant to convey—they had found me.

But was I the only one out here to find?

"Elaine," I said as Martin and Lorenzen eased me into the back seat of the Humvee.

"She's fine," Martin assured me. "She's back in town."

"Cap wouldn't let her come on the patrols sent out to find you," Lorenzen said.

Warm air from the vehicle's heater washed over me, but still I shivered as I managed a chuckle.

"I imagine that went over well," I said.

"Two alpha females," Martin said, grabbing a blanket from the seat and wrapping. "We married into trouble."

A soft, distant thud rumbled across the landscape, followed by a timpani of small popping sounds.

"The other team responded!" Quincy shouted from near the truck.

"Let's get him back to town," Lorenzen said, eyeing me with more than a hint of concern. "He looks shaky."

Martin nodded and reached to close the back door, stopping when Nick approached and leaned halfway in to give me a quick hug.

"Damn glad we found you, Fletch."

I looked the longtime Bandon resident in the eye, all bout me telegraphing confusion before any words came out.

"What happened, Nick?"

"There'll be plenty of time for that later," Martin said, closing the door before climbing in the passenger seat. "We need to move."

Quincy got behind the wheel, Lorenzen and Withers hurrying back to the truck. In a minute we were moving, pulling ten point turns to get the vehicles heading back the way they'd come. I pulled the blanket tight and let my body collapse against the Spartan seat.

"Martin."

The man who'd led Bandon through the worst of the blight was already looking back from the front seat, watching over me.

"Yeah?"

"Seriously...what happened?"

He didn't answer right away. Thinking, instead, it seemed to me. Searching for some reply that might satisfy my wondering, and calm the vague fear that I could see on his face.

"I wish I knew," he said.

I asked no more as we headed west. Toward home.

Five

In the brief time I'd been gone, Bandon had changed.

What had been a relaxed town by the sea, just beginning to thrive, creeping toward a sense of normalcy, was now an armed camp much like the hardened community of survivors we'd arrived at after fleeing my Montana refuge. Checkpoints, abandoned after returning from Skagway with new life blooming in our absence, were once again manned. Residents who had fallen back into a sense of some new normalcy held rifles and scanned the roads and terrain with binoculars. Patrols moved about the woods to either side of the road we followed from the east.

"Where's Elaine?" I asked as we were waved through a checkpoint.

"I'm not sure," Martin said.

I looked through the thick side windows of the Humvee, past droplets of mist condensing on the blast resistant glass. Friends and neighbors gawked at our mini convoy, surprise and relief plain on their faces. My return had not been expected, it seemed.

"How long was I gone?"

Quincy steered us around a corner, taking us north along familiar streets.

"Three days," the private answered. "Elaine looked for you around the cottage and down the coast before she came back to town."

"There was no sign of you," Martin said.

"Three days," I said, almost gasping at that fact. "How can that be?"

"I don't know," Martin said. "Once the doc gets a look at you we may have a better idea."

I noticed the route we were taking now, driving quickly into town. Toward what had become the town's administrative buildings.

That wasn't where I wanted to go.

"Take me home," I said.

Martin looked back at me as the town blurred past the windshield in front of him.

"The doc will be waiting," he said. "The cap—"

"Home," I interrupted. "If Elaine knows I've been found, that's where she'll go."

The town's former leader offered no resistance. In a time past, when his son was still alive and he felt responsible for the lives of all those who'd aligned themselves with the fragile boy's genius, Martin Jay might have told me that we were going where it had been decided I should go. This was not that time. Not anymore.

"Take him home," Martin said without looking to Quincy.

"But—"

"She's your commander," Martin said, half smiling as his gaze angled toward the private. "But she's my wife. I'll take the heat for any detour from plans."

Quincy drew a breath and made her decision quickly, slowing the Humvee and pulling a wide turn at the next intersection. The truck followed the maneuver, and trailed us as the private steered us into the neighborhood and to the simple yellow house.

I was home.

Six

Martin brought me a cup of coffee. I took the mug from him with one hand and cinched the blanket tight around my shoulders. The worst of the chill that had nearly killed me was gone, beaten down by the fire I'd built, the remainder fading now in the warmth of drink, dry clothes, and the concern of friends.

"Drink," he said.

Behind him, at the front window, Lorenzen stood, looking out to the damp street. Quincy and Nick Withers had left with the vehicles, leaving the street out front vacant but for a few concerned friends and neighbors who Martin had shooed away, sharing that I needed a little time to decompress.

I knew there was more to the near privacy he was seeking than that.

"Cap is gonna be pissed," the sergeant said.

"Yes, she is," Martin said as he set a pile of kindling to blaze in the fireplace, small logs catching. "Sergeant, can you give me and Fletch a minute?"

Lorenzen looked away from the window, his gaze shifting between us. It might not have puzzled him that two men, two friends, might want a moment of privacy to discuss something, particularly after one's enforced absence. But it did. And he hesitated, puzzled and wary, it seemed.

"Just a minute," Martin prodded and promised all at once.

Lorenzen moved from the window and stepped out onto the front porch, saying nothing as he pulled the door behind to ensure our privacy. When he was gone, Martin came to where I sat and stood close.

"How'd they know you were at the cottage?"

His question was clear, even if the answer was not.

"How did anyone who wanted to grab you know you'd be there?"

"Wait," I said, seizing on one implication in his questioning. "You think I was targeted?"

"From what Elaine remembered after they knocked her out, the bunch that took you was professional. And uniformed. Black from head to toe, tactical gear. And they had what they needed to subdue the both of you. But they left her behind."

"Me..."

I spoke the word not with any disbelief based on the facts at hand, but simply because I couldn't fathom what purpose snatching and then releasing me, or anyone, would serve.

"They took you, kept you, and dropped you twenty something miles from Bandon," Martin said, recounting the bare particulars. "And from that I return to what worries me—how did they know you, the person they wanted, was going to be where you were?"

Martin glanced to the door, and the window, Lorenzen's shadow hovering beyond, out of earshot.

"That team had to know where you'd be, and when you'd be there," Martin told me.

"You think..."

I didn't have to finish what I was about to suggest. Martin nodded, fully aware where my mind was going with this. Maybe it was influenced by what we'd faced on our journey to Alaska to find Martin and the others. Infiltrators. Moles. Spies. People who were not who they said they were. Who feigned friendship and loyalty to aid an enemy.

"You think we have someone who's passing information outside the town?"

"I don't know how they would do that, but it makes sense," Martin said.

Now I glanced to Lorenzen's dark silhouette on the porch outside.

"You haven't told Angela your suspicion," I said.

"She may have the same thoughts," Martin said. "But I don't want to add to them if she has."

Now I wasn't certain where he was going with this. Where his thoughts, his worries, were leading.

"You don't think she needs to know?"

Martin shook his head.

"We have an adversary out there," he said, pointing east, though threats could come from any direction, we both knew. "If we start looking inward, we lose focus on what may be a real danger."

The man was no longer the leader of Bandon, but he had been. His concern for the town he'd guided through the blight, and so many things that spun from that, still resonated, whether he wanted it to or not.

"Angela is a soldier," Martin said, with cold admiration apparent in his voice. "She, all of her people, they'll aim themselves at anything, at anyone, who might harm us."

"You're afraid of a witch hunt," I said.

Martin shook his head.

"I'm afraid of a disaster."

I thought on what Martin had suggested, and on his reasoning for keeping his suspicions quiet. All that he was thinking was sound. I could see myself making the same assumptions, and coming to similar conclusions.

But, still, I was uneasy.

"One of us?"

My words were born of pure disbelief, not doubt.

"I think there's a more telling question," Martin said.

He was right. Both of us knew precisely what that was.

"Why me?" I asked, giving that curiosity voice.

Before either of us could muse on any possible answer, the roar of an engine sounded and tires squealed on wet pavement. A flash of headlights swept across the front windows then went dark. Vehicle doors opened and closed. Footsteps raced urgently up the walkway and onto the porch.

Then the front door swung fast inward and she was there.

"Eric," Elaine said, my name half breath as she spoke it.

I rose from the chair and let the blanket slip from my shoulders. She came toward me, and I toward her. No frantic rush to drive us together. Just a gentle union, arms wrapping each other. Embracing. Tears welled in my eyes as she sobbed softly against my shoulder.

"I'm okay," I said.

"I was terrified you wouldn't..."

"I'm back," I said, trying to ease, if not erase, the worry that had pained her. "I came back."

She eased back and looked up at me. I leaned in and kissed her softly. Briefly.

"They wouldn't let me come look for you."

"I'm sure you were fine with that," I said, eliciting a quick, thin smile beneath glistening eyes.

"Good to have you back."

I looked up and past Elaine to who had offered the greeting. Schiavo stood in the doorway, Private Quincy just behind her on the porch, the Humvee that had carried them all nosed toward the curb in front of the house.

"Captain," I said.

She glanced toward her husband, then behind to her sergeant still waiting on the porch.

"Thank you for looking for me," I said.

Schiavo nodded, a sternness about her. She'd always been a capable leader, from the first moment Elaine, Neil, and I had encountered her on Mary Island. The traits that allowed that had only blossomed since her promotion from lieutenant to captain, and since her arrival in Bandon to lead its garrison.

But amongst those very laudable characteristics, a sternness had subtly emerged. It exhibited itself not with directives or diatribes, but as I was seeing it now—silence. A quiet that might have been simply a momentary burst of contemplation, but, I sensed, was not. The seriousness with which she took her position, her responsibility, was hardening her. Perhaps that was why Martin was reluctant to share his concerns with the woman he'd married.

She'd changed. We all had. But, in her case, I feared not all of that which was different was for the better.

"We need to get you checked by the doc," Schiavo said, looking to me.

I didn't want to leave my home. Not so soon after returning to it, and to Elaine. But the choice wasn't really mine.

"She's right," Elaine said, taking the blanket from the floor where it had fallen and draping it snugly around my shoulders again.

"You need to be looked at," Martin agreed.

Schiavo flashed him a look, then focused on me again. "Let's go," she said.

Elaine kept an arm around me as we walked to the Humvee. Those neighbors and friends who'd stood out front after my return smiled joyfully and spoke soft welcomes to me as I slipped into the Humvee, Elaine next me, Schiavo riding shotgun as Quincy drove us away from the place I called home.

Martin did not come with us.

Seven

He didn't look like a Navy man. Much less a full commander.

"Your core temp will rebound fairly quickly," Clay Genesee said, tipping my head back and lifting each eyelid as he examined the whiteness of my sclera. "Plenty of warm liquids. But take care not to overheat. Don't overdo it on the blankets tonight."

The last direction he said to Elaine, who stood to the side in the exam room in the town's clinic with Schiavo next to her.

"You mentioned a bad taste in your mouth?"

I nodded at the doctor's question as he eased his hands back from my face.

"Yesterday," I confirmed. "When I woke up on that road."

"Almost certainly from some anesthesia that was used on you," Genesee said. "It's a common aftereffect."

Elaine crossed her arms and shifted nervously.

"So after they knocked him out at the cottage, they gassed him?"

"Yes," Genesee told Elaine.

She looked to me, worried.

"I'm fine," I assured her.

Schiavo, though, eyed me with some doubt as to that certainty.

"Why grab him and put him under, commander?"

Genesee looked to the woman who he outranked when their military classifications were placed side by side. Here, though, Captain Angela Schiavo was in charge.

"I'm not on the spook side of things, captain. Never have been. And this sure seems like some black bag guys dreamed it up."

There was no outright derision toward Schiavo or her question. Just a vague dismissiveness. But it made clear to me that the rocky relationship between the captain and her superior subordinate had not improved in the few days I'd been away. From the moment Commander Clay Genesee had stepped off the transport which had brought him ashore from the *Rushmore*, an undercurrent of tension had existed between him and Schiavo. At first I'd wondered if some ember of misogyny smoldered within the man. At first. But as time wore on it became clear to me, and to anyone who took the time to notice, that what afflicted him was not distaste for his leader, but distaste for the institution. The military. He'd been ordered to Bandon, just as other medical personnel had been sent to the known survivor colonies. Yuma. San Diego. Edmonton.

His internal clash with the assignment he'd been given spilled out ways subtle, such as his quiet clashes with Schiavo, and in a manner impossible to miss—his refusal to wear anything resembling a uniform.

Commander Clay Genesee, originally from Allen, Texas, was a prisoner without shackles. That was how I sensed that the man saw himself. And me, and the other residents of Bandon, to him we were work product. Assignments he had to complete on a daily, sometimes nightly, basis.

He was no Doc Allen, to put it mildly.

That comparative thought was eerily prescient, I realized, as the door to the exam room opened after a quick, soft knock. It was a gentle tapping that I knew. That I recognized.'

That I missed.

"I heard you found your way back to us," Everett Allen said as he stepped in, flashing a quick smile Genesee's way. "Doctor."

Mayor Allen, formerly Doc Allen, had seen the residents of Bandon through the worst of times. He'd tended gunshot wounds and broken limbs and heart attacks. He'd treated Micah Jay, Martin's boy, through the unlikely heart procedure that had kept the boy alive—for a while. Now, at an age when most in the old world would have retired to days of fishing and reading and napping, the man had been asked to take over for Martin as leader of the tight knit community of survivors.

But, despite the change in role, he could not entirely let go of the vocation which had occupied the majority of his life.

"He checks out okay?" Allen asked the man who'd replaced him.

"Slight hypothermia and some post anesthesia effects, but he'll be fine."

Allen nodded at the report. A slow, thinking gesture that ended when his attention shifted to me.

"So you're feeling all right?"

He was *Doc* Allen again. Stepping into his old shoes in an unfamiliar place. His office had been in his home, not at the downtown clinic which had opened next to the garrison's headquarters. But the manner, the concern, was the same.

"I actually feel pretty good," I told him.

A foot to my left, I felt Doctor Genesee turn half away and slip his hands into the wash basin, water flowing as he scrubbed down after the examination.

"Good," Doc Allen said, his warm gaze narrowing down at me. "You're sure?"

"He's fit, Mayor Allen," Genesee said, some edge to his tone, and certainly in his obvious use of the man's current title. "I checked him from top to bottom."

Doc Allen considered this.

"You had him strip down?"

Genesee finished at the sink and turned back to face the man he'd replaced.

"There are ladies in the room," Genesee said, gesturing to Elaine and Schiavo. "And he presented no issues. No complaints other than a taste in his mouth yesterday."

"From anesthesia," Doc Allen said.

"Yes," Genesee said, his irritation simmering now. "He's fine."

Doc Allen looked to me again. Weighing something. The situation in total, maybe.

"I guess the question is, why did they anesthetize him?"

Genesee wiped the last of his hands' dampness on his jeans and came around the table I sat upon so that he was talking with Doc Allen over me, as if I was the disputed land in the battle of their clinical abilities.

"As I told our esteemed captain, you're going to have to ask the operators who grabbed him to find that out."

"Maybe," Doc Allen said, allowing the possibility. "Maybe."

The old man looked to me again, serious and comforting all at once.

"So the only effect from your forced excursion was some cold and a medicinal taste in your mouth? Nothing else?"

I shrugged.

"Some soreness," I said. "That's just from being in the elements and..."

I stopped there. Remembering. Recalling that at least one bit of discomfort I'd experienced hadn't come from the hours I'd spent walking barefoot and barely clothed in the rain and cold.

"What is it?" Doc Allen probed.

"Eric..."

Elaine's quiet burst of concern brought me out of the recollection.

"My arm," I said, reaching with my left hand to the back of my right arm, behind the bicep. "This was really sore. A bit of a sting to it. But I almost can't notice it now."

Doc Allen looked to Genesee. The navy commander in civvies absorbed the revelation and stepped close again.

"Let's get your shirt off," Genesee said.

A moment later it was, both he and Doc Allen standing behind, staring, but not silent.

"Angela, come look," Doc Allen said.

"What is it?" I asked.

Schiavo joined the men examining me. Elaine, though, didn't move, a worry building in her gaze. Fear as well.

"What did you find?" she asked.

Schiavo studied what the medical men had pointed out to her.

"Someone did a little work on you, Fletch," Schiavo said.

"Work? What do you mean *work*?!"

Doc Allen put a calming hand on my left shoulder and looked to Elaine.

"We'll deal with this," he said, the words as much a promise as they were informational. "He'll be fine."

"I thought I *was* fine," I said.

Elaine stepped close and took my hands in hers.

"Doc..." she implored the older man gently.

It was Genesee who answered, though.

"You have a puncture," he said.

"Very small," Doc Allen added. "But it's there."

"And there's a slight bump beneath the skin," Genesee continued.

"A bump? What kind of bump?"

Again, Doc Allen held back, letting the man who was charged with my care give the diagnosis.

"It looks like something was inserted," Genesee answered. "It's beneath the skin."

I didn't panic. There was no need to do so, and no point in such a reaction even if I'd been inclined to let fear overwhelm reason. Elaine squeezed my hand and looked into my eyes.

"It's all right," she said. "They know what to do."

Schiavo took half a step back from where she'd stood to see what the doctors had discovered.

"What are you going to do?" she asked.

Genesee glanced to his predecessor, then fixed on his leader.

"We've got to get in there and see what it is," he told her.

"Surgery?" Elaine asked.

"Minor," Genesee said, a surprising calmness to his manner now. "We could even do it with a local. Or light sedation."

Doc Allen thought for a moment, unsure.

"I'd think sedation," the older man said, agreeing. "No discomfort at all, Fletch. You'll sleep right through it."

"Wonderful," I commented, the sarcasm biting in my tone. "I get grabbed and knocked out, then I come home and you're going to do the same."

"It won't be a long procedure," Genesee said, shifting his attention briefly to the man whose learned probing had led to the discovery. "Doc Allen and I will take good care of you."

There was no decision to be made. It was obvious I was going to let the men do what needed to be done. Something had happened to me during the time I'd been gone. Something unknown that had to be made known.

"Let's get it over with," I said, looking to Elaine.

She nodded, agreeing, but not happy that this was a road we had to travel.

"All right," Doc Allen said. "Let's get you prepped."

* * *

Twenty minutes later I was lying on a gurney in the clinic's modest surgical suite. Elaine stood with me, mask and gown hiding most all of her. But not her eyes.

"They said I can stay if you want," she said, holding my left hand gently, an IV line already inserted into the back of it.

"You want to see this?"

"I won't be looking," she said, the mask stretching over the building smile I could not see. "But I want to be close."

Those eyes. How harsh they'd seemed, how determined, when we'd first met under very different circumstances. Now, as determined as they still were, there was a sweetness and a vulnerable beauty in them.

"Thank you," I said.

"We're going to get started now," Genesee said as he stepped close, Doc Allen approaching as well.

The men who would cut into me wore surgical scrubs and masks and clear face shields. And confidence. Whatever friction existed between them, it had been set aside. They were men of medicine. That was all that mattered at the moment.

"Ready for a nap?" Doc Allen asked me.

I nodded and squeezed Elaine's hand as Genesee brought the syringe up and inserted its needle into a port in my IV line. He depressed the plunger and I fell into blackness.

Eight

I remembered no dream. No green world as it was, or how we were making it that way once again. But when my eyes began to open I was certain that I was dreaming. That I had to be.

Where am I?

Again, in as many days, I was waking in a place I knew I should not be. But this place was not like the other. It was not outside. Not in the cold. There was no rain. There were walls and a door and furniture and there was something else.

Familiarity.

I shifted where I lay in the small bed. Not my bed in my home. But a bed I knew. A bed I'd last seen with a dead child resting peacefully upon it.

I was in Micah's room.

"Don't freak out."

The voice, too, was familiar. As was the breathy rasp that distorted it. I looked toward the sound and I saw Martin, looking and sounding as he had when I'd first laid eyes upon him. He wore a full bio hazard suit and respirator, eyes staring out at me through thick plastic lenses from where he stood at the door to his late son's bedroom. When we'd reached Bandon after a treacherous flight in search of Eagle One, Martin had greeted us in the town's meeting hall covered just as I saw him now. That had been a precaution, we'd learned, to protect his son's compromised immune system from any germs or contaminants he might unwittingly transmit to the child from outsiders.

But here, now, he was wearing all the same gear. And, more worrisome, as I glanced past him to the room beyond, I could make out the clear plastic divider in place once again. Used to bisect Micah's radio and computer room from a visitor's gallery, Martin had pulled it down in the moments after his son passed away.

"What's going on?" I asked, my voice wet and thick. "What's happening?"

Martin stepped close and reached a hand down.

"I'll help you sit," he said.

I took his hand and began to shift my position on the bed. My right arm ached sharply. I looked to it and saw a clean gauze bandage circling the bicep.

"All the way up," Martin guided me, his grip firm and comforting. "Just let your senses catch up, then we'll all talk."

All?

He wasn't referring to just the two of us. I leaned a bit, looking past him again to the space beyond the open door. Through the mild distortion of the plastic room divider I could make out a pair of feet, their owner blocked from view by the edge of the door frame.

"Who's out there? What happened? Where's Elaine?"

My questions weren't frantic, despite the rapid fire manner in which they came. But I was concerned. What I was seeing before me, what surrounded me, was not normal. Was not right.

Something was wrong. With me.

"Elaine's in the next room," Martin told me. "Doc Allen and Commander Genesee are, too. And Angela."

The medical, political, and military brain trust of the town was waiting for me just a few yards away. Along with the woman I loved.

"Martin," I said, pushing off the small mattress and willing myself to stand, "how bad is it?"

Beyond the fat round lenses of his mask I saw the muscles beneath his cheeks bulge, hinting at a smile I could not see. An expression of reassurance. But in his eyes I saw nothing that matched that calming gesture.

I saw uncertainty.

"Let's go see everyone," he said, gripping my left elbow lightly for support as he helped me into the next room.

* * *

They sat there, the four of them, in folding chairs, staring through the plastic divider.

"It's good to see you up," Schiavo said.

I gave a half nod as Martin helped me to a chair, Micah's old chair, already placed to face those who'd been waiting to see me. As I settled into it I looked through the divider and focused on Elaine. She wore a manufactured smile which did little to mask the worry which was plain just beneath the expression's thin veneer.

"Will someone please tell me what's going on?"

I asked calmly, but with my desire for a quick and certain answer more than clear. Martin let his hand rest on my shoulder for a moment, then stepped a few feet to the side to look at me as Commander Genesee began to speak.

"We found a capsule beneath your skin."

A capsule?

I glanced toward my right bicep and reached with my left hand to gingerly touch the bandaged spot at the back of my arm.

"It was very small," the Navy doctor went on. "Extremely small."

"Precision machined metal," Doc Allen added.

I stared at them, massaging the tender spot where they'd found the foreign body which had been placed in mine.

"There were micro fine holes in its surface to dispense its contents," Genesee said.

"Dispense?"

I posed the question by reflex, mildly shaken by what the medical men had just revealed.

"That's why you're in here," Martin said.

I looked to him, then out to Elaine. The smile was fully gone from her face now. A harsh wash of angry fear had replaced it.

"Just until we know if you're contagious," Genesee explained.

That word chilled me, even as it explained all that I saw around me. The isolation I'd been placed in. The precautions Martin was taking, now meant to protect *him* from what existed on this side of the barrier.

"You think they grabbed me to, what? Act as some unwitting Trojan horse?"

"We don't know," Schiavo said.

Elaine hadn't stopped looking at me. Her gaze was fixed with mine whenever it shifted her way. She wasn't even listening to what was being said, I thought, some clear sign that they'd all discussed the facts and fears of the discovery before I'd come out of the anesthesia.

"Just a minute," I said, forcing myself up, standing to face those who were bringing me news of my own potential and impending mortality. "You can't just hand me 'I don't know'."

"We don't know, Fletch," Doc Allen responded, stamping his approval on the reality Schiavo had stated. "So we have to take precautions based on the possibility that you might become infectious."

I didn't sit again. Not immediately. But hearing the term 'infectious' tossed out sent a ripple of queasiness through my knees.

"If I could infect others, that would mean I'm already infected."

No one said anything to counter what I'd suggested.

"Okay, all right," I said, the weakness causing my body to teeter suddenly.

"Hold on," Martin said through his respirator as he took hold of my arm and eased me back into the chair. "Just take a few breaths. Do you want some water?"

I shook off the offer and looked out at those eyeing me like a specimen under glass.

"What was in the capsule?"

"We don't know," Genesee said. "We really don't have the equipment to test it, and keeping it stable was too big a risk."

"We had to destroy it, Fletch," Schiavo said. "Incinerated it. Just in case there was anything left inside. Any pathogen or virus or...anything."

There was no arguing with the logic of what they'd chosen to do while I'd been under sedation. I would have made the same decision, had it been mine to make.

"But some of whatever was in it got into me," I said.

Doc Allen nodded without hesitation.

"Without a doubt," the doctor turned mayor affirmed.

I drew a breath, the air spilling sick and warm down my throat. My stomach churned as the reality of what I faced set in.

"Quarantine," I said.

"Just until we see what signs you show," Genesee said. "If any."

"If any? They didn't put that in me just for kicks. Something's going to happen."

Again I looked to Elaine, trying to dial my burst of panic down. It was one thing to face an external threat, one you could shoot at or run away from. But this...

"It's going to be okay," my wife, my love said. "Everyone's focused on making sure you're going to be fine."

"She's right," Schiavo said, gesturing to Doc Allen and Commander Genesee. "Every doctor we know is on your case."

It was an attempt at humor, and it elicited a smile from the older of the two men she'd made note of. But Elaine's expression didn't change. Not one iota. It hovered somewhere between terrified and stoic.

"Right," I said, acceptance, gratitude, and doubt expressed together in that single word.

Elaine, I should have suspected, would not miss the gallows sarcasm mixed amongst the other emotions.

"Hey," she said, and I looked to her. "You're going nowhere. Understand?"

I wanted to. I truly did. But a bleakness had risen within, and, as hard as I willed it, would not recede.

Nine

I asked for some time alone.

Martin shed his protective gear in the makeshift airlock to the left of Micah's old radio and computer room and departed with the others.

The others, except for Elaine.

"Please," I said, watching her fix an almost angry gaze upon me. "Just a few minutes. You can come back after that. I want you back after that. But I need...to think on my own for a little bit. Okay?"

She said nothing to my quiet plea. Just stared at me. Then, acquiescing to my wish, she turned and disappeared down the hallway.

I was alone.

I stepped close to the plastic divider and put a hand upon it. Micah had existed with this same barrier, had thrived behind it, and he was just a child.

A very special child, I reminded myself. Brilliant. Precocious bordering on arrogant. But arrogant with a reason. With a purpose. He had saved his town. Had saved me, and Grace, and Krista.

And Neil.

I turned toward the bank of electronics arrayed against the wall facing the barrier, walking to them after a moment's consideration. With a simple flip of a switch the entire collection of devices powered on. Computer screens hummed. Hard drive lights flickered. Radio display screens glowed.

It all still worked.

My attention focused on the radios. I'd watched Micah manipulate the controls on occasion, and recalled using Del's similar amateur equipment back at my refuge in Montana. I knew how to adjust frequencies, but that wasn't necessary, I knew. All I needed to do was turn the volume up.

"Ranger. Ranger. Ranger."

Neil spoke to me over the airwaves. His recorded voice was clipped and official. As if he was robotically performing some vital task. I'd wondered since first hearing his voice over the radio why it was him broadcasting at all. He'd left us, for reasons I still could not fathom, and some months later had turned up speaking to us, to everyone, in the way I now heard him.

Why?

The question nagged. Perhaps I was allowing this maddening curiosity to invade my thoughts if only to push out the wonderings, the fear I had about my own situation. Maybe. That was a true possibility.

But the need to find some rational explanation to at least this part of his very irrational act gnawed at me. Why was it him? Was he being used? And if so, for what purpose? Anyone could have read the simple repetition.

"Ranger. Ranger. Ranger."

"What are you doing, Neil?" I asked the radio.

The broadcast repeated again and again without any answer coming to me. Finally I turned the volume down, then flipped the switch which powered off every device at Micah's workstation. A thick silence filled the space around me as the last whirring fan stopped and the humming displays went dark.

I was alone.

"You're going to be okay," I told myself, turning to look through the clear barrier to the empty side of the space. "You are."

Without any conscious effort my eyes closed and I found my way to the chair a few steps away. My body settled into it. A steady throb built on the back of my arm where I'd been cut open to remove what had been put inside me. It pulsed to the beating of my own heart in a hypnotizing rhythm. I let the discomfort come. Let it settle me.

But with it came thoughts. Questions.

Why me? Why had I been taken? Not Elaine, not anyone else, but me?

"Enough!"

I half shouted the admonition to myself in the solitude of my quarantine chamber. There had been enough questions already. Too many. Musing on possibilities, torturing myself with unknowns, would do nothing to better my mental state at the moment. For a while, at least, I had to let go.

My eyes opened and I stared at the empty space beyond the barrier. Just stared and waited for this new nightmare to end.

Ten

Commander Genesee came to check on me a few hours after I silenced the radio. Martin returned not long after that, with Schiavo. She was dressed down, in civvies, holding her husband's hand. They sat with me and talked for a while through the antiseptic transparency that bisected the space, sharing that Doc Allen had returned to his duties as the town's leader and was, at that moment, coordinating with Sergeant Lorenzen a further increase in Bandon's defensive posture.

Elaine did not return with them.

Each told me that they hadn't seen her since she'd left to allow me my desired privacy. And as Martin and Angela departed, with night falling and darkness closing in on the room's lone window, permanently nailed shut, I was alone again.

But not for long.

"You're going to tell me this is stupid."

It was Elaine's voice. The sound of it was wonderful, and close, and unfiltered by the barrier and the electronic intercom in place to allow clear communication through it.

I turned away from the window and saw her, standing near the exit of the corridor which led to the airlock. She was on the same side of the plastic as I was. In the same space. Breathing the same air.

My air.

"Elaine..."

"It's already done," she said, a very faint but very, very real smile upon her face.

"You have to get out of here," I told her, backing away. She stepped toward me and shook her head.

"It's already done. I'm here."

There was nowhere I could run to put distance between her and myself. Between whatever had been put inside me and the woman I loved.

"I'm not leaving you," she said, her hand taking mine. "We're going through this together."

I shook my head. She put her free hand to my cheek and stopped the gesture. Then she rose slightly on her toes and kissed me, ending any chance that, if I were contagious, she could avoid becoming infected.

She settled back onto her feet and looked me in the eye.

"And we're going to come out of it fine," she promised me. "Together."

* * *

None of those responsible for quarantining me were even remotely pleased at what Elaine had done. But, aside from turning back the clock with magic and preventing her from joining me, there was no way to fix what had transpired.

So we waited. Together.

Commander Genesee had informed us that ninety-six hours would likely be the window in which some symptoms of what I'd been infected with would appear. Four days. That was how long we might have to wait.

Two days into our quarantine we heard the gunfire.

Elaine had been on the bedroom floor, expending nervous energy by doing fast pushups, and I'd been occupying myself with a bit of nostalgia, reading through Micah's voluminous old notes on everything from the food cache lockers he'd learned of, to estimates on how far his signal would travel when he would broadcast as Eagle One.

I might have continued exploring the writings of the late child genius had the rapid crack of distant weaponry not invaded the bored silence of our morning.

"Where is that?" Elaine asked urgently. "South? To the south?"

She'd leapt from her position on the floor and come fast into the space where I sat near Micah's workstations. For a moment I didn't move, taking in the bursts of gunfire, my head angling left and right like a weather vane, attempting to discern their point of origin.

"Yeah," I agreed with Elaine, rising. "South. Maybe just outside of town."

"There's a checkpoint there, now," she told me.

When Elaine and I had left on our brief getaway where I had been taken, there had been no armed outpost on the coast road. One that had been there during the wary months after our arrival in Bandon had been reactivated just before my return, along with others on the town's perimeter, with roving patrols to fill in the gaps between. All eyes searching for threats.

By the sounds coming from the south, a threat had been found.

"Where's our gear?"

Elaine knew what I was asking, and what I was suggesting, and that might have been why she didn't answer me quickly enough to stop my agitated follow up.

"If there is a fight out there," I began, "it could spill into town. Breaking quarantine will be the least of our—"

I stopped abruptly as her gaze shifted toward the hallway beyond the plastic barrier.

"You hear that?"

I listened for a moment, then nodded at her question.

"It's quiet," she said.

The shooting had stopped. But not all sound had. Quickened footsteps, just shy of all out running, came from the front room beyond the hall, and a moment later Bryson

Hunt rushed in, his chest heaving and color flushed. The young man, just shy of his twenty-fifth birthday, had been assigned during daytime to keep watch over the entrance to the place of our quarantine. In the old world he was a fisherman, plying the sea with his father. In the new world, our world, his father was dead and he was playing babysitter to us, ready to respond to us if we called out to him.

"What's going on out there?" Elaine asked.

Bryson took a few seconds to catch his breath, bending forward, hands on his knees, then he looked up to us with widened eyes.

"I don't know," the young man told us. "Sarge raced by in a Humvee and I ran after to find out what was happening, but I couldn't catch up."

"Go find out," I said. "We'll be okay here."

He turned to leave, but only made it a few steps.

"Bryson," Elaine called to him, drawing his attention. "On your way back, stop by our place and get our weapons and gear."

Her request kept him from moving.

"You can't—"

"I know," Elaine said. "Just in case."

"You can leave it in the front room out there," I said.

After a moment's consideration and a quick nod, Bryson Hunt was gone again, racing out into daylight.

I paced away from the barrier and rubbed at the still bandaged spot on the back of my right arm where I'd been cut open.

"I should be out there," I said, frustrated.

The silence behind me reminded me I was nearing a line I'd once crossed. I looked back to see Elaine's beautiful gaze turned harsh.

"I know, I know," I said. "*We* should be out there."

She let my unintentional slight pass without saying anything. I'd made a far more overt and awkward attempt to shield her from harm on our trek north to Skagway, and doing so had almost cost me my life. It was her, my wife, certainly of the fairer sex, who'd saved me when I was staring down the barrel of an assault rifle wielded by a merciless Russian. She'd buried her knife into his brain with cold, silent precision. That necessary and terrible act had taught me one thing with crystal clarity—Elaine Morales Fletcher could not only take care of herself, she could take care of me.

I went to her and pulled her into a gentle hug. Our arms wrapped each other as we listened to the sounds beyond our quarantine. Vehicles speeding on nearby roads. Distant, muffled shouts. For twenty minutes that was all we could do.

Then Martin came to see us. His expression was beyond grim.

"The Hunt kid gave me your things," Martin said, his face screwed tight, anger and regret working every muscle. "I left it in the front room."

"Martin, what happened?" Elaine asked.

His gaze dipped a bit and his head shook slowly.

"Mike Riley and Sarah Fredericks are dead."

Elaine's hand gripped my left arm tight, shock rippling through her. And through me.

"They were on patrol moving from the woods toward the south checkpoint on the coast road when..."

I had a terrible feeling what he was about to tell us. It turned out I was right.

"There was confusion at the checkpoint with the patrol schedules," Martin explained. "They thought that sector should be clear. When they saw movement, they thought enemy."

"No," Elaine said, and she turned to press her face against my shoulder.

"Friendly fire," I said.

Martin nodded, looking up now, a skim of tears over his eyes.

"We should never, ever lose anyone like this," he said. "Never. There's been too much death already. If we have to lose people it can't be for stupid things like this."

"It's an accident, Martin," I said.

"I know."

He did know that. And I knew that he accepted it. But, regardless of his position now, having stepped away from a leadership position in Bandon, he still felt responsible in some way. I was certain that in his head he was running over scenarios of things he might have done when he was in charge. Things which could have prepared those at the checkpoint, which could have prepared everyone, to better handle the uncertainties of such a situation.

That, though, was but a wish wrapped in a dream. He'd done a remarkable job keeping all of Bandon safe, and together. But he couldn't work magic, or turn back time.

"I have to go," Martin said. "The kid will be back in a few minutes if you need anything."

He turned, the darkness he'd dragged into the space seeming to envelope him.

"Martin," I said.

He stopped, but did not look back at me.

"This isn't on you."

Still he did not turn to face me, but the words he spoke were plain and painful.

"Everything's on me," he said.

Those were the words he left us with. For the moment I knew he believed them. In time, though, he would not. The realities and randomness and dangers of our world, and our current situation, would nudge him back toward some acceptance that his role in this tragedy was not even minimal—it was nonexistent.

"I thought we could just live again," Elaine said, easing back from my shoulder and looking up to me. "Just live."

I knew what she meant. What she wanted. It was all anyone in Bandon wanted. Just to be allowed to move forward, with the new hope we'd found, and fought for. That was it. A chance at some new, acceptable normal.

It seemed, though, that we weren't done fighting for the future we wanted to make.

Eleven

We were sprung from isolation two days after the terrible incident on the coast highway. Ninety-six hours of total quarantine for me, and a bit less for Elaine.

For nothing.

"It doesn't make a lot of sense," Genesee said from his position on the 'safe' side of the barrier. "I don't know what to make of it."

Neither did Schiavo, or Martin, or Doc Allen, all of whom had gathered to mark the end of the time period during which something had been expected to manifest. A sneeze. A sniffle. A rash. An ache. Fever.

But no symptoms arose. Not a one.

"I doubt we're looking at something with a longer incubation period," Genesee said.

"I agree," Doc Allen concurred.

"What about smallpox?" Schiavo asked. "Or something similar? A weaponized agent?"

"You don't need an implant to infect someone with anything like that," Genesee said. "A simple injection would suffice."

"One we might never have noticed," Doc Allen said. "Just a prick in the skin."

I looked to Elaine, puzzled. A mix of relief and confusion similar to mine formed her expression.

"We're okay," she said, though there might have been the slightest hint of a question in how she delivered the simple statement.

Martin stepped to the barrier and gripped the seal that held it in place, peeling it downward so the entire wall of plastic fell into a long, low heap on the floor.

"Welcome to Bandon," Martin said, smiling.

I hesitated, glancing to the mound of plastic which had sealed us off from the rest of the town for four days. Days in which we'd talked, and slept, and held each other. And worried. About what would, what *could,* happen to us.

This was not what either of us had imagined.

"So what was it?" I asked, holding position on my side of the barrier. "What did they put in me?"

No one offered any answer. Because no one could.

"Come on," Martin said, reaching out and taking me by the arm. "Time to get out of here."

I felt Elaine grip my hand and watched her step past the fallen barrier before us. With her urging, and Martin's, I made the crossing myself.

Our first journey outside was to the cemetery.

* * *

Mike Riley and Sarah Fredericks were laid to rest in a quick and simple ceremony, their bodies encased in crude metal burial boxes which had come in on the most recent supply delivery by the *Rushmore*. Dirt was shoveled in by hand, and the few dozen who'd come to pay their respects strolled slowly out of the greening cemetery.

Eddie Lang was among them. Among us. He'd pulled the trigger, loosing a few bursts from his AR. Fifteen rounds it turned out, three of which had found Mike and Sarah. She was killed instantly. He lived a few minutes after the distraught crew from the checkpoint reached them. Since that moment, Eddie had been inconsolably silent. He'd shut down. Even here it took friends and neighbors to guide him to and from the burial site.

He was a tractor salesman. Not a soldier. Yet, thanks to the blight, he was neither anymore.

"I'm going to request some help for him when the *Rushmore* arrives," Schiavo said as we reached the edge of the cemetery. "It might be possible to evacuate him to somewhere he can get real help."

"Genesee can't help him?" Elaine asked.

Schiavo shook her head.

"He's as much a psychiatrist as you," the captain said. "Or me."

"He can't leave," Martin said. "He can't. This is his home."

"He needs better treatment than we can give him," Schiavo told her husband.

"She might be right," I told Martin.

But he was having none of it.

"Every person we lose is a failure," he said. "No matter the reason. We don't have people to spare. Every life matters here."

For a moment we walked in silence, down the path from the cemetery and toward the road to town. There was grass everywhere. Trees had grown. Fruit hung from low limbs. In the near distance, without much effort, you could hear the calm mooing of cows, or the frantic crowing of penned chickens mixed amongst the crash of waves rolling in from the Pacific. If we could get past this new situation, whatever it was, we had a chance, a good chance, to reach a point where we could thrive again. Grow. Build the world back up from this one speck on the Oregon coast.

So I knew what Martin meant. Every single life did matter. This was a numbers game. The more we had, the more chance there was to grow. And not just in the question of procreation. There was work to be done. Every willing and able body would be needed to keep making progress.

A willing body, though, required a sound mind.

"Who's going to make the decision?" I asked.

It was directed to no one in particular, but Schiavo was the logical choice to answer among the three fellow residents who were with me.

"I'll talk to Commander Genesee, and if he thinks it would be prudent I'll have a message sent in the next burst transmission to see if it's even a possibility."

We were still reliant on quick transmissions bounced off a satellite at very precise moments of the day for both outgoing and incoming communications. As the White Signal had ended, and the Red Signal before it, there was always that chance that the Ranger Signal would cease someday soon and free up the airwaves for more robust and frequent contact with the outside world.

What that would mean for the man who had recorded the current transmission, my friend, and for us, I had no idea.

Twelve

Elaine and I settled back into the life that had been interrupted by my abduction and return. But that life, like the town, had changed.

A wariness had begun to build. In the first days after we'd been released from quarantine that uneasiness had been directed at us. Neighbors and friends who'd been warm and welcoming were hesitant to approach. Their fear, wholly understandable, soon faded when no sickness materialized, allowing all anxiousness to focus where it should be—on the unknown.

We were all in the dark. The perpetrators of my taking had to be out there. Somewhere. Men in black with some agenda none of us could yet fathom. That uncertainty had returned our recovering town to a posture of defense. All were involved. Everyone was affected.

The town's school, opened in the weeks after our return from the tribulations in Skagway, was closed again out of an abundance of caution. Children met in small groups with either of Bandon's teachers, in private homes so as not to have all together in the same place in case of an attack.

Fuel was being rationed, as the well which produced oil that was processed into diesel was beyond the town's border and difficult, if not impossible, to protect. It still ran 24/7, but the reality was it could cease its flow at any moment, either through mechanical failure or outright sabotage.

One positive, though, had been spawned by recent events. A bit of the old world's technology, silenced since soon after the blight struck, had been brought back into operation. The ringing phone in the living room reminded me of that.

"I'll get it," I said, rising from where I'd planted myself on the couch and crossing the small room to where the phone sat on a side table. "Hello?"

There was no interconnected exchange linked to an outside source which the Ranger Signal could interfere with, as the Red Signal had while the world was crumbling. A pair of former telecom engineers had scrounged enough material from Bandon and nearby abandoned communities over several months, working feverishly in recent days to complete a rudimentary direct wire system with simple phone numbers. Elaine and I were the impossible to forget ninety-nine.

"Fletch, what are you doing?"

It was Enderson, third in terms of rank in the six-person garrison assigned to Bandon.

"Elaine and I have a shift on the north perimeter in a while," I told him. "She's changing."

"I'm changed," she said from the hallway, overhearing my half of the conversation.

"What's up, Mo?" I asked, the 'never Morris, only Mo' directive having taken hold long ago where the young man's name preference was concerned.

"Can you two step outside and...just listen?" Enderson requested.

I took a few steps toward the front door, lifting the phone and dragging its long cord with me. The Ranger Signal could still overpower and interfere with a simple cordless handset, so going old school was the order of the day when needing to converse at any distance from where the phone was wired in.

"What are we listening for?"

"Just listen and tell me if you hear anything."

"Okay," I agreed, looking to Elaine. "He wants to know if we hear anything outside."

Elaine didn't ask for any clarification on the request. She moved to the door and past me as she pushed it open. I followed and a moment later was standing with her in the front yard, stars twinkling above and a hush thick upon our street, and our town.

"Put the phone down and just listen," Enderson told me.

I lowered the phone handset without a word, holding it and the unit's base low near my waist. Then, as he'd asked, I listened. And listened.

"Do you hear that?" Elaine asked.

I didn't. Glancing at her I saw her gaze cast up into the night sky. My hearing had never been as acute as my eyesight, but Elaine could detect footsteps in a darkened forest, or mumbles of mine from a room down the hall. If she was sensing something where we stood, I knew there had to be something there.

"What is it?"

She shushed me with a shake of her head and kept listening. I tried to tune in to whatever had caught her attention, focusing on the vast heavens above. Letting all other sounds fade until there was just that looming nothingness.

That was when I heard it, too.

"An engine," I said.

"Aircraft," Elaine added. "Small and at altitude."

She was right. The distant, steady whine could have been a small plane akin to the one that Neil, Grace, Krista, and I had arrived in so long ago. That could mean that there were more survivors inbound.

Or it could indicate something very, very different.

"Mo, we hear an aircraft," I said, bringing the handset back up.

"So I'm not crazy," Enderson said. "I was coming on watch at HQ and the sound just was there. It would come and go."

"I still hear it," Elaine said. "It's moving south to north."

"Elaine—"

"South to north," Enderson said, prompting that he'd heard what had been reported. "That's what I hear."

"Is there any way we can get eyes on what kind of aircraft?" I asked.

"I could break out the night vision binoculars, but I doubt we'd be able to zero in on a target," Enderson said. "It sounds awful high to me."

"It has to see us," Elain said. "Whoever's on it."

She was right. There were enough lights burning in town, including a good number of streetlights which had been put back into use after an additional hydro generator was installed in the Coquille River. The town, for now, had enough power from hydro, solar, and diesel generators to power almost anything it needed.

But all the power we had couldn't give us what we needed at this very moment—a good look at what was up there.

"If they see us, they have to know we have an airstrip," Elaine said. "It's on every map and chart of the area. They wouldn't be flying that blind."

"No, they wouldn't," I agreed.

On the other end of the call, Enderson was thinking the same thing, and coming to a similar conclusion that I and, I suspected, Elaine was as well.

"They're not planning to land," Enderson said. "They're on a reconnaissance flight."

They...

It was safe to assume that the 'they' looking down on us from above were at least related to what had happened to me. In the hollowed out world as it was, there weren't enough of our kind to make coincidences even possible.

"I've got to inform the captain," Enderson said, then he ended the call.

I nodded with the phone against my cheek and listened for a few minutes more until the sound of the aircraft faded to nothing.

"What do you think they want?" Elaine wondered aloud. "It can't be the cure for the blight. We already passed that along. It's no secret."

"Maybe they don't know that," I said.

"You don't sound convinced of that."

"I'm not," I told her.

"Then what? Why spy on us?"

I thought for a moment. A half dozen answers rattled about in my thoughts, but one kept sticking.

"To look for weaknesses," I said.

Elaine looked to the sky again, nodding.

"Only one reason to do that," she said.

She was right.

"To prepare for an attack," I said.

Thirteen

I hated being apart from her.

"I think we should hold here," Nick Withers said to me, his voice hushed.

I nodded and stopped behind the splintered trunk of a tree, most of its limbs snapped off and turning to pasty dust on the still barren forest floor. Nick moved a few yards further and lowered to one knee next to a mound of beefy, jagged rocks.

"I've got east and north," I said.

"East and south," Nick replied.

We were on the eastern perimeter of the town, a half hour past sundown, enough light remaining that we could see a hundred yards or more through the thinning woods beyond our position. Behind us, to the west, was Bandon, and an array of checkpoints to provide a more robust defense than the roving patrols could manage. Patrols like the one I was on.

And Elaine.

She was somewhere to the north, paired with Private Quincy, doing much the same that Nick and I were—staking a forward position for a while and scanning our slice of the pie. Observing. Searching. Hoping to find nothing, but almost certain that something was out there. Some*one* was out there.

A lot of someones.

Elaine and I had worked every patrol together until now, the luck of assignments catching up with us. Or, maybe, it was Schiavo and Lorenzen deciding that a husband and wife should not be placed together on every occasion. The captain and her sergeant were taking very seriously the needs of the town as a whole, with that paramount over personal wishes and aversions of the residents as individuals. Reluctant as I was, I had to yield to whatever they believed was best.

Just a few minutes after Nick and I took up our position, I was as thankful as could be that Elaine was not with me when muzzle flashes blazed in the woods to the east and south, bullets whizzing over our head, rounds chewing into the wasting stand of fir and pine that surrounded us.

"Contact!" I shouted out of habit, though no warning was necessary. "Covering!"

My AR came up, no suppressor on the muzzle, the sight picture I found in the distance just a mix of vague shapes and hellish incoming. I squeezed off three bursts and rolled to the right to a nearby tree, its trunk more stout than the one I'd chosen before. It was then that I saw Nick huddled against the rocky mound he'd been planted himself at, tucked into a ball as rounds splintered off shards of rock.

"Nick!"

He didn't respond. The twenty-seven year old grease monkey, who was more at ease with a ratchet in hand than the grip of an AK-47, simply shivered, his weapon pulled tight to his chest.

"Nick!" I shouted his name again. "Lay some fire!"

The young man's eyes came up, finding mine, his body trembling, from a cold that was not external. This shiver that afflicted him came from a wave of utter terror that had drenched him, penetrating to the bone. He was nearly catatonic.

I knelt behind the tree and fired the rest of my mag toward the muzzle flashes, too distant and obscured by the darkening woods to give me any clear sight picture. I dropped the empty and inserted a fresh magazine, chambering the first round and squeezing off a series of single shots before dashing to the rocky covering which shielded Nick. Incoming rounds kicked up dust and dirt a yard or two behind me.

"Nick, can you hear me?"

I hunkered down in the shelter of the sharp boulders and grabbed him by the coat collar.

"Nick!"

Finally, he showed some response, his gaze angling up at me as a flurry of rounds pecked at the far side of the rocks. I looked into his eyes and saw none of what I needed to at that moment. There was no fight in them. Nearly no life at all. Just a blank window to what the sudden eruption of terror had done to the man.

He was helpless.

I leaned left and fired to the east at the extreme north end of the force that was out there, muzzle flashes defining the limit of their line. Or the limit they were allowing me to see. In minutes they could move further north and flank the position we held. There would be no cover from such a move. No tactics to thwart it. We'd be overrun.

"Nick, we've gotta move," I told the young man, shaking him by the collar. "Due west. You hear me? We've got to run. Right through the trees."

He didn't react at all. I grabbed the AK from him and tossed it aside. I was going to have to drag him clear of the attack we were facing, and all his weapon was now was dead weight that I would have to move with us.

"We're moving, Nick. Do you understand?"

Again I shook him, with no effect, then I drew my hand back and swung the gloved palm across his face. The impact jolted him, his body shuddering as though some electric shock had run through it. His head swiveled left and right, his gaze finally settling on me. There was life in his eyes again, I could see. At least partially, Nick Withers was back with me.

"We're gonna move, Nick, okay?"

He looked left and right, cringing instinctively as incoming fire bracketed our position, already dead trees threatening to topple as their wasted trunks were chewed away by the unrelenting streams of bullets.

"Nick?"

Again he fixed on me and nodded.

"Stay down and when I grab you we move west, got it?"

"Got-got-got it."

The fear-induced stutter at least told me that he was processing what I'd said to him, which meant, hopefully, that I wouldn't be hauling dead weight through the woods back toward town.

More fire shifted north. The force out there was moving to flank us. And I was beginning to hear voices in the distance. Commands being given. In English. For a moment I was grateful that the Russian force we'd decimated along the Alaskan coast hadn't reconstituted and followed us home seeking revenge. But I quickly realized that American bullets would make us dead just as quickly as Russian ones, and it was time to make our move before that happened.

A final time I leaned left past the rocks and fired off bursts at the enemy's northern advance. My AR ran dry and I let it drop to hang from the sling across my chest.

"Now!"

I grabbed Nick and pulled him away from cover, pushing him ahead, his own feet propelling him through the trees as we weaved left and right around the trunks, chunks of decaying wood spraying down from above as incoming rounds struck high.

"Move!"

Thankful that I wasn't having to drag a catatonic friend away from the danger zone, I urged him on, reloading as I ran nearly alongside. A hundred yards into our retreat, with sporadic fire still whizzing past, I halted briefly, motioning for Nick to keep moving. I brought my AR up from where I stopped next to a knot of young pines that would never reach maturity. By the time I had it aimed in the direction of the enemy, the incoming fire stopped. Just ended. As if a cease fire order had been given.

I held that position, ready to cover any pursuit, not hoping to stop any such advance by the enemy, but to delay it until reinforcements could arrive. There was no doubt in my mind that the firefight had been heard, at least on the eastern end of town. The three checkpoints there, all hardwired into the phone system, would have reported what was happening. Help would come.

As it turned out, none was needed.

Five minutes after I'd halted my retreat the first backup arrived, Sergeant Lorenzen and Private Quincy, with a half dozen armed civilians in tow.

"Where are they?" Lorenzen asked.

I pointed east and drew a sweeping arc to the south.

"Some were moving north when we broke contact," I said. "I sent Nick Withers toward town. He was—"

"Pretty shaken up," Lorenzen said.

"We sent two shooters back to town with him," Quincy said.

"How many are out there, Fletch?"

I looked to the sergeant before answering his question. "Too many."

Lorenzen stood with me for a moment as Quincy directed the civilians to form a defensive line. We waited for five minutes, then ten, the sound of more reinforcements arriving behind us rising. Twenty minutes after the last bullet had been fired we were a force of fifty, including Schiavo.

"Enderson has a reaction force in town ready to move if this was just a feint," the captain said.

Lorenzen thought for a second, then shook his head. "The truth is, Captain, I don't know what this is."

Schiavo walked past her sergeant a few yards, into the no man's land ahead of our line.

"Fletch," she said, and I walked forward to join her.

"Yeah?"

"Do you think they were waiting for you, or do you think they were on the move first?"

"I have no idea," I answered. "It just became a lead throwing contest, and they were the winner."

Schiavo nodded and surveyed the darkening woods to the east.

"Good."

"Captain," I said, not understanding her appraisal of what had just happened. "How is any of this 'good'?"

"Because we know they're out there now," she answered. "And they know we know."

Fourteen

"We're forming a town defense council," Mayor Allen announced to those he'd gathered in the conference room at the town hall. "I'm asking everyone here to be part of it."

The message had come by phone. A simple request early in the morning, when Elaine and I were sitting down to breakfast after a full night's sleep, which followed a six-hour shift at an eastern checkpoint, together this time. After the engagement I'd been involved in, with Nick Withers at my side, I suspected that Elaine had initiated some contact with either Schiavo or Sergeant Lorenzen, and arranged, through begging or force of logic, that she and I should be paired on any assignment going forward. The latter, a carefully and forcefully presented argument, was the catalyst, I knew. Begging was not in her nature.

I had to say I was pleased. The incident with Nick, where his presence became more hindrance than help, had driven home the already known reality that we were only as strong as our weakest link. Out there, in the dead woods, he'd been the liability that could have gotten us both killed. If that had been the intent.

I didn't believe for a moment that it was.

"What are we going to defend against?"

The question I posed seemed to take Schiavo, Martin, Mayor Allen, and even Elaine by surprise.

"You were out there, Fletch," Mayor Allen said.

"I was. And there was a good force in the woods shooting at us."

The puzzled gazes zeroed in on me, as if I was speaking from a place where amnesia had robbed me of recollections of recent events.

"Do you want to clarify your thoughts on this for us?" Schiavo asked,

I clenched my right hand into a fist atop the table, the contraction forcing an annoying throb to stab at the place where my arm had been violated.

"This is Bandon," I said, then tapped with my free hand to points around my fist on three sides. "And we've had movement reports from here, here, and here and the exchange in the woods. Multiple contacts over the past few days."

"Indicating testing of our defenses," Schiavo said.

I nodded. And they waited, not following where I was going. To be honest, I hadn't even considered the possibility of the conclusion I had come to until Elaine and I were just arriving at the meeting. Outside, Nick Withers stood, pistol on his hip, guarding the entrance to the town hall. Mayor Allen had asked for him to fill that position I knew, not wanting the young man's failings in the firefight to beat down his morale. As Martin had said, we needed everyone, even those who might not perform at the highest standard. To that end, Nick Withers, mechanic extraordinaire and lackluster soldier, was being given a task through which he could contribute, and feel as though he was contributing to the town's safety and security.

Looking at him as we entered, as he smiled and nodded and held the door open for Elaine and me, I thought very plainly that he should not be here. That I should not be here. The both of us should have died in the woods.

But we didn't.

"How many do you think there are out there?" I asked. "Realistically."

We'd battled our way up the coast of Alaska against a force of Russians that numbered fewer than two dozen.

This was a world where armies, however mighty they once had been, were reduced to units only a fraction of their intended size. We were a town of just over 800, with maybe 100 that could be considered battle worthy at some level, with another 75 or 80 who could take up arms in a reserve capacity if things became desperate. But we were stationary, in a fixed position, and reasonably well supplied. Whoever was out there, in and beyond the woods and hills, was mobile. They'd come here, and whatever supply line they had was certainly extended. I knew this, and so did Schiavo.

"Seventy, maybe eighty," the captain answered.

"We outnumber them," I said.

"They have some support and better arms," Schiavo reminded me.

"And air assets," Elaine added, curious along with the others as to where I was going with this.

"Right," I said. "So why am I alive? Why is Nick Withers alive and standing guard at the door to the town hall?"

I could see the first spark of realization dance in Schiavo's gaze.

"Nick and I were stationary targets out there," I said. "We were making no move and they opened up on us, and missed us with every shot. *Every shot.* They were aiming high and wide. Even when I was running with Nick in the open between the trees their fire was still off."

"You were *perfect* targets," Elaine realized.

"More than once," I said.

"They didn't mean to kill you," Martin said.

"If they had, you'd be talking to an empty chair," I agreed.

Just below the tabletop, Elaine reached to my lap and gripped my knee. I was here, but I sensed she wanted to physically feel my presence after what I'd just said.

"Okay," Schiavo said, allowing the possibility of what I'd suggested. "They're just feigning an attack posture? That's what you're thinking?"

"Maybe," I said. "Or maybe it's psychological. To let us know they're out there. To ratchet up our stress level."

"You're talking about a siege," Martin said.

"Good Lord," Mayor Allen reacted, shaking his head.

Schiavo thought on the situation for a moment.

"If that's their purpose, what's the end game? All sieges end. Either the besieged give up or fight to the death, or the outsiders are driven off."

"What do they want?" Elaine asked.

"It would help if we knew who they were," Martin said. "Where they've come from, who they answer to. That all would speak to their motivation."

His wife, though, didn't seem certain of his appraisal.

"There's no secret here," Schiavo said. "Or at least there won't be for long."

"What do you mean?" Mayor Allen asked.

"She means they'll make contact," I said, and Schiavo gave a slight nod.

"And it won't be a genial greeting," Schiavo said. "It will be an ultimatum."

That word, that near certainty, hung there for a moment, each of us processing what it might mean to Bandon. To our home.

"They'll try to weaken us," Schiavo said, her gaze shifting to me. "You might have been their first attempt at that."

"The Trojan horse," Martin said.

Mayor Allen thought for a moment, nodding.

"It's possible we got that capsule out of you just in time," the old doctor said. "If it was time release meant to spread some sickness after you'd been back in town for a while..."

Elaine squeezed my knee again and shook her head.

"What's the ultimatum going to be?" she asked, glancing my way. "What are they going to want? What do we have that they just couldn't ask for?"

No one had an answer that made any sense.

"Why not attack?"

It was Mayor Allen who posed the question, a suggestion that seemed so out of place coming from the peaceful, almost sedate old man.

"We have the advantage in numbers if Angela is correct," the mayor said. "Why not use that? Right now?"

He focused on Schiavo. We all did. Though I knew before she spoke that her answer was not going to be in concert with what the mayor was envisioning.

"Because I could be wrong," the captain said. "They could have a thousand troops out there on the other side of the hills. The aircraft they have could bear armaments. But the bottom line truth is that I have six real soldiers who've been trained to execute attacks. I can't lead them and the few townspeople who could keep up into a lopsided battle. It would be suicide."

Mayor Allen sat back in his chair, accepting the counter to his suggestion.

"There is one hope to better our situation," Schiavo said in the brief silence after she'd gently shot down the idea of charging at our unseen, and unknown, adversary. "The *Rushmore*."

"Can they bring in reinforcements?" Elaine asked.

"They would have already departed for their supply run," Schiavo said. "But I can ask if they can spare some of the crew so I have a few more shooters. If the Navy is amenable, we might pick up a dozen troops. That would triple the size of the garrison."

"Our friends out there might be made to think it's more than that," I said. "If we play it up big. Make it seem like we're getting five times that. Six. Ten."

"They might think twice about making any move," Elaine said.

"The barbarians at the gate could just slink off, back to wherever they came from," Schiavo said, agreeing.

"When is the *Rushmore* due in?" Mayor Allen asked.

"Three or four days from now," Schiavo said.

"Can you get a burst transmission to them?" Martin asked.

His wife nodded and was about to say something more when the door to the conference room opened with sudden urgency, Sgt. Lorenzen coming through, his gaze sweeping the room before landing on his commander.

"You're not going to believe this," he said.

Schiavo knew her second in command well enough that his tone, and his amped manner, pointed to something profound having occurred. She rose slowly, her chair sliding back as she did.

"What is it?"

Now Lorenzen looked to me, gaze widened over quickened breaths.

"She's back."

I stood now, as did Elaine, neither of us with near as smooth a motion as the captain. Our chairs screeched noisily away from the table, mine nearly tipping from my haste.

"Who?"

Asking the question was natural. But so was suspecting the answer. There was only one 'she' whose return would elicit such an announcement.

"Grace," Lorenzen said. "And she's not alone."

Fifteen

Grace Moore had simply walked into town from the east, Krista at her side and a baby in her arms. They'd approached a checkpoint and were being sheltered there from a morning rain as we raced across town in a pair of Humvees to pick them up.

We took her and the children to their house. To what had been the house she shared with Neil. For six months it had sat vacant, but not empty. All that they had abandoned, minus the weapons, had been left undisturbed. A neighbor had come by one day soon after my friend's inexplicable departure and made the beds. Once a week after that the same neighbor had entered the silent house and dusted, keeping the home as clean and tidy as possible, maybe in the hope that the family would someday return.

That hope had been realized in part.

"I need to feed the baby," Grace said, shedding her coat and settling into a comfortable chair in the living room as if she'd just returned home from a trip to the market. "Can you hand me that blanket?"

The request was directed at Elaine, who noted the nod Grace gave toward a small, fuzzy throw neatly folded over the back of a high backed rocker. She retrieved it and handed it over.

"I'm just not one of those women who can let it all hang out when I'm breastfeeding," Grace said, slipping the blanket over her shoulder and opening her blouse beneath as she began to feed her son.

Their son.

"A boy," I said.

Grace looked up, some incalculable distance in the expression.

"His name is Brandon," Grace said, gazing down at the infant in her arms. "Neil wanted that name. He said it was the closest to Bandon that wouldn't get him beat up in kindergarten."

She tried to smile at the mild joke. We all did. But the confusion that reigned over her sudden reappearance muted any natural reaction. Questions swirled without being asked. Doubts raged. Pity simmered as we looked upon those who had come back to us. Those who had come home.

I turned away from Grace and looked to Krista. She sat on the couch, ill at ease, as if she was visiting a stranger's house and was afraid of offending her hosts.

"Hey sweetie," I said, taking the space next to the child. "How are you?"

She didn't verbalize any answer, but responded with a quiet nod. A child's backpack sat on the floor near her feet, pretty and pink, its top zipper open to reveal a collection of toys and colored pencils inside.

"All your things are still in your room," Elaine said. "Nothing's been changed."

Krista looked up to Elaine and let a small smile form, as if allowing the expression despite what she felt within. She clutched a small, hardbound notebook on her lap, its blue fabric cover bare, thumb and fingers rubbing nervously at the spine.

"What's that?" I asked Krista.

Her gaze dipped to the notebook.

"My drawings," Krista said.

She opened the cover and flipped through several pages of colorful, fanciful pictures. Animals drawn from memory. Horses. Elephants. Giraffes. Creatures that, almost certainly, existed only as recollections in the child's mind.

"Those are very good," Martin said.

"Micah showed me a lot of pictures of animals on his computer," Krista said, closing the notebook, the smile she'd managed now fading.

"He had pictures of everything," Martin said, his own smile building. "He loved showing them to you."

Krista didn't respond to Martin's kind, bittersweet words. Her attention shifted, instead, to the front door. I looked and saw that the crowd which had gathered outside was growing, Lorenzen and Schiavo working to part the phalanx of townspeople so that familiar faces could make their way through.

"I hear we have a baby," Mayor Allen said, Commander Genesee at his side.

Grace looked up and nodded. The gesture was slack and subdued. No feeling in it whatsoever. Almost robotic. Without any training to back up my assessment, it seemed to me that she was in a state of mild shock.

"Grace, how are you?" Mayor Allen asked.

"I'm okay."

The old doc tipped his head toward Krista.

"Is it all right if we give big sister a quick checkup?"

"Sure," Grace said, her flaccid gaze shifting to her daughter. "Krista, Doc Allen is going to examine you."

Krista, too, nodded almost without thought. Just a motion, head tipping up and down, because that was what the moment required.

"This is Commander Genesee," Mayor Allen said, offering the introduction. "Trained in the Navy, so he must know what he's doing."

"It's good to meet you," Grace said, adjusting the baby against her breast.

"It's very nice to meet you," Genesee responded.

"Why don't we give Krista a quick look in her bedroom," Mayor Allen suggested, smiling at the young girl. "I'm sure Elaine would come along to keep you company."

"Absolutely," Elaine said, reaching her hand out toward Krista.

"Can I bring my notebook and my backpack?"

"Of course," Mayor Allen said.

Krista slid her small hand into Elaine's and stood, slipping her notebook into the open backpack and lifting it by one strap. She and Elaine led the way down the hall and into her bedroom, Allen and Genesee following them in.

That left Martin and me with Grace and the son she'd had with my friend.

"Grace..."

She looked to me, a skim of tears glistening on her eyes. There were questions, too many questions. The both of us knew this. We also knew that answers would not change things. Would not turn the clock back.

Not while there was still one person missing.

"How is Neil?"

The simple question, so ordinary in another time, now carried with it pain, and disappointment, and worry.

"I'm so sorry," Grace said, her gaze shifting to Martin. "I didn't know this was all going to happen."

Was she sidestepping the question, or was the answer she might give something she could not give voice to? I instantly wondered if something had happened to my friend.

"Did something happen to Neil?" I pressed her.

As she hesitated for a moment, Schiavo came in, leaving her sergeant outside to manage the wondering crowd. She stood close to Martin, and he let his hand come up and rest against the small of her back, a simple show of caring, maybe all either would allow while she was in uniform.

Grace, I saw, noticed this gesture, this warmth between man and wife, and loss already plain in her eyes seemed to double on itself.

"Is Neil okay, Grace?" I asked again.

"He's...not hurt. He's doing what he thinks is right with the Unified Government."

The conversation stuttered there as she uttered those unfamiliar words.

"The what?" Schiavo asked, the slightest abruptness in the delivery of her question.

Grace shifted a bit, pulling her infant tighter against her body and regarding the captain with sudden wariness.

"The Unified Government," Grace repeated, taking in our puzzled reaction for a moment. "The new government. You don't know about this?"

"No," Martin said. "We don't."

"I didn't know we needed a new government," Schiavo said.

"Nothing was working," Grace said, trying to explain. "You know that. They've got it working again. Neil promised me that. Neil promised..."

Her words trailed off there, as if the meaning that drove them was too tenuous to sustain. Too convenient in the face of what she knew, what she believed, in her heart, in her mind, and in her soul.

"We're doing all right here, Grace," Martin said. "Before you left we were on a good footing. It's only gotten better."

She looked to each of us, confused. Then her gaze shifted abruptly, cast downward to the new life held close against her breast.

"Grace," I said.

She looked up at me, and for a moment all I could think that I was in the presence of someone lost on the outside, and broken within.

"Why is Neil's voice on the signal?" I asked.

"It was an honor," she answered, almost timidly. "That's what he said. To give the command which would unite the country."

Schiavo looked to Martin, and then to me.

"Unite by force," the captain said.

Grace, though, took quiet, almost confused exception to that. She shook her head.

"No, that's not it at all," she protested, patting her baby gently on the back as he fussed while feeding. "That's not true. I'm the proof of that. The three of us are."

"What do you mean, Grace?" Martin asked.

"We're a goodwill gesture," she said. "To show you that no one wants conflict."

"We've been shot at, Grace," Schiavo said. "Our people, including Fletch here, have been shot at. Two people died because everyone is on edge about the threat facing us."

"No," Grace countered. "Neil told me everyone would be safe. That we'd all be okay."

The promises she'd been given weren't meshing with the reality we were sharing with her. That part of her which I'd sensed was broken seemed on the verge of shattering outright now. Scattering pieces of the woman, the mother, the survivor that she was to some foul wind which had swept over her.

"No," she said once more with fading disbelief.

Soon after arriving on the *Rushmore*'s first trip to Bandon, Schiavo had told of factions vying to be the sole authority over the devastated nation. Now, it appeared, the enemy on our borders, presumably one of those entities, had a name. And even a motive, if the news Grace had brought to us was to be believed. We still needed more. Information about their numbers. Their supply line. Command structure. But we weren't going to get that from Grace, I suspected. And not at that moment I knew as Mayor Allen and Commander Genesee returned to the living room, coming out of the hallway together, the look about them almost identical, hinting at something unexpected. Grace took note of their almost puzzled demeanor immediately as emerged from the emotional fog which had enveloped her.

"Is Krista all right?"

"She's fine, Grace," Mayor Allen said. "She's showing Elaine her drawings. We just wanted to check something."

"Check what?"

Genesee stepped past his older predecessor and crouched close to Grace.

"Can I just have a look?" Genesee asked, his hand reaching to the right sleeve of her loose sweater.

Grace nodded and Genesee slipped the garment upward until it was well above her elbow. He leaned a bit and checked the back side of her bicep, then looked up to his elderly colleague.

"The same," Genesee said.

"Let me just have a peek at your boy here," Mayor Allen said, easing the blanket covering the infant just a bit to perform the same check on the child.

When he was done, both he and Genesee looked to us. To me in particular.

"Krista, Grace, and the baby all have it," Mayor Allen said.

"Have what?" Schiavo asked.

"What Fletch had," Mayor Allen said.

"An implant," Genesee specified.

Sixteen

"They said it would protect us," Grace said. "Like a vaccination."

We looked to one another, all thinking the same thing. It was Martin who voiced the obvious.

"Vaccination against what?"

"No one said," Grace answered, looking to the hallway as Elaine joined us again.

"Krista's still drawing," my wife said. "Do they have it, too?"

Mayor Allen nodded. Elaine took my hand and stood close, her gaze angling up toward me. I felt it in her touch, what she was thinking. The fear suddenly welling—*if it was meant to protect, we took it out of you.*

"It will be all right," I said, squeezing her hand gently.

I was expressing hope. As I had many times since the appearance of the blight. The sense of belief in the future, in a better future, had been instilled in me by my friend. My absent friend. Who was trying to look out for me from afar. That could be the only explanation for my being taken and implanted with the same thing meant to protect his family.

"He's a good man," Grace said, the sentiment rising without prompting. "You have to believe that."

I did want to believe that. I always had. If there was some way to see through all my friend had done since leaving, to a place where his actions made sense, I simply could not. Not without some deeper understanding of his motives. His true intentions.

"Will you excuse us?" Schiavo said, looking to Elaine, Martin, and me as she nodded toward the exit.

* * *

The four of us left the medical men with Grace and her children and stepped out the front door.

"They're planning a biological attack," I said, quiet enough to keep my prediction unheard by those inside and the crowd lingering on the sidewalk.

"No," Schiavo countered. "They're preparing for one."

"There's a difference?" Elaine challenged her.

"We'd better hope so," Schiavo said, looking to the people gawking at us from beyond the dirt patch where a lawn had once stretched lush from porch to picket fence.

"If this Unified Government thing is real, we're stuck in the middle," Martin said. "We're the girl that two guys want to take to the prom."

"The choice is still ours," Elaine reminded him, and all of us

There was some boast in her words. Some determination. But also a truth for which we might pay a heavy price. And, because of which, difficult, even impossible, decisions would have to be made.

What Commander Genesee told us when he joined us on the porch a moment later made that beyond clear.

"This may give us some options," he said.

"This?" I asked. "You mean Grace coming back?"

"Options for what?" Elaine asked.

Genesee hesitated for an instant. As if he knew what he was about to suggest pushed some boundary, either medical or ethical.

As it turned out, it was both.

"If we hadn't destroyed what we took out of you," Genesee began, looking to me, "it might have been possible to make a diluted vaccine from what it contained. Enough to give everyone in town at least some defense against whatever we're going to face."

After those words, it was clear where his thought process had taken him. And where he was trying to lead us.

"Those implanted capsules use time release to dispense the contents over weeks," Genesee said. "Maybe months. If we remove—"

"No."

The answer was simple and abrupt, and it came from the one person whose opinion the Navy commander had no chance of changing.

"You're not cutting them open," Schiavo told the doctor. "Not a mother and her children. I won't allow that."

Genesee was up against the immovable object, and he knew that he was no irresistible force. But I could see in the man's look, in the way his neck muscles drew suddenly taut, that he was unwilling, maybe unable, to simply accept such a decision without offering any counter to it.

"If we don't, if what's in them will offer protection, then you're sentencing people to a fate we could avoid," Genesee told his superior. "And that might be death. For some, for the sick, the old, the young, that may be a certainty."

Schiavo let him finish. But she said no more. Used no words to chastise him or repeat her decision. She let what she'd said stand. If there was any other way to stoke the animus in Genesee right then, I could not imagine it. The Navy man who had never showed fondness for either his uniform, nor the chain of command it reflected, turned without uttering any further rebuttal and left the porch, moving down the walkway and abruptly through the crowd.

"Is what he's suggesting possible?" Elaine wondered.

Schiavo's gaze shifted to my wife, as if she was facing another challenge to what she'd decided. But in that instant of contact between them, the very real façade of command, of leadership, softened. With a man such as Genesee, unlike her troops, unlike any of us, Captain Angela Schiavo had to exert her authority. Whether there was some distrust of his superior because of personality, or because of gender, he had never given her the full measure of respect she deserved. His challenges toward her were mostly subtle, quiet, often internal, with only glimpses escaping for others to witness.

Here, on this day, he'd let more than a hint of his simmering disdain toward Schiavo show.

"I'm not agreeing with him," Elaine said.

Schiavo nodded and drew a breath.

"I know."

The moment, whatever it might have become, had defused itself. At least amongst us. How Genesee would react in any further conflicts was yet to be seen.

"Cap," I said.

She looked to me, a tiredness about her. We'd returned to Bandon just hoping to live our lives. The garrison, led by Schiavo, had joined us, all wanting the same, I knew. But now we were facing another external threat, and it was wearing on her. Wearing on all of us. Exchanges like the one she'd just had with Genesee did nothing to lighten the burden she bore 24/7.

I was afraid what I was about to ask would only add to it.

"Do you even know who you're getting your orders from?" I asked Schiavo.

"What do you mean?" Martin asked.

His interception of the question spoke to his protectiveness. He could not stand before her on any battlefield, but here he was seizing what might seem like yet another challenge directed at her.

"It's all right," Schiavo said, nodding to me. "I know what he means."

"You get coded messages over a brief transmission a couple times a week," I said.

The secure burst transmission relay, which bounced off a passing satellite at specific times, was not always reliable. Just over half of the communications sent were acknowledged, requiring a repeat transmission. The issue could be easily explained by the complex nature of the attempted communication, requiring many moving parts to all work without losing synchronization. In the real world, that was not possible.

And, when the actions of our own kind were thrown into the mix, simple issues led to fears of manipulation for purposes at odds with our own, and with the government we believed was working to bolster our survival.

"Do you have any way of knowing that it's our side you're talking to?"

Our side.

That term used to hold such clarity. Not anymore. Not since the blight, and certainly not since the residents of Bandon were forcibly relocated to Skagway in the government's, in *our* government's, attempt to assist our survival. That endeavor had gone horribly wrong. But, to me, it demonstrated that there were times when the actions of an ally and an adversary were difficult to distinguish.

I was beginning to wonder if our contact with the outside world should not be viewed with the same level of skepticism.

"Fletch," Schiavo began, a calm confidence about her, "the people in the woods, they're not who I've been talking to. I don't know a lot about this situation, but I know that. Okay? You have to trust me."

She was right, even if she was wrong. I did have to trust her. We all did.

Schiavo quieted and thought for a moment, then did something that I did not see coming. That none of us did, in particular her husband as she leaned in and gave him a very quick, but very deliberate kiss on the cheek. His gaze seized on her, and hers on him, as she eased away. In that moment, where I saw love, pure love, I felt an immense worry rise.

"I need to get a message out and find out just what the hell is going on," Schiavo said.

She left us alone on the porch, Martin and Elaine standing with me. A few yards from us, the captain pushed through the crowd and climbed behind the wheel of a Humvee, speeding away, leaving her sergeant to deal with gathering of the curious and shocked.

I glanced behind, through the front doorway. Mayor Allen was sitting with Grace, Brandon in her arms and Krista on the floor, sitting at her mother's feet. I stared at them for a moment, wanting to flush the fear that had risen with Schiavo's very tender gesture from my thoughts.

But I couldn't.

"Eric..."

I turned to my wife, who'd looked at me as Angela Schiavo had her husband on many occasions. During good times and bad. But those connections, those moments, I expected of her. She'd never held them back since we'd become one.

This was the first time I'd seen such a display from the captain while in uniform.

"What's wrong?"

Her question hung there, with Martin wondering what she'd noticed. His own puzzled look mirrored Elaine's. I could have lied, I knew. Held back what I felt. Maybe share it with Elaine when Martin was not around to hear what I had to share.

But I didn't. Because neither of the people in my presence would hold back from me.

"She's worried about something," I said, gesturing with a nod toward the spot on the porch where Schiavo had stood.

To my surprise, Martin nodded without hesitation.

"Yes," he said. "She is."

"What?" Elaine asked.

For what might have been a tense, grim moment, Martin surprised me yet again with a subtle, true smile as he answered us.

"She's worried about bringing a baby into all this."

Part Two

Silence

Seventeen

The phone in our house rang at eight in the morning. I scrambled to it, thinking how odd it was that we'd willingly brought back a bit of the old world's technology whose primary function was interrupting what might be happening at any moment.

"I've got it," I said as Elaine hurried out of the bathroom after her shower, towel pulled quickly around her.

I slowed a bit and let my gaze linger on her dripping beauty.

"Yeah, yeah," she said, scolding me mildly. "Answer it already."

She darted into the bedroom and I continued on to answer the call, savoring the very ordinary, very natural moment for an instant before lifting the handset.

"Hello."

"I'm sending a car for you."

It was Schiavo. There was impatience, maybe frustration in her voice, but no urgency.

"All right," I said. "Elaine was going over to help Grace for a while."

"You can fill her in later," Schiavo said.

That meant that something consequential had occurred. That it wasn't earth shattering enough to warrant telling me immediately was good. That the captain had decided to hold the information close until we could be face to face was likely not.

* * *

Twenty minutes later, three of us stood with Private Westin in the communications center which had been set up in the garrison's portion of the town hall, Schiavo next to her private, who was responsible for the devices which connected us, in a very limited way, with the outside world.

"So the radio is malfunctioning?" Mayor Allen asked, seeking clarification of what the young soldier had just told us.

"You don't understand," Westin said, looking to Mayor Allen, and then to me. "We're sending. But there's nothing receiving. There's no carrier signal."

Schiavo drew a breath and eyed the town's leader.

"It's like a dial tone on a phone," Schiavo explained. "You pick up the handset and hear that, and you know the system is functioning."

"There's no signal from the satellite," Mayor Allen said, hinting at an understanding.

"Maybe no satellite at all," Westin suggested.

"Let's not go there yet," Schiavo said.

"It could be a simple malfunction," I said. "Right?"

Schiavo nodded, though there was little conviction in the expression.

"Those things are built to be robust," Westin told us. "You'd have to shoot it out of orbit."

For an instant, Schiavo was silent. Until the alternative to what her soldier was suggesting rose to the level of possibility in her thoughts.

"Or shut it down," the captain said.

"Can that be done?" Mayor Allen asked.

All eyes shifted to Westin, and without any hesitation he nodded.

"If authorized," he answered.

"We're way past the powers that be worrying about proper authorizations," I said. "If there's a switch somewhere that can cut us off, and someone wants us cut off, they'll throw it."

"It appears they may already have," the mayor said.

No one had said it yet, but the ramifications of this development had effects both near and far.

"We can't reach the *Rushmore*," I said.

"No," Westin confirmed.

"There goes giving them any warning about our needs," Schiavo said.

She thought for a moment, and I watched her as she did. Watched her too closely, as my interest drew her attention. Her gaze shifted and met mine, some unspoken question in it. Since Martin's revelation earlier that day that he and his wife were expecting, I hadn't been able to stop thinking about her. About the very real fear he'd told us she felt. To make the world whole again there would have to be children, but with the burden Angela Schiavo already carried, the weight of command and leadership and lives depending upon her, the addition of a new life to the mix could very understandably add almost crushing stress to her existence. I was concerned for her, and it showed.

"Is there a problem, Fletch?"

It was more than a question she posed. It was almost a challenge.

"Just trying to understand our com issues," I said, deflecting her concern with a partial lie.

"There's not a whole lot to understand," Mayor Allen said, catching on fully now. "We're cut off."

"By our side or theirs?" I asked.

"Or some other faction we don't even know about," Mayor Allen suggested.

Schiavo eyed me for a moment more, then shook her head.

"No," she said. "It's our friends out there. The Unified Government. This is coordinated, not a coincidence."

Coordination such as this implied planning, on a scale and over a distance which indicated sophistication. And determination.

"They're starting to turn the screws," Mayor Allen said.

No one in the communications center could disagree with what the town's elderly leader had said.

"So what's their next move?" Westin asked.

Schiavo shook her head, the frustration I'd sensed on her earlier phone call plain now, right before me. Before us.

"I have no idea," she said.

Eighteen

Three people stood on the beach at dawn on a Friday and stared at the ocean. I was one of them.

"How late could it be?" Martin asked.

His wife, the captain at this particular moment, shook her head slightly, her gaze fixed on the calm and clear Pacific to the west.

"A day," Schiavo said. "Two."

It had been four days since the *Rushmore* was scheduled to return to Bandon with more supplies to sustain our recovery. Four days with no sight of her on the horizon. With no contact at all, thanks to the sudden disruption of the satellite we'd used for burst communications. With the Ranger Signal still overwhelming all normal transmissions, we'd lost our only link with the ship, and the wider world. As Mayor Allen had said, we were cut off.

And now, it appeared, our supply line had been severed.

Martin took a few steps off the shoulder of the beach road where we'd come to look one last time for the ship, his shoes sinking slightly in the soft sand. He turned to look at us.

"How are we supplied?" he asked, slipping back into the role of town leader, if just for a moment. "Including the animals that we could slaughter, how are we on food?"

"That won't matter," Schiavo told her husband.

"We're surrounded and our delivery service just quit on us," Martin said. "We have to know how long we can last if not a single can of preserved beans makes it to us again."

"This won't go on long enough for that to be an issue," Schiavo told her husband.

She still expected some direct contact from the Unified Government. Some clear and unambiguous ultimatum to surrender and join. But join what? What were the principles of this new government, other than intimidation by force? How could we possibly go willingly into the arms of an entity we knew so little about?

Martin, though, had lived through uncertain times before Schiavo had arrived. He'd seen attacks, and starvation, and had to lead the town's residents through it all. He'd had to make difficult decisions. Weigh the good of the town over the wishes of the individual. The survival of the town, even if he'd stepped away from being its leader, still was beyond important to him. And that survival he'd shepherded hadn't just happened. It had required planning. Calculation. And he wasn't seeing that sort of precision even considered as his wife spoke.

"You can't just wing this," Martin said.

"I'm not."

He stood there, staring at his wife. The captain. The senior military officer in Bandon. Maybe the last officer left holding allegiance to the United States of America as it had once existed.

"Almost everyone in this town has watched someone starve to death," Martin said as he stepped close to his wife. "Have you?"

He walked past, leaving her with that question as he made his way up the coast road toward town.

"He's not wrong," I said.

Schiavo looked to me. Studied me. That moment when I'd locked eyes with her in the communications center days before came rushing back. That sense that she was probing me. Seeking some understanding of what I was thinking.

Then, her gaze softened. The edge that seemed ever-present about her when she was functioning in her military capacity evaporated as some realization came to her.

"He told you," she said. "Didn't he?"

There was no point in pretending, or in seeking clarification as to just what she was referencing.

"He did," I confirmed.

Schiavo took a breath and nodded, the combination seeming to release something that had been pent-up within.

"Who else knows?"

"Elaine was there when he let on what the situation was."

She smiled, an almost girlish expression, too awkward to not be among the most honest reactions she could offer.

"Situation," Schiavo repeated. "I guess that's a word for it."

"It's not a bad thing," I reminded her.

"No, but it's definitely not how I saw myself at this point in my career, and at this age."

"Did you talk to Genesee?"

She shook her head, reacting with mild horror at the thought.

"Doc Allen," she said. "I don't want Genesee knowing. Not until there's no choice."

I could understand her desire for at least a modicum of privacy on the issue, particularly where the Navy commander was concerned. He'd never seemed fully accepting of Schiavo, as either a person or a superior. It was possible that he saw those two things as inseparable, and, in many ways, they were. Schiavo inhabited her role as a military officer. That she had to do so as a woman with a male subordinate who might hold her gender against her seemed to tighten the grip with which she held onto her often strict expectations and behaviors. She was a hard ass unafraid of being one.

And she was going to be a mother.

"It wasn't supposed to happen," she said, a fair amount of resignation in her voice. "We were being careful."

"If that's possible," I said.

Nothing was as easy as pharmacology used to make it in the world before the blight. I wondered if that was a feature, not a bug, of this new reality. Humanity needed to expand if the species, our species, was to survive. The difficulty of preventing new births might be just one way that we would claw back from the brink of extinction.

"I'm not sure how Martin feels about it," she said.

To our east, maybe a hundred yards, we could see the relief shift, eight strong, moving across a field toward the southern checkpoints. They saw us and waved a greeting. I returned it, but Schiavo did not.

"After losing Micah..."

She was trying to express some imagined doubt. At least I hoped it was just an errant, misplaced reading of what her husband truly felt.

"He's been distant, Fletch. Since we found out, it's like his mind has been working on overdrive. Trying to figure out just what a child means for him. For us."

"When did you find out?"

"The day you and Elaine set off on your getaway," she said.

The intersection of events, both personal and public, were at play here, I suspected. To be certain, Martin was experiencing unexpected feelings about the sudden news that he was, again, going to be a father. But when thrown into the mix of my being taken, and our town, the town he held dear in his heart, being surrounded, to merely brand his reaction and demeanor as linked only to the child they were going to have was not an accurate read of the man.

"He has a lot on his mind," I reminded Schiavo. "You, a child, the town, our enemies. Do you want my opinion? My honest opinion?"

She nodded.

"He's coping," I said. "Throwing himself into what he can control. Into a way to contribute. The Defense Council, worrying about supplies. The child you two are expecting is going to come. That's out of his hands. I think he's concerned about the town it's going to be born into."

My words didn't soothe every worry she had. But she seemed to at least allow the possibility that any distance her husband was exhibiting was tied to what I'd said, and after a moment she let out a small, refreshing chuckle.

"You know what you described, right?"

"No," I said.

"He's nesting," Schiavo said. "The way a guy would."

I laughed. As severe as she could be at time, the Army captain had an insightful wit about here when she chose to show it.

"The town is the nest to him," I said.

"It has been for a long time," Schiavo agreed.

The moment we shared was good. But it was just a moment. As the jovial exchange faded, we both looked out over the ocean again, the empty ocean, no sign of the ship we'd hoped against hope to see.

"If they come at us, Fletch, we've got nowhere to run," Schiavo said, eyeing the waters that were beautiful and vast and blocked any chance of retreat. "We're going to have to fight."

"Do you think we can win?"

Schiavo stared out at the Pacific, considering my question in silence for a moment.

"I don't know," she answered, with calm and brutal honesty.

"We've been up against long odds before," I reminded her.

She turned and faced me now.

"This is different, Fletch," she told me. "Despite what those people out there call themselves now, they were us. They were Americans. Maybe even some people I trained with. People I might know."

She fell silent for a moment, but never looked away from me.

"And I think we're going to have to kill them to survive," Captain Angela Schiavo said, making plain what almost certainly lay ahead for every single one of us. "All of them."

Nineteen

Mayor Allen sat at the head of the table in the conference room in the town hall.

"We're on our own," he said.

The defense council sat with him. All but Martin, who'd chosen to stand, staring out the window at splashes of green against the grey woods in the distance. We'd kept Bandon alive, and set it on the road to thrive. All that, now, was in jeopardy.

"There's no point in making any announcement to the town," Schiavo said. "It's already filtered out there. People know."

"And they're scared," Elaine said.

The loss of communications, and the failure of the *Rushmore* to return as expected, had only increased the sense of dread among the longtime residents.

"What are our options?" Mayor Allen asked the group, looking to Schiavo when no one offered a response to his question. "You said you believe they'll contact us with an ultimatum."

"I do."

"Perhaps we should reach out to them first," Mayor Allen suggested. "There has to be a way to do that."

Schiavo shook her head with little consideration of the possibility.

"If we do that, we advance the timetable of conflict," she explained. "They'll give us their demands, which we can expect will be unconditional surrender."

"Join or die," Elaine said.

"The longer we hold out, the greater the chance we can prepare," Schiavo said. "Bolster our defenses. Train more to fight. Even learn about their numbers, equipment, and so on."

"You just want to wait," I said. "Let them dictate events."

"Yes," the captain said, again without hesitation.

Mayor Allen settled back into his chair at the head of the conference table.

"I don't like waiting," the doctor turned leader said. "If I see a disease, I treat it."

"Different worlds, doc," Schiavo said. "Different rules. But one does apply to both of us—*primum non nocere.*"

He smiled at her recitation of the familiar phrase in Latin.

"First, do no harm," Mayor Allen translated.

"As troubling as our situation may be right now, we're still free," Schiavo said.

"Free..."

The comment came from Martin where he stood at the window, still staring out at the glaring contrast between landscapes, old and new.

"You have something to add, Martin?"

The former leader of Bandon turned and faced the mayor. Faced all of us.

"What sort of authority do we have here?" Martin asked.

"I'm not sure I understand," Mayor Allen said, speaking for all of us, it seemed. "What sort of authority?"

Martin came back to the table, but didn't take a seat. Instead he stood, looking down at us from a place just to right of his wife.

"I mean, what laws are we functioning under? Normal everyday law? Martial law? We really need to get a grasp on that."

"Martin, what are you going on about?" Schiavo pressed him.

He took a breath, as if he needed to fuel himself for what he was about to say. To propose.

"Before the blight, if the country was facing what we are now, with an enemy on its borders, certain laws would be suspended. We would be able to take certain actions."

"Such as?" Mayor Allen asked.

"Warrantless searches," Martin answered. "Look, I know we don't function like a normal society. Not yet. There hasn't been a need for trials and proceedings and legalities. We've just made things work. But I don't think we can do that anymore."

"Searches for what?" Elaine challenged him.

He looked to me, and I knew. He was still concerned about a mole. A traitor. An infiltrator. In my living room immediately after I'd returned from being taken, Martin had expressed his fear about just such a possibility to me. At that point he wanted to hold his suspicions close. Wanted to keep them from others, particularly his wife.

It appeared to me he wasn't willing to do that anymore.

"We have a traitor among us," he said.

He explained his suspicions, relating the accurate knowledge necessary for me to be taken. Knowledge that could only have come from within our community.

"You want to rifle through peoples' houses in search of a spy based upon that?" Schiavo challenged her husband.

"No," he said, shaking his head. "Not only that."

He left his spot next to the table and walked to the door, opening it and waiting.

"Come with me."

* * *

We followed Martin to his house. His old house. The one he'd shared with Micah. To the boy's workstation in particular.

"I like to come here," Martin said, looking to his wife. "Sometimes I go for walks and I end up here."

She regarded him with quiet pity.

"I just like to be here. Where he was. The cemetery...that's not where I knew him. Where I loved him."

The distance between them that Schiavo had referenced while we talked at the beach, I suspected that this might be one factor influencing why she felt as she did. Unexplained absences. Withholding of reasons for such. There was pain here, in this relationship, and it flowed both ways, swirling in the space between a life gone, and one yet to begin.

"I'll sit here, and I'll turn on his computers and his radios, and I'll just listen and look," Martin went on. "It makes me feel close to him again."

Schiavo reached out and put a hand on his arm. He reached up and put his hand on hers.

"I have a wonderful life now, I do," Martin said. "But I miss my boy."

No one burst into tears, but there were no dry eyes in the room. After a moment, Martin sniffed away the emotion bubbling from within and gestured to one of the radios.

"Last night, late, I came here," Martin said. "It was two in the morning. I turned on the radio and I listened. I know how pointless that is, with the Ranger Signal blaring. Except..."

"Except what?" I asked,

"Except at five minutes after two that signal stopped," Martin told us. "There was clear air for thirty seconds. And in that short window I heard another transmission."

"What?!" Schiavo reacted.

Martin looked to her and nodded.

"What was in the transmission?" I asked.

Martin stepped close to the workstation and powered up the devices as I briefly had while in quarantine, radios and computers coming to life.

"Micah had it set up so anytime the radios were on, a recording was being made on a hard drive," he said. "What I heard was saved."

He reached to a mouse and clicked an icon on a computer screen, activating a sound file.

"Ready?" Martin asked.

"Go ahead," Mayor Allen said.

Martin clicked *play* and sound rose from the speakers. The familiar at first.

"Ranger... Ranger... Ranger..."

The same repeated again, and again, and then the speakers went quiet, only the hush of a white noise static hissing from them. And then, a few seconds into the silence, a fast and sharp *bee-ee-eep* sounded, followed by more nothingness until my friend's voice returned.

"Ranger... Ranger... Ranger..."

"What was that?" Elaine asked.

"I don't know," Martin said.

"Play it again," Schiavo said.

Martin repeated the transmission a second time. Then a third. And a fourth.

"It's just a high pitched beeping sound," Mayor Allen said. "It sort of stutters a bit."

"Maybe it's just an anomaly," Elaine suggested.

Martin nodded, allowing the possibility.

"Maybe," he said. "But if it's not..."

Schiavo thought for a moment, then looked to me.

"Go get Westin for me, Fletch."

* * *

Ten minutes later the garrison's communications specialist sat at the workstation, the five of us standing behind him as he played the transmission over and over, first through the speaker, and then through headphones.

"It's local," he said, slipping the headphones off.

"How local?" Schiavo asked.

"Very," Westin said. "It's low power, probably within a mile of where we are right now."

"That puts it in town," Martin said.

Mayor Allen looked to Martin and nodded.

"You were right," the town's current leader said to his predecessor.

Westin puzzled mildly at the exchange, and at what it might indicate.

"Ed, I need you to keep anything you hear right now confidential," Schiavo said, addressing the private almost maternally.

"Absolutely, ma'am," Weston agreed.

"Is there any way to pinpoint the source?" I asked.

Westin thought for a minute, his face twisting as he considered the possibilities.

"If we know when it's broadcasting, possibly. But the power is so low and the transmission is brief. We'd also have to have multiple direction finding units, and we don't even have one."

"Could we build them?" Martin asked.

"Sure, possibly, but there's something else," Westin said. "This transmission is recorded."

"You can tell that?" Elaine asked.

"Yes. It has the same acoustic signature as the Ranger Signal, which we know is a looped recording."

I was starting to understand his reluctance to embrace the search idea.

"You're saying this could be transmitted from a remote spot when no one is there," I said.

"Precisely," he confirmed.

"Okay," Schiavo said. "Finding it might be pointless because the transmitter could be low power, small, and

highly mobile. So let's focus on the other big question—
what sort of use would our enemy get from a beep?"

Westin smiled, getting into his role as com sleuth.

"That's just it," the private said. "It's not a beep. It's a
series of beeps compressed. Listen."

Westin dragged the audio file into a simple processing
program which Micah had used and slowed the playback
down by a factor of sixty. When the transmission was
played at this much reduced speed, the singular stuttering
beep became a minutes' worth of long and short tones
whose purpose was unmistakable.

"Morse," Martin said.

With its universally recognized auditory dots and
dashes, what we were listening to was some message that
had been condensed, much like the burst transmissions
we'd been bouncing off a satellite. Here, though, the
recorded message was being broadcast locally. From within
our very town.

"Can you decode it?" Schiavo asked her com specialist.

Westin nodded and slipped the headphones back on.
He faced the computer screen and watched the sound
pulses on the display as he listened, no pen or pencil in
hand to jot down the words he was deciphering. When he
was finished he removed the headphones and looked to
those of us standing behind.

"Supply ship not arrived. Resident anxiety growing.
Patrols increased in northern sector."

The private's recitation of the message hung there for a
moment, absolute confirmation that we had a traitor in our
midst.

"That patrol increase order went out at the morning
briefing to residents yesterday," Elaine said.

"Anyone at the briefing could have turned on us," I
said. "Or anyone who heard it second hand."

"Meaning everyone in town," Mayor Allen said.

Schiavo said nothing at first, looking to her husband, the man who'd seen this development before anyone, then turning to her private.

"Ed, absolute silence on this," Schiavo said. "I'll get Sergeant Lorenzen up to speed."

"Yes, ma'am," Westin affirmed, then rose from his place at the workstation, took his weapon in hand, and left the room without further prompting.

"What about the searches?" Martin asked once the private was gone.

It wasn't Schiavo who answered. She looked to Mayor Allen, under whose authority any such decision would have to be made. After a moment, he looked to Martin and shook his head.

"Practicality dictates my answer," the town's leader said. "By the time the first search was happening, the whole town would know. Including the traitor."

"They'd ditch or hide any incriminating devices, transmitters, whatever," Schiavo told her husband.

To his credit, Martin didn't protest. But he wasn't pleased.

"We can't just do nothing," he said.

Schiavo looked at him with a thin, almost knowing grin.

"Somehow I think you haven't been."

Martin did not react to his wife's subtle accusation. He simply let that unspoken truth exist between the five of us.

"There is something we do need to do," Schiavo said. "This is also courtesy of Martin. I want to do an inspection and audit of our supplies. We need to see what we have, and what's vulnerable."

"You think this may drag on now?" I asked the captain.

"If they have someone inside, that's a force multiplier. They may feel that they don't need to push. That they can peck away at our preparations. Weaken us without destroying us."

"That's what they want," Mayor Allen said. "It's what they need. A live colony to add to their ledger."

"The term subjugated comes to mind," Elaine said.

"Unified," I corrected her. "Unification is all the rage."

My wife chuckled. It might have been that, by marriage, she felt obligated to laugh at my attempts at humor. I doubted I was that funny. In any case, I liked hearing her express silly joy. I loved the look of her when she was happy, especially in times that worked against that emotion.

The fact was, I simply loved everything about her.

"Tomorrow we start our survey," Schiavo said, looking to her husband next. "And you continue with your project."

Martin smiled and nodded.

"Yes, ma'am."

Twenty

We returned to our house after stopping in to check on Grace and the children. A pair of neighbors had stepped up and were helping her, cooking and tending to Brandon when Grace needed to sleep. It was impossible to say that she was doing fine. But she was alive, and with us. She was home.

I wished I could say the same for my friend.

"Fletch!"

It was our neighbor, Dave Arndt, calling out from the front yard of his house two down from ours. He jogged the short distance and met us at our front gate, holding a sheet of paper in his hand.

"Dave," I said. "What's up?"

"Have you seen this?" he asked, holding the paper out to us.

"What is it?" I asked.

Elaine reached out and took the item. It was a flyer, crudely printed, with a very clear message in the words upon it.

"Residents of Bandon, we are your brothers and sisters in liberty," Elaine read from the paper. "Join us. Cross your borders unarmed and you will be welcomed."

"The Unified Government," I said, reading the final mark upon the page.

"Propaganda," Dave said, irritated bordering on angry.

"Where did you find this?" I asked.

"A lot were found on the routes between town and the checkpoints," he explained.

"They're sneaking inside our perimeter," Elaine said, crumpling the flyer in her hand and tossing it into the street.

"Were these reported?" I asked.

"Sergeant Lorenzen found one, too," Dave said.

"I'm going inside," Elaine said, turning abruptly and leaving me standing with our neighbor.

When the screen door slapped shut, Dave took a step closer to me and spoke in a quieted tone.

"Fletch, some folks are taking this offer seriously."

"It's bait," I told him. "Just one part of their plan to weaken us. They get ten, twenty, thirty people to cross over and we lose people who can stand up and fight."

"People are tired of fighting," Dave reminded me. "Everything since the blight hit has been a fight."

Dave Arndt was a Bandon original. He'd lived here before the world fell apart. A realtor by trade, he now helped repair abandoned houses when he wasn't standing watch with a Remington 12 gauge in hand and a Smith & Wesson .50 caliber hand cannon holstered on his hip. I knew that he didn't share the sentiment that some might be considering, but that didn't lessen the truth behind it. Even in a tight knight community which had overcome so many obstacles, there would be some who would seek a simpler path—even if it was an illusion offered by strangers.

"I just wanted to make sure you knew about this," Dave said, nodding toward the discarded flyer.

"I appreciate you telling me," I said.

He looked past me to the house.

"I'm not sure Elaine does," he said.

I shook his hand and joined Elaine in the house, closing the door and putting my weapons down next to where she had already stowed hers near the closet just off the living room.

"Elaine," I called out quietly, waiting for her to reply from the kitchen, or the bedroom, or the bathroom.

But silence was all I heard.

I looked down the hallway. A soft light spilled out from the bedroom.

"Elaine..."

Again I heard nothing. I might have been worried, even frightened that something had happened in the few moments we'd been apart since returning home. I flashed back to the morning I entered Neil's house and found it empty, abandoned, he and his family gone.

This was not that.

"Hey," I said as I reached the bedroom door.

Elaine stood inside the room, between me and our bed, wearing a sheer half robe and nothing else, the thin garment leaving little to the imagination of what it only vaguely concealed.

"I don't want to think about anything out there," she said. "Not tonight. I just want to think about you, about us. I want everything else to stop for a while."

She stepped toward me then, peeling the robe back and letting it slip to the floor. Her hands reached to my shirt and began undoing the buttons, slowly, one at a time. She leaned forward and planted a soft kiss on my exposed chest, then looked up, into my eyes.

"Make love to me and don't stop," she said.

I reached around her waist and lifted, kissing her as she wrapped her legs around me. I carried her to the bed and eased our bodies down upon it, together.

Twenty One

No!

> *Eric, wake up...*
> *Stop!*
> *Eric...*
> *Don't!*

"Eric!"

My eyes snapped open, Elaine hovering over me. Around her, around us, was familiarity. Curtains. Furniture. Wallpaper.

Our bedroom.

"You were having a nightmare," she said to me.

Sweat drenched me. Soaking the sheet beneath me. Beading cold on my face.

"You're okay," she assured me.

I pulled myself up so that was sitting against our headboard. Elaine put her cool palm against my head and brushed the damp hair from my brow.

"What were you dreaming about?"

There was no trouble recalling the imagery that had tormented me as I slept.

"Neil," I said.

How was it that he had invaded my dreams? This night? After the wondrous time I'd spent with my wife, holding her and knowing her as I'd known no one in my entire life. So close we'd become during our time of passion that I'd truly, ignoring any cliché attached to such an impossibility, felt as though we were one body. One soul.

And yet, after that, after the beauty and the love and the intense physical and emotional connection we'd shared, it was my absent friend who'd come to me in my sleep.

"He was running away from me, toward a cliff," I said, recalling the vivid imagery of my friend, my oldest friend, sprinting toward his death, willingly and with some impossible joy. "And he was smiling. He kept getting closer and I kept screaming for him to stop. But he wouldn't."

Elaine said nothing, her hand softly stroking the side of my face.

"And he ran off the edge of the cliff," I said. "And he was still smiling as he fell."

I fell back against my soaked pillow.

"You can't choose your dreams," Elaine said. "Not the ones while you sleep, at least."

Her words, simple as they were, soothed me, entirely because she was the living embodiment of the statement she'd just made.

"I should be dreaming about you," I said, not embracing her words of wisdom just yet.

"You don't have to," she told me. "I'm right here."

She eased in and kissed me, soft and quick. But time was no determining factor in the effect she had on me. A look. An innocent touch. A calming kiss. All made me want her. I reached out to pull her closer once again.

That was when we heard it.

"Another flyover," she said.

Yes, another one, but this time it was different.

"That's a lot lower," I commented.

We got out of our bed together, slipping into clothes and making our way to the yard behind our house. A fog had rolled in from the Pacific as we slept. Above us and all around us, the thick, cool mist obscured everything, from the unseen craft above to the house we'd exited, just a few yards away.

"It's flying west to east," I said.

Elaine nodded as we tracked the aircraft's progress, heading inland from the ocean. It did sound different than the one we'd been alerted to by Corporal Enderson. At a reduced altitude, yes, but the engine propelling it had a higher timbre. Almost a whine.

This was a jet.

"They have more than one plane," Elaine said, picking up on precisely what I was.

"Yeah," I said.

But that realization only held a paramount place in our thoughts for a moment as the same baffling question arose.

"Why are they flying in this?" Elaine asked, the whitish weather shrouding everything above—and below. "They can't see anything down here."

"The plane could have sensors," I said.

"Maybe," she said. "Maybe."

She wasn't convinced of my suggestion. Neither was I.

"There's nothing we can do, is there?"

I shook my head and stared up toward the aircraft as its sound receded, growing faint as it cruised toward the hills east of town.

"Not right now," I said.

The enemy could fly over us with impunity, it seemed. We weren't protected by any anti-aircraft weaponry. That simply hadn't been a worry. And, even if the garrison had come so equipped, shooting down one of the Unified Government's aircraft might do nothing more than ignite a conflict that was being held in abeyance for the moment.

"That was low."

The voice, clear and familiar, came from behind us. We both turned to see Martin standing at the end of the narrow walkway that ran down the east side of our house.

"Martin, what time is it?" I asked.

The man looked at his watch.

"Three thirty," he said.

Sunrise was several hours off, yet the town's former leader had found it necessary to seek us out. Something was up.

"There was another one," he said. "Another message. The Ranger Signal went down for thirty seconds at the same time as the night before, and in that quiet was a compressed Morse transmission."

"We need to get Westin to decode it," I said.

"Already did," Martin said, holding a small slip of paper out to us. "Micah had books on Morse code, and I watched Westin decompress the message yesterday, so I did it."

Elaine looked to me, then reached out and took the slip of paper.

"Confirm psyops delivery. No supply ship. Defenses scattered."

"Pysops?" Martin wondered aloud after Elaine had finished reciting the decoded report.

"I think I know what that refers to," I said, telling him about the propaganda leaflets found just hours earlier, items that could easily fit within the definition of psychological operations.

"This person inside is important to them," Elaine said.

"They have eyes above us," Martin said, the skies fully quiet again. "And eyes on our very backs."

"Do you have any ideas on who the traitor is?" I asked.

Schiavo had de facto blessed her husband's hunt for the turncoat working with the Unified Government forces beyond the town. I sensed that Martin Jay was taking that role he'd adopted as serious as anything since I'd known him.

"Some," he said.

"You care to share?" I asked.

He shook his head, eyeing both of us with an appraisal that was not born of suspicion, but caution.

"No," he said, then turned and made his way back through the fog.

"Do you have any idea?" Elaine asked me when Martin was gone.

I nodded, the chill of the misty night clinging to my sweaty skin.

"Who's new here and wants to be anywhere else? Who came in on the Navy ship which has disappeared? Who has the medical expertise to manage an epidemic so that we stay sick?"

There was no doubt that I was talking about Commander Clay Genesee, United States Navy.

"That's one hell of an accusation," Elaine said.

"So you disagree?"

"I don't know," she said.

In the distance, the sound of another aircraft, prop driven, began to rise, coming in low like its just departed, speedier cousin, this time from the south. Our thoughts shifted from Genesee as a suspect to the thing cruising north toward us.

"I just wanted one night," Elaine said, her mood souring by a few degrees. "One night with you and none of this."

I pulled her into a loose hug, understanding what she meant. Her night, our night, had been defiled by the reality of the enemy we faced. Mine, also, by my friend's invasion of my dreams.

"We're okay," I told her.

"I know," she said.

We both felt that. Both knew it. Both believed it.

For now.

Twenty Two

The Defense Council visited the animals on the northeast edge of town. Private Sheryl Quincy had been drafted to join us, providing additional firepower to what we carried with us. Only Mayor Allen was unarmed.

"This is too exposed," Schiavo said.

She was right. Cows and goats and various other livestock wandered about the fenced field, smaller animals in more contained pens. In quickly constructed buildings on the far side of the field, chickens spent their days laying eggs, unafraid of foxes or coyotes who would have preyed upon them in the time before the blight. The only predators of note were those on two legs in the woods just beyond the fields.

"The grass is growing out here," Mayor Allen said. "And the processor needs water from the creek to make the supplemental food for them. Particularly the cows."

He pointed to a small shed standing next to the perpetual creek that spilt off from the Coquille River upstream, before rejoining it nearer the northern bridge. Within, powered by an array of solar panels, was the pulp processor which had come in on the *Rushmore*'s first visit to Bandon. Fed by an endless supply of dead wood, harvested from the grey forests that bordered the town, the processor combined the almost chalky remnants of what the blight had wrought with moisture to form, through heat and pressure, edible loaves which the animals could subsist upon until the meadows and fields beyond town became self-sustaining. It was a marvel of technology developed by unknown engineers in a far off place, and it was vital to our continued survival.

It also could not be moved.

"We're secured out here pretty well, captain," Private Quincy told her commander. "I've made sure we have six sentries backing up when the ranchers are on site."

Ranchers...

Two men and one woman from town who'd had experience with livestock. They were wholly responsible for the health and care of every beast, winged or hooved, that we'd been provided with. Along with the 'Farmers', they were key to our ability to provide for ourselves.

We just had to get past this threat for that to matter.

"I check the coops on the far side of the field myself every afternoon while we're out here," Quincy told her commander.

The coop was the closest structure we had to the presumed enemy lines. Having personnel traverse the open terrain to inspect and tend to the chattering mass of fowl could be seen as inviting some response by our unseen adversary.

"Is there any way to at least move the chickens closer to town?" Mayor Allen asked.

"I can ask the ranching crew," Quincy said.

"Do that," Schiavo told the newest member of her unit.

"Will do, ma'am," Quincy said.

Martin walked along the fence, stopping and surveying the herd of cattle. We had thirteen now, plus fourteen milking cows. Thirty goats. Twenty-five pigs. The chickens numbered in the hundreds.

"Maybe we should strengthen this area," Martin suggested. "Put a strongpoint here."

"That might just draw more attention," I said.

"It would be one more fighting position to supply if bullets start flying," Elaine said.

Schiavo nodded at her observation. We'd run into this issue before, when errant movement reports came in. Invariably those residents drafted into service would respond with members of the garrison, bringing their personal weapons and ammunition, the latter of which had raised questions about effective distribution during any prolonged engagement.

"We need to do something about our ammo issue," Schiavo said.

"We have a good supply, ma'am," Quincy told her.

"We do," Schiavo agreed. "But what doesn't belong to the garrison is scattered all over town in a couple hundred houses. People respond ready to fight, but only with what they can carry. Their reserves remain at their houses."

Her concern was valid. Resupplying any force would mean multiple trips to dozens of houses to retrieve individual ammo caches. That would take too many people out of the fight.

"We need to centralize," Elaine said.

"No one's going to like having their ammunition seized," I told the captain.

"Not seized," Schiavo said. "Temporarily repositioned. And not all of it. Only half. We just need to make sure there's a central store of ammo. One collection point, one distribution point."

It made sense. But I knew of several residents who would resist anything that even appeared like an infringement of their rights.

"Some won't go for that," I said. "At all."

"We're not going to confiscate anything," Schiavo said.

"Voluntary?" Mayor Allen checked.

"Recommended," Schiavo clarified.

As long as there was no threat of forcibly taking ammunition, the action might only send a ripple through the community. But ripples, down the road, could build to crushing waves, I feared.

"Ma'am, the garrison armory is jam packed," Quincy told her commander. "There's no room."

The storage room in the town hall, which had once been used to keep banners and decorations for the kind of community events which were common before the blight, could hold no more of the ammunition which had been stuffed in its confines. Schiavo, I knew, had been leery about keeping the supply of armaments and small explosives there in the first place. Too many people came and went. The town hall was the administrative hub of the town. To have so much potentially volatile material there was not wise, in her mind.

"I'd like to get everything but our personal supply out of the town hall," Schiavo said, looking to Mayor Allen. "Can you think of a new location for a town armory?"

The mayor thought for a moment, instinctively glancing back toward the town, only the peak of the church's steeple visible from the distance we'd traveled.

"There's an old auto shop just north of downtown," he said. "I was told the man who owned it left early on after the blight started. During the building inventory it was considered for a food storage location, but it's not the cleanest space."

"We can clean," Schiavo said. "How secure is it?"

"Steel doors," Mayor Allen said. "A big rollup door at the front."

Schiavo looked to Private Quincy.

"When we get back to town, talk to Sgt. Lorenzen about getting this space readied for use as the town armory."

"Yes, ma'am."

The captain looked to me next.

"Fletch, will help Mayor Allen with the request for residents to transfer part of their ammunition to the town armory? People respect you."

"Meaning we need to balance the presence of a dirty politician," Mayor Allen said, smiling.

"We'll be the first to bring half of our supply," Elaine said.

"That's a start," Schiavo said.

Everyone had been heard on the idea. Almost everyone.

"Martin..."

The man turned toward me as I spoke his name.

"A centralized town armory sound good to you?" I asked.

He nodded an acceptance of the idea, but said nothing. He was preoccupied, some thought, or series of thoughts, filling his head right then.

"What is it?" Schiavo asked her husband.

"I was just thinking that this might not be such a good thing we're doing," Martin answered.

"What?" she asked.

He looked to her, to Mayor Allen, then to the dead woods beyond the green fields.

"The town's political and military leaders are standing right here," Martin said. "And we're probably being watched right now."

Eyes shifted slowly to the still dense forest, grey and tall. The enemy could be right there, as Martin suggested. A single sniper of moderate skill could eliminate the town's power structure in a few seconds. It was unlikely they would make such an overt move.

But not impossible.

"We need to get you two out of here," I said.

Martin backed away from the fence and stepped close to his wife.

"Mayor," Elaine said, gently placing her hand on the elderly man's elbow to guide him away from the open space.

"Ma'am," Private Quincy said, bringing her M4 up to a ready position.

"In a minute, private," Schiavo said.

Elaine looked to me and I signaled with a nod to keep moving and get the mayor clear of the area.

"Angela, let's go," Martin urged his wife mildly.

Still she didn't move. She stood her ground, staring out across the fields, past the livestock, to what was unseen in the distant woods.

"Private..."

"Yes, ma'am?"

"You stay sharp when you're out here," Schiavo instructed.

Quincy nodded and kept her eyes on the line of dead trees.

"Will do, ma'am."

With that, Schiavo turned away and began following Elaine and Mayor Allen back toward town. Martin and Quincy trailed her, but I hung back. For just a minute. Scanning the shadows between the trees for any movement. Any sign of presence. I could see none.

But I could feel it.

Twenty Three

Fog shrouded the town the morning the stranger arrived.

He came from the east, overland, ignoring roads and trails as he slipped through the barren woods and was spotted by Sergeant Lorenzen and Private Westin walking along the street two blocks from my house. The patrol escorted the man to the garrison's offices downtown. That was where I first saw him after receiving a call to get there ASAP.

In fact, it wasn't the first time I'd laid eyes on the stranger.

"Who is he?" I asked Schiavo in the center's lobby, glancing past the captain to an interior room beyond a window, the stranger sitting and chatting with Lorenzen.

"You don't know him?" Schiavo asked.

I fixed on the man and shook my head.

"But I've seen him," I told her.

On the table before him lay a weathered Cattleman. The same hat and the same man I'd seen at the cabin in the woods.

"When I was out there," I said. "He was stalking me. Or stalking someone."

"He was carrying that," Schiavo said, gesturing to the corner of the room where we stood.

I looked and saw what she'd directed me to. Leaning against the wall was a Winchester lever gun. The same .30-30 I I'd seen him carrying at the cabin. A small shoulder bag sat next to it on the floor, top flap open after some obvious search.

"He had a bigger pack when I saw him," I told the captain.

"He's travelling light," she said. "Probably has a camp somewhere close by."

He'd cached his supplies and come to town with only the minimal amount he'd need. But need for what?

I looked from the man beyond the one-way glass to Schiavo again, seeing immediately that her attention was focused hard on me, not on the visitor.

"And it was you he was stalking," the captain said. "He asked for you when we brought him in. By name. Said he was looking for Eric Fletcher."

Once more I looked to the stranger. To the man who had been seeking a very specific prey—me.

"He won't tell us anything about himself," Schiavo explained. "There's nothing identifying in any of his possessions. He said you're the only one he wants to speak to about why he's here. Hell, he's talking baseball with Paul in there right now."

It didn't appear that the man was worse for wear. Not wasting away, or even thinned out, as one might expect of a lone stranger appearing out of nowhere. He'd appeared well supplied when I'd seen him at the cabin, and, looking upon him now, from a closer distance, I thought it almost certain that he'd been supported somehow. Supplied by others.

"You think he's part of the group that grabbed me?"

Schiavo thought for a moment, then shook her head.

"I don't see how that makes sense. They take you, release you, then have this guy shadow you until, for some reason, he decides to make contact? To what purpose?"

She was right. I hadn't asked the question with any surety that what I was suggesting had been the case, but the man's appearance here, in search of me, made no more sense than anything we could imagine at the moment. And there would be no understanding until I did what I knew Schiavo had summoned me here to do.

"I'll talk to him," I said.

I removed my belt, the holstered Springfield heavy as I passed my rig to Schiavo. She set it on a desk behind her.

"We'll be right out here," she said. "Watching and listening."

* * *

A moment later I sat where Sergeant Lorenzen had been, facing the stranger. Alone with him.

His hands rested atop the table, folded, a slight smile on his lips as he seemed to study me.

"You're a hard man to find."

"Not really," I said. "Chances are I'm the only Eric Fletcher left alive."

"Could be...Fletch."

He spoke my nickname with such knowing, such familiarity, that I felt a brief chill ripple up between my shoulder blades. The kind of iciness that comes both from within and far away at the same time.

"Yes, I know a lot about you, Fletch. Pretty much everything. Up until the blight, that is."

It was my turn to appraise the man, the stranger. To seek some clear understanding of the who, and the what, and the why of his presence before me. Nothing showed on his face but that thin, almost smug grin.

Then, he glanced away from me, to the window. Light in the room and near darkness beyond the glass mostly hid the space from which I'd come.

"The cavalry is close," he said. "They don't trust me."

"They don't know you," I said, adding almost too quickly. "*I* don't know you."

For a few seconds the stranger just looked at the glass, as if meeting the stares he could not see boring into him from the far side. His gaze then shifted to me and he sat back in his chair, hands slipping easily to his lap. Out of view. I knew he'd been searched before being placed in the room. There would be no weapon on him. But still I was wary. Something about those hands, and not being able to see them, unnerved me.

"Tyler Olin," the stranger said.

"Excuse me?"

"Now you know who I am," he said.

Tyler Olin. If he was being truthful, it offered me no insight into who he really was. The name meant nothing to me.

"Okay, Tyler—"

"Ty," he interrupted. "People call me Ty...Fletch."

Again, he wielded the familiarity like a scalpel, carving shallow cuts in my defensiveness. As much as I hated to admit it, this man, in an inconceivably short time, had found a way to push my buttons simply by uttering a nickname given to me by—

"Neil," I said, and Olin's grin deepened.

"Good old Neil," he said.

"You know him."

"*Knew* him," Olin corrected. "Or I thought I did."

"Who were you to him?" I asked, some fervor to my question. "Friend? Colleague?"

Olin sniffed a quiet chuckle.

"Colleague," he repeated selectively. "That makes us sound so...ordinary. Like bankers, or doctors."

"So you did work with him at the State Department," I said, zeroing in on what had to be a certainty.

As it turned out, I was more wrong than I could have imagined at that moment, or at any in the span of time that I'd known my absent friend.

"I didn't work for the State Department," Olin said.

I stared at him, wary and confused.

"And neither did Neil Moore," Olin added.

The silence I responded with opened the door for him to continue. To set my head spinning with foul revelation.

"Your friend wasn't some low level diplomat lackey," Olin said. "That was his cover."

"What the hell are you talking about?" I pressed the man. "I've known him since we were kids. I know what he did for a living."

The grin was gone. Now Olin managed something that might have been a smile, though it seemed more an involuntary expression that was part bitter, part sweet.

"My wife thought I worked for the Department of Agriculture the entire time we were together," Olin said. "From the day I first asked her out until the moment she took her last breaths in my arms."

He stopped there for a moment. Seizing on memories from old, dark places, it seemed. When his attention refocused on me there was no hint of a smile.

"Your friend and I both worked for the CIA," Olin said.

Twenty Four

My world didn't come crashing down around me. Just a portion of what had been, that place held only in memory, crumbling now, beliefs peeling away, like a building whose foundation had just been compromised.

"Yes," Olin said, answering the doubt my slack silence expressed. "The Central Intelligence Agency."

I shook my head, slowly. There might have been dispute in the gesture. Or just denial.

"You don't have to believe me, but that won't change the reality of what I just told you."

"The CIA," I said. "The CIA?"

"Langley," Olin said, with just a hint of nostalgia. "The Company. Whatever you want to call it. Den of spies. Black Ops Central. All of those things are true and false."

Black is white. White is black.

Neil's parting words came to me without warning, the flash of memory bursting like a thunderbolt.

Neil...

For a moment I thought of my friend. Just thought of him. Of our simple times. I pictured his dumb smile. Imagined his almost impish laugh. That was how I remembered Neil Moore.

The Neil Moore *I* knew.

"This makes no sense," I said, coming up from the recollections.

"Doesn't have to," Olin said.

I fixed on the man now. As calm and knowing as his gaze had regarded me, mine now bore at him with the opposite intensity.

"So you're some master spy, I guess," I challenged Olin.

The clumsy jab bothered him not at all.

"You can insult me, but your friend is what he was, and what he still is."

What he still is...

"Are you saying he's...performing some mission? That his leaving us was planned?"

At that instant, if only for a few seconds, the tables turned, with Olin in the dark without any apparent way to throw light upon what he'd been tripped up by.

"What do you mean 'leave'?"

I could have easily withheld information, which he clearly was doing, maintaining as much of a one-way flow of information as possible. But I needed to know more. I needed to know what he knew. For my own benefit, and, maybe, for everyone else's as well.

"A stealth helicopter came down one day and took him and his family away," I said.

"Family?"

I explained about Grace, and Krista, and the child that they would have had by now, but did not reveal details about the baby, wanting to hold close the fact that my friend's family had since returned. I shared the tale of how Neil had reached my refuge north of Whitefish, our journey together continuing from there in search of Eagle One. Then to our trek across the wasteland to find the salvation in a greenhouse. And on to our mission north to Skagway, and then south again to our adopted home in Bandon.

"That explains a few things," Olin said as he processed what I'd just shared.

"To you, maybe," I told him. "So what the hell is he doing? Why did he leave?"

Olin considered the question for a moment. Then he, too, seemed to summon some memory, a quick glint flashing in his gaze. He smiled at me.

"I don't know what he's doing," Olin said. "I know what he was supposed to do before he took off and joined up with you."

In that statement I found part of an answer to the question that had nagged since I'd first laid eyes on the stranger by the cabin in the dead woods.

"You were looking for me to find him."

Olin might have nodded. Or his head might have just shifted as he crafted a response. His momentary hesitation, though, was all the confirmation I needed to my query.

"Why are you looking for him?"

The man, the spy, didn't answer.

"Why are you looking for him?" I repeated.

"You won't understand," Olin told me.

"I'm a fairly bright guy."

"Intelligence has nothing to do with it," he said. "Some things people just won't accept."

"Try me."

Olin sized me up for a moment. Not in any physical sense, but in the way I looked at him. My seriousness. It seemed as though he was looking inside me.

"I'm looking for him because he called out to me," Olin said.

"Do you want to try being a little less vague?"

Olin drew a shallow breath. His gaze dipped to the tabletop.

"Ranger," he said.

Ranger. Ranger. Ranger.

He looked up after a moment.

"Exactly what you're hearing on the radio," he said. "What anyone with functioning com system is hearing."

"What does Ranger mean?"

Olin hesitated. If what he had said about himself was true, then revealing information was far from second nature to him. The exact opposite, in fact, might very well be the only mode of operation he knew how to function within.

Even for him, though, the realization that times had changed, inexorably and forever, could not be ignored.

"It was our code word," Olin said. "Whenever we were on missions. It had a specific meaning."

"And what meaning was that?"

"Danger," Olin answered.

"So it was a warning?" I pressed. "And you think it still is?"

To these simple questions, Olin offered no response. No direct response, that is.

"The security of a secret increases exponentially as the number of people who know it approaches zero," he said.

In his own way, Olin was telling me to tread no more on that path of questioning.

"You want me, want *us*, to believe that the message he's repeating is meant for you? Just for you?"

Olin sat in silence for a moment, glancing once or twice to the darkened window and the people he knew to be beyond the reflective glass.

"I thought you could help me," Olin said. "Neil's movements were traced to your Montana place, then here with the transmissions from the plane you flew in."

"All while the world was falling apart you people and your technical wizards were tracking him," I said. "Tracking us."

"To a dead end, it seems," Olin said, as if admitting defeat.

He might be doing so, but I was not. I wanted more. I needed more if I was going to fill in the blank spots of my understanding. But snippets of some previously impossible possibility were beginning to form in my thoughts.

"He was on a mission before this all started, wasn't he?"

Olin didn't satisfy me with a reply.

"You both were," I said, letting my supposition encompass him now.

The man's silence lingered. As it did, my frustration simmered.

"What was your mission?" I asked, some force now in my tone and manner. "The last thing that you did? That he did?"

"You think it's that easy?" Olin challenged me. "You just say pretty please and I violate an oath I took?"

"I haven't said pretty please," I told the man. "And I'm not going to."

Olin eased back in his chair, relaxing it seemed. Maybe he felt himself freed of the restraints his vocation had placed upon him. Or, possibly, he suspected that I wasn't up to the task of extracting answers from one who was unwilling.

He was wrong about the latter, if that was his estimation. I'd crossed my own lines of morality in Skagway to pry what was needed from a Russian infiltrator. That bit of me, which I'd long ago thought rock solid, had turned malleable. Our grip on existence was so tenuous that extreme measures, however ugly, were sometimes necessary. I could live with that, even if it made me less of the man I'd always prided myself in being.

Here, though, I doubted any violent coercion would be necessary.

"Look, you're already keeping secrets," I told Olin. "You won't answer some questions, so answer this one. The world your missions were carried out in is gone. The men who sent you on it are probably turning to dust already."

"The woman," Olin said.

"What?"

"A woman sent us on our last mission," he corrected me. "Allison Milbank. And she is dead. I know that because my friend, your friend, he killed her before he headed off west to Montana."

So, according to this man, my friend was not only a spy, but a murderer.

"Neil Moore is not who you think he is," Olin said. "He never has been."

I leaned forward, elbows on the table.

"What was the mission you two were on?"

Olin's body tilted forward, his own forearms on the table now, the distance between us narrowed to almost nothing.

"We were sent to get samples of the biological agents," Olin said. "The blight and its cousin."

"What do you mean? What cousin?"

The man smiled at me and sat back again, appraising me as one might a child who'd just asked the most precious, obvious question.

"Please tell me you don't think that dead plants were the intent of this," Olin said.

"Dead plants have done a number on the neighborhood, if you haven't noticed."

"But there are still neighbors," Olin reminded me, an ominous suggestion in his words.

For an instant I flashed back to Ben. Colonel Ben Michaels. He'd said something, about the Legionnaire officer and the possibility that something more than the blight had been developed by the Iraqi scientist he'd coopted.

"Borgier *did* have something else," I said.

Olin reacted visibly as I spoke that name.

"Yeah," I said, realizing I'd played a card he didn't imagine in my hands. "Also known as Gray Jensen. An American who was an officer in the French Foreign Legion in Iraq during Desert Storm."

"So Neil did tell you."

"No," I said. "He didn't."

I shared the story of our encounter with Michaels, an Air Force officer on his own desperate mission. And of our escape through a hell fire unleashed upon a swath of Wyoming prairie.

Olin absorbed what I'd just told him and shook his head.

"Madness," he said.

"There's a lot of that going around," I agreed with him.

"Neil knew all this," Olin said. "He knew it long before your colonel friend told his tale."

In another time, in the world as it was, I would have denied the man's statement any quarter in my thoughts. But my friend had held secrets. I knew this. His leaving was for reasons I still did not understand. If he was part of our nation's intelligence apparatus, as unbelievable as that might have seemed to me, then accepting that he'd known all along what Ben Michaels had told us would not be beyond the possible.

"What else did Borgier have?" I pressed, returning to the line of inquiry which mattered most at the moment. "I deserve to know. We all deserve to know."

I wasn't certain if the manner in which I'd implored Olin for an answer had worked, or if he'd already decided the secret was no longer worth keeping. Whichever it was, he held nothing back when he began to speak.

"Your friend and I were tasked with obtaining pure samples of what Borgier had gotten his hands on. BA Four Eleven and BA Four Twelve."

"What does that mean? Those acronyms?"

"BA," Olin repeated. "Biological Agent. Four Eleven was the blight."

"And Four Twelve?"

He hesitated, a half cough, half chuckle filling the void of explanation.

"What do you think?" he asked me.

He knew what I thought. The possibility had been hinted at by both of us earlier in our exchange. BA 412 would be an agent which would affect humans. A blight for our species.

"How bad?"

"If you bury yourself in a salt mine for fifty years while everyone else is dying up top, not so bad," Olin said. "But if you're up top..."

Find a hole and bury yourself...

That had been among Neil's final directives to me. His final warnings. Was this what he'd been referring to? This cousin of the blight and the ravages it might bring to Bandon? To all of us?

"There's no immunity? No vaccine?"

Olin shrugged and gave a half shake of his head at the likelihood of anything I'd suggested.

"Who knows? Maybe there's some Yak herder in Siberia whose genetic makeup will leave him as the loneliest man on earth. Except his Yaks are all dead, so he's already dead."

I thought on this revelation for a moment. It was no more fantastical than the blight would have been branded a few years before it ravaged the planet. Mother Nature, with a little help from a man of science, had opened her bag of tricks on the whole of humanity. But, if Olin was to be believed, one trick still remained to be used.

"So you and Neil were trying to get samples of the blight and this four-twelve thing so the government could work on a cure," I said.

Olin's silence was as far from a confirming reaction as I could have imagined.

"What did you do?"

He took a moment to craft his thoughts. To make them palatable. As it turned out, that was not possible.

"I was assigned to get an original sample of Four Eleven," Olin said.

"The blight."

"Right. Neil was attached to a SEAL team that raided a location in the Caribbean where a supply of Four Twelve was supposed to exist."

"So he got one part of this, and you got the other."

"I have no idea what he got," Olin said.

"What do you mean?"

"He delivered his sample to a military lab, and then he split. A few days later the virologists there determined that what Neil had handed over wasn't anything resembling a viral agent."

"What do you mean?"

"It was colored water with some dissolved organic compounds," Olin explained. "Our director, Allison, personally went out to his farm to find out what went wrong. She was thinking that the team had grabbed some other sample by mistake. The next day when our operators raided the place they found his father, offed by his own hand, and Allison Milbank dead with two bullets in her head."

"Why would he kill her?" I asked.

"What, you think your old friend isn't capable of cold blooded murder?"

I flashed back to the sight of Neil executing the trio of cannibals we'd come across near my Montana refuge. In that, as disturbing as it was, I'd seen a righteousness. A violent and necessary response to a reprehensible new reality.

But to kill a woman, a superior. There must have been a reason. At least one that he could live with.

"Why would he kill her?" I repeated.

"Fear," Olin said, holding nothing back on this subject. "It was death. Like nothing the world had seen. We had intelligence that the Iraqi scientist had tested it on an isolated village. Everyone was dead within days of one resident being infected. The whole place was incinerated after the test. Neil was truly scared of what the government might do with four-twelve."

"Why would he think the government would use it?"

Once again, Olin was quiet, the silence telling.

"He had reason to think they'd use it," I said.

"You can't understand what that time was like there, in Washington," Olin said. "With this slow motion death machine rolling toward the US, there were power grabs. Internal fights. Factions struggling for the little influence they knew would remain after all hell broke loose. The only way to get a handle on it was to get some control."

"Control?"

Olin nodded.

"Control of what?"

"Of when the blight would explode here," he said.

For the briefest instant I didn't comprehend the subtlety of what he was saying. The simplicity. And then, like a bright light flashing once in a dark room, I saw it. I understood.

"We released the blight before it actually got here? In the States?"

Olin cleared his throat. If there had been a pitcher of water and a glass before him, as there might have been at any congressional hearing men like him, and his superiors, were once subject to, I expected he would have taken a long, slow drink to compose his thoughts.

"There was a belief that remnants of society would survive a sudden collapse better than one that crept along," he explained, though the conviction he held in his own words seemed dubious. "Less time for rioting, the breakdown of order."

"How'd that work out?" I challenged the man.

"Doesn't really matter," Olin fired back. "By the time the worst of the blight was taking hold, the government was

fracturing. There were competing orders. Mini coups.
Assassinations. You lined up with who you believed in, or
who you believed could keep you alive."

"And who did you throw in with?"

Olin let out a breathy, brief chuckle.

"I stayed with the red white and blue. The home team.
The masters who'd engineered the disaster."

"And Neil went with the Unified Government," I said.

I'd surprised Olin again, knowing something he'd
suspected I had been in the dark about. Grace had
enlightened me, had enlightened all of us, upon her return,
to the extent she was able.

"How do you know about that?" Olin asked. "He
wouldn't tell you that. Not if he kept everything else from
you."

It was my turn to withhold, and after a few seconds of
silence on my end, Olin chose not to press the question any
further.

"That name came later," Olin said. "But the players
now were the players then. And your friend, my friend, he
chose to walk the path with them. He thought that my side,
which used to be our side, might already have Four Twelve,
and he couldn't accept that. Not after realizing his
paymasters had advanced the timetable of the blight
reaching the U.S."

"So what did he do with BA Four Twelve?"

Olin's face shrugged.

"The only man I know who can answer that is Neil
Moore," he said.

"But you have a suspicion."

"I'm trained to be suspicious," Olin said.

"You think he took it to the Unified Government," I
said.

To my surprise, Olin shook his head at that suggestion.

"I think he planned to," Olin said. "To counter what he thought Uncle Sam already had. A sort of germ equivalent of mutually assured destruction."

MAD. It had been the cornerstone of deterrence in the nuclear age. Using a weapon of such immense destructive power on a similarly armed enemy would bring an equally devastating retaliatory strike. That such a mentality and strategy survived into this new age did not surprise me. That my friend Neil was somehow involved in such machinations did.

"I believe he intended to go all in with the other side," Olin explained. "Until he saw that they were no different than our side."

Their side. Our side. Every side. I'd always been a proud and loyal American, but knowing just what that would entail in a world just inching out of the ravages of the blight was almost impossible to know.

"I think he brought it with him," Olin said without any prompting from me.

"Here?"

Olin shrugged a 'why not?'

"Or he cached it somewhere along the way," Olin theorized. "Maybe in one of those empty supply lockers that are sprouted like daisies all across the country."

The lockers, filled mainly with food, had been intended for the elite to use in escaping chaos as the blight exploded. But with its rapid spread, the 'how' of which was no longer a mystery, the plant killing organism had sent the country spinning out of control. Many of the buried lockers remained untouched, and several had sustained our expedition on its way to and from Cheyenne.

"Or at your Montana place," Olin said.

"If it was there, it went up in smoke."

Olin thought for a moment, then shook his head slowly as he eyed me.

"No, he wouldn't have taken it to you. Or here. He wouldn't have risked involving you...or infecting you."

It was my turn to study the man with a look. A long look. As my attention dragged on, Olin began to smile.

"You're wondering if I'm really here because Neil signaled me, or if I'm now on the hunt for Four Twelve."

"It's not a stretch to wonder," I said.

Olin chuckled and shook his head.

"Mass murder isn't my game, Fletch."

"Don't call me that," I said. "You haven't earned that right."

"Whatever you say," Olin agreed, then glanced at the reflective window behind me again. "Since the reason I came isn't actually here, I think I'd like to be on my way."

I waited for a moment, trying to imagine anything more of use I could get from the man. But to do that I would have to know what to ask. Olin himself was a mystery, and lived in a world of lying truths. Any further discussion with him would likely be circular in nature, and a waste of breath.

Maybe. Or maybe not.

"Tell me one thing, Ty."

"What's that, Eric?"

"We seem to be surrounded here, yet you made it through the Unified Government's lines."

"Yes, I did."

"How'd you do that, Ty?"

Olin slid his chair back from the table and stood now, that smug smile back in all its maddening glory.

"Maybe I'm just that good."

* * *

After a quick discussion with Schiavo while Olin remained in the interview room, the man joined us in the outer office and was given his gear and weapons. Lorenzen stood behind the man, his presence impossible to ignore.

"A shadow indoors," Olin said. "I feel special."

"I'll drop you back at the checkpoint," the sergeant informed our visitor.

Olin nodded and headed for the exit.

"Olin," I said.

He stopped at the open front door and looked back to Schiavo and me.

"How did you track me?" I asked. "Out there. By the cabin."

He smiled and slung his lever gun on one shoulder, small bag hanging on the other.

"I didn't," he said. "Blind luck. I was walking up that road when I came across signs of travel. It just happened to be you."

If what he was saying was true it was...

"Incredible," Olin said. "I know. Almost like it was meant to happen."

"You're welcome to stay in town," Schiavo said.

Olin shook his head politely at the offer.

"No, this isn't my place," he said, looking to me. "If he comes back, I'll be close by. You make sure he knows that."

"You think he'll want to see you?" I asked.

"He called out to me," Olin answered. "He's already made his choice."

Then he walked out. Sgt. Lorenzen trailed him to the Humvee which would transport him to the edge of town. From there, I suspected, he would disappear, as simply as he'd appeared.

"What do you think?" I asked the captain.

Schiavo walked to the door and held it open, watching the Humvee drive off.

"I think your friend's life is catching up with him," she said. "And we might be the ones who pay for it."

Twenty Five

Elaine took Grace and the children to our house while I searched for what Neil might have hidden in theirs.

After hearing what Olin had revealed, there was the thought that what had been put in me, and what still remained in Grace, Krista, and Brandon, might be some protection against the BA 412 virus. Through love for his family and some loyalty to me it was possible he'd leveraged his Unified Government brethren to have us protected should the weapon be released.

But released by whom?

"Fletch."

I looked back through the open door to where Martin stood on the porch. Beyond him, Enderson and Quincy stood where the walkway met the sidewalk, keeping any curious neighbors moving. If these minimal procedures could be considered effective against what Olin had described, we were fooling ourselves.

"Yeah?"

"Angela thinks this is necessary," Martin told me.

"But you don't," I said.

"No."

"Neither do I," I agreed with him. "Olin was right—he wouldn't have kept something that dangerous here with his family."

"And if he didn't take it with him to the Unified Government..."

What Martin was suggesting was just a small nightmare scenario amongst many.

"It could be anywhere between here and his camp in Virginia," I said.

His 'camp'. Rolling acres of farmland. My friend's refuge, not unlike what I'd manage to maintain north of Whitefish. If the truth of the stories both Neil and Olin had told were to be meshed, it was the place where Neil had killed his CIA controller, and where his father had left the world by his own hand. Once a bucolic getaway, it became a place of death.

"I'm sure Olin's friends turned that place over and ran it through a sieve," Martin said. "Which only leaves the whole country as a place where he could have hidden it. If he hid it at all."

I scanned the living room, giving cursory attention to the myriad of places where one might stash something small. Behind me, Martin entered. My gaze shifted quickly to his closer presence.

"It's not here, Fletch," Martin said. "We're not going to be infected."

I faced the man and shook my head, though not in disagreement with his pronouncement.

"I just don't get this, Martin. They put something in me, something in Grace and the kids, presumably to protect us, but from what?"

Once more I looked to the room, and to the hallway, and the adjacent spaces. Out the side windows. Through the front door. I was trying to make all the pieces fit. Every sliver of information from every source.

"Neil leaves, takes his family, has me snatched, sends his family back. Then some old spy buddy of his shows up looking for him because the Ranger Signal is some code word only the two of them know."

"I'm not sure you're ever going to understand why it happened," Martin said.

"But it should," I said, facing Martin again. "Something that...monumental in our lives should make absolute sense. So why doesn't it? Why did Neil do it all in this cloak and dagger style that matches a life I knew nothing about."

"Olin could be half right," Martin said. "Or half wrong, actually."

I didn't follow where he was going with this line of reason. Martin stepped inside now, just a few feet past the threshold. He seemed uncomfortable in the space. Not because of any fear, but, I suspected, for a reason similar to that which affected me. The house, the home, felt tainted. Even with Grace and the children returned, some stain remained on the place. A stain that was the shadow of my friend's absence.

"What if the Unified Government already has Four Twelve," Martin suggested. "And they threatened Neil to get back with the program or they'd use it on Bandon. On us."

Black is white... White is black...

That admonition from my friend as he departed flashed in my thoughts yet again. That world of shifting contrast was a place where what Martin was proposing could easily exist.

But did that make it true? Or even plausible?

"Why would they need him at all, then?" I asked.

"Maybe he's more important to them, to their plans, than even Olin knew," Martin said.

"Or that he told us," I said.

Olin was a creature of deception. Entire portions of his life were based upon people accepting lies he told about himself, or about others. And a lie did not have to be told to have impact. Some truth simply needed to be withheld.

Like some further truth about my friend.

"That's just another question, Martin."

"I said you may never understand," he reminded me.

I nodded. To him. To myself. That the one reality about all this was I might never know the truth, the whole truth, about the man who'd been my best, my closest friend, sickened me. The place I stood right then sickened me. All reminders of the man sickened me.

But some things in the home could not elicit such a feeling of revulsion.

"What are you doing?" Martin asked.

I'd bent and picked something up from the coffee table near the couch. Colorful pencils and markers were scattered about, all having been used to craft what lay within what I held.

Krista's drawing book.

"I'm surprised she left the house without it," I said, smiling as I flipped it open and paged through the silly, wonderful drawings. "She's been pouring herself into this. Everyone who's stopped in has said this is all she does. Draw."

"Art can be therapy," Martin said.

I was glad the child had that. Some way to help her process all that had occurred. We had no such outlet. We had only the reality that we faced, out there, ill-defined and ominous all at once.

"We have to do something, Martin," I said, placing the book back precisely where it had rested.

"We don't have many moves to make," he said. "If any."

I hated this. Hated the not knowing, and the not doing. I was no military man. No soldier. I'd picked up my fighting ability out of necessity in the new world. Conflict had been thrust upon me, and I'd learned to give as good as I got. So it burned me to just wait. To do what soldiers were taught not to do—be a stationary target.

"We have to wait, Fletch. We have to trust Angela and get everything we can in order for whatever might come."

"You know what's strange about all this?" I asked.

"What?"

I gave the space a long look, that sickening feeling rising again.

"Neil would know what to do," I said.

Twenty Six

There were more flyovers. Louder. Lower. Crisscrossing the town, from north to south, west to east. Always at night. On one such crossing, with clear skies above, Corporal Enderson was able to snap a grainy image through the night vision binoculars.

Elaine and I stood with the captain and Mayor Allen in the garrison's office, the image downloaded onto a laptop screen. Its shape was unmistakable, long, slender wings and a bulbous, stubby nose where a cockpit should be.

"Drone," Schiavo said.

"Observing us," I said.

Schiavo's silence indicated that she wasn't convinced.

"What's to observe?" she asked. "The number of flights seem excessive for reconnaissance."

Elaine reached out and put a single finger to the image, directing her attention to something below the wing. In the distorted picture it appeared little more than a black smudge, but that it was there at all is what mattered.

"Missile?" Elaine asked.

The deadly ability of drones armed with Hellfire missiles had been made plain through news reports and declassified footage from past battles in the Middle East and elsewhere. It was possible that we were facing the same threat here.

"It could be waiting for a target of opportunity," I said.

"Or it could just be a message," Mayor Allen suggested. "I assume they know we might have the ability to see it."

"A demonstration of their airpower?" Elaine wondered.

It could be that. Or what I'd thought. Or something else altogether.

"Where is Martin?" Mayor Allen asked, the question interrupting the matter of the moment. "He got the message about this, yes?"

The question was posed to Schiavo. His wife. And the soon to be mother of his child.

"He said he had something to take care of," she said.

His project. The hunt for the traitor. That was what she wasn't speaking of with any openness, but which those of us on the Defense Council understood to be taking much of his time. Mayor Allen, too, remembered as soon as Schiavo's oblique reply was given.

"Of course," the mayor said.

"So the aircraft don't have pilots," Elaine said.

"Not aboard them," Schiavo said.

"The Unified Government forces are showing an impressive level of sophistication," Mayor Allen commented.

Schiavo nodded her head as she stared at the photo on the screen. The gesture continuing as some spark seemed to rise in her gaze.

"David and Goliath," the captain said, smiling now as she looked to us.

"We're David," I said, anticipating the reference she was making, even without understanding how it applied to us in any useful way.

"Yes," she said. "And they're Goliath."

She closed the laptop screen.

"And tonight, we're going to throw some stones."

* * *

Every checkpoint was at double strength by sundown. Every patrol had three times as many shooters as the night before. Two reserve groups, each twenty strong, waited in the northern and southern parts of town, ready to react in any direction should the need arise. Should there be any reaction to what we were about to do.

And at the center of town I stood with Lorenzen, Quincy, and Westin, our weapons held low as we waited. And listened. A few yards away, Schiavo stood with Corporal Enderson, wired phone in her hand, his eyes scanning the night sky above through the bulky night vision binoculars.

"You're our David," Lorenzen told Westin.

The communications specialist, holding a SAW, or squad automatic weapon, at the ready, nodded. A boxy magazine hung below the light machinegun, a hundred rounds within to feed the weapon. I couldn't see inside, but I knew that every bullet was red-tipped. There for a specific purpose.

And that purpose was about to play out.

The phone in Schiavo's hand, connected to a nearby house by a seventy foot cord, rang.

"Go," the captain said into the handset, listening for a moment before hanging up. "Sounds coming from the east, moving west."

Enderson was first to shift his position, bringing the binoculars up to scan the eastern sky as the rest of us, the fire team, readjusted to face the same direction.

"I've got it," Enderson reported, dialing in on the target spotted through the night vision optics. "About five hundred feet altitude. Prop driven. I see weapons beneath the wings."

Westin glanced at our spotter to get a general idea of the unseen drone's place in the sky, then brought his SAW up to match and track the anticipated movement. The sound was reaching us now, a fast whine, engine spinning a propeller as it chopped through the cool air, pushing the craft toward us. Closer. Louder. Closer.

"Five hundred yards," Enderson reported.

Westin steadied his aim, pulling the SAW's bulk tight against his upper body. The rest of us brought our weapons up, matching Westin's aim. If this didn't work, we'd be doing nothing more than taking a shot in the dark. Hundreds of shots in the dark. But if it did work, it would be our first blow against the forces arrayed around us.

"Ready," Enderson said, the angle of his binoculars putting the drone about to pass just to our south. "FIRE!"

Without hesitation, Westin opened up, firing long bursts of tracer rounds which dragged a streak of fire into the sky.

"Up and to the right!" Enderson shouted, giving firing directions, trying to guide the stream of glowing rounds to an imaginary intersection in the sky.

As Westin followed the directions, the intersection was imaginary no more.

"Hit!" Enderson reported.

In the sky above and just to our south, the effect was unmistakable. The red hot tracers had impacted some part of the drone's airframe, sending a starburst of sparks into the night, marking its position as it trailed a thin stream of fire behind.

"Open fire!" Lorenzen ordered.

He and Quincy and I squeezed our triggers almost simultaneously, aiming just ahead of the damaged drone, firing as Westin kept up a stream of tracers from his SAW.

"Good hits!" Enderson reported.

We maintained our rate of fire, on full automatic, changing magazines once. Halfway through that second volley we saw a satisfying bloom in the sky, the trail of fire from the drone increasing and the path of its flight altering severely.

"Going down," Enderson said, lowering the binoculars.

We ceased fire, our barrels steaming. High fives were exchanged for a mission expertly executed. Instinctively I looked for Elaine, realizing after a moment that she wasn't with me. Wasn't within half a mile, actually. She'd gone to wait with Grace and the children as our attempt to bring down one of the Unified Government's drones took place, there to assure them that the fire they were hearing was planned and not some attack.

"That had to come down near the coast," Schiavo said.

"If not in the ocean," Lorenzen said. "Let's go confirm the kill."

Schiavo looked to Quincy.

"Bring the Humvee up," she said. "Private Westin, get back to com and monitor reports from the checkpoints. Corporal Enderson..."

Schiavo hesitated there, a sudden cough interrupting her orders. The congestion cleared after a few seconds and she continued.

"Tell the fire crew to stand down."

The town's small fire department had been put on alert, prepared to respond if a successful shoot down had resulted in a crash and fire amongst the town's widely scattered structures. As it appeared, though, any impact with the ground was beyond inhabited spaces.

"Fletch, you coming?"

Schiavo's invitation was not unexpected, and I didn't hesitate to accept. I climbed in the back seat of the Humvee as it pulled up, Lorenzen next to me and the captain up front with Private Quincy.

"Get us there, private."

"Yes, ma'am."

* * *

Five minutes later, guided by a glow to the west seeming to emanate near the coast road, we found what we'd come looking for, the wreckage ablaze on the sand, just shy of the lapping waters of the Pacific.

"Private Quincy, keep people back," Schiavo ordered, noting a half dozen curious residents making their way toward the crash site.

Quincy headed off from where she'd stopped the Humvee on the beach and prevented those approaching from coming any nearer.

"It came apart," Sergeant Lorenzen reported, his flashlight sweeping the shore and lighting up various pieces of debris. "Midair."

I looked to the spot of the largest fire, the remnants of the drone's fuselage crumpled and burning there, maybe ten yards from the water. Nearby were smaller blazes, pieces of wire and electronics smoldering. Amongst all these were chunks of the aircraft, some scorched, but most seeming to have been ripped from the airframe by a final, violent explosion as it neared impact with the ground.

"Wing," Lorenzen reported, focusing his flashlight beam on the long, slender piece of debris. "Uh, Cap..."

Schiavo hadn't said a word since dispatching Quincy to handle crowd control. She'd just walked amongst the bits of aircraft parts scattered along the shore, not even bothering to use her own flashlight. But at her sergeant's call she finally activated its beam and joined him where he stood. I followed her a second later.

"That's not any Hellfire missile," Lorenzen said, lighting up what was still affixed to the underside of the wing, although bent and cracked.

"What is that?" Schiavo asked.

I approached the sliver of wing and used my own light to examine the slender cylinder affixed to what had been its underside. Its front end, near the leading edge of the wing, was bulbous, and had been a perfect half sphere before the crash deformed it. At its rear, the shape tapered to almost a teardrop configuration, with a slender tube extending from it, some mechanism wired to it as if it were a...

"A valve," I said, realizing what I was looking at.

"What?" Schiavo asked, seeking clarification.

I stood and took a step back, away from the wreckage. Lorenzen noted my sudden wariness.

"Fletch, what is it?"

I looked to the sergeant, and then to the captain.

"That's a nozzle," I said, centering my light on the valve and its actuator. "This whole thing is a spray tank."

Schiavo stifled another cough that came without warning, looking to her hand as she brought it away from her mouth.

"They haven't been watching us," she said.

I shook my head in agreement.

"They've been dosing us from the air," I said.

Twenty Seven

It started without anyone realizing that it had even begun.

Sniffles were the initial complaint, though most had dismissed them. Then coughing, much as had happened for Schiavo. When the fevers began, mid-grade, hardly anything over 101, Commander Genesee sounded the warning that the biological attack we'd expected, feared, and confirmed by downing the drone two days earlier, had taken hold.

"We have thirty cases now," Genesee told the assembled defense council. "Including yours truly."

The man looked like death on two feet, skin pale and brow glistening. Elaine had begun to exhibit symptoms the night before, stuffy nose and an infrequent cough keeping her from a restful sleep. When I'd tried to feel her forehead just before we'd entered the town hall she'd gently blocked my hand, signaling with avoidance that her temperature was on the rise.

"I expect we'll see double that in a couple days," Genesee said. "And another doubling a few days beyond that. And so on."

"Until everyone is sick," Schiavo said.

Genesee nodded. But it was not the gentle bob of his flushed face that drew my attention. His right hand, resting on the table where he sat, tapped nervously, absently upon the wooden top. Soft little pecks, quick and slow, the cadence familiar.

Too familiar.

And I was not the only one noticing. Seated across from me, on the same side of the table as Genesee, Martin's gaze was angled hard left, fixed very plainly on the doctor's softly drumming fingers.

"There haven't been any overflights since we downed their drone," I said.

"They don't need any more flights," Mayor Allen explained. "They've introduced enough virus already. The rest will be spread person to person."

"How bad is this going to get?" Elaine asked through thick sniffles.

"No way to know," Genesee said. "Some may have few if any symptoms. Most, I believe, will be flat on their back by a certain point."

"They'll be incapable of participating in any defense," Mayor Allen said.

"Then the Unified Government forces just walk in and take us," Schiavo said. "Without much of a fight."

"They have to have some treatment for the virus," Genesee theorized. "Something to bring people back to health. Otherwise they'd just be taking a town of dead people."

At the head of the table, Mayor Allen agreed. He'd not yet been affected by the sickness. His decades around sick people, perhaps, had granted him some tiny modicum of resistance, though expecting anything such as that to last, if it existed at all, was foolish.

"We have to find some way to weather this outbreak," Martin said.

"Palliative care is all we can do," Genesee said, looking directly to Schiavo next. "Without undertaking more drastic measures."

Her refusal to allow any removal of the implants still inside Grace, Krista, and Brandon, had been based upon a moral code which, to me, seemed unwavering.

"We keep people hydrated," Mayor Allen said, laying out a course of treatment. "That and rest. The sickest we'll monitor either in the clinic, or on home visits."

Genesee's fingers stilled atop the table and he regarded both Schiavo and his predecessor with a look of plain disagreement, shaking his head as he stood.

"Just so you know, people are going to die from this," the Navy doctor said. "They will die. And we could stop that, maybe, if we introduce a diluted vaccine. The effects could be lessened."

"We've already discussed this," Schiavo reminded him, her reddened eyes fixed on the man as she fought to suppress still another cough.

Genesee looked away, just standing there for a moment, trying to summon some argument, it seemed. But after a few seconds he simply turned and made his way along the conference table's long edge and through the door past its end, leaving us, the Defense Council, to deal with the issue on our own.

"Would that work?" Elaine asked, repeating the question she'd raised when Genesee first proposed his idea after examining Grace and the children upon their return.

We looked to Mayor Allen, who was clearly stepping back into his role as Doc Allen during this medical crisis.

"It could work," the mayor said, his gaze fixing on Schiavo. "But I agree with the captain. Some things just aren't right."

I didn't disagree with her decision, or the mayor's concurrence. The possibility of a diluted vaccine did, however, leave me wishing that what had been implanted in me was still in place so I could volunteer its removal and use.

"So we treat the symptoms," Martin said. "Keep people comfortable."

"Yes," Mayor Allen confirmed.

"Our fighting ranks are going to suffer," I said, directing the appraisal at the one person I knew had already come to that conclusion.

"We do the best with what we have," Schiavo said, stopping when a wet coughing fit prevented any further discussion for the day.

* * *

"Genesee," I said, cornering Martin outside as the others drifted away from the town hall.

"What about him?"

"You saw the same thing I did," I reminded the self-appointed spy hunter. "The way he was tapping the table."

"Maybe it was just tapping."

"There was a rhythm to it," I said. "Like he's used to doing that."

"Fletch, let me handle this," Martin chided me mildly. "I told you early on that I was afraid of a witch hunt, so let's you and me not start our own."

I understood where the man was coming from, but that didn't negate the oddities which cast suspicions on the man.

"And let's not forget," Martin began, "he's sick."

"He's also a doctor," I said. "He could have the vaccine stashed somewhere so he can give himself occasional shots. Just enough to not get too sick. He wouldn't even need to have an implant."

"He wanted to cut the implant out of Grace and her children," Martin reminded me. "Why do that to make a vaccine if you're here to help bring us to our knees?"

"He would control it," I said. "He could make it ineffective. Look, if things get bad enough, people will be clamoring for a vaccine, even if it's a longshot. Do you think Allen and Angela will be able to stop a mob from demanding that they take the implants out of Grace? Out of the children? There are other children here. Children whose parents will be desperate. Genesee knows that, and he could negate any helpful effects by controlling any vaccine that would be made."

Martin nodded, accepting what I was theorizing. Mostly.

"Fletch, even if you're right, we need proof," he said. "I need proof. Absolute proof. And you know why that is."

I did.

"Because Angela will have whoever it is shot," Martin said.

That sober reality gave me pause for a moment. I had to consider that my personal feelings toward the generally unlikeable Navy doctor might be clouding my assessment of him as a possible traitor. He was most definitely a difficult man to like, or even get close to. That, in itself, didn't make him a traitor. And his actions, the tapping of his fingers, was that really enough that I could say, with any level of certainty, that his persona fit the profile of one who would turn against his countrymen?

"Maybe I'm overreaching," I said.

"Maybe. That doesn't necessarily mean you're wrong."

"But you think I am."

To that, Martin nodded.

"I watched him most of yesterday," Martin said. "He was dealing with sick people for twenty hours. If somewhere in there he was able to slip away, record a Morse message, then get it to a hidden transmitter, then he's some super being."

"There was another message?"

"Reporting on the sickness and the progress in shifting our ammunition supply to the new armory," Martin said.

"He couldn't have managed sending that?"

Martin shrugged.

"It's possible."

We were fighting a mostly unseen enemy, a virus, and a shadow. And we were losing to all three.

"So if it's not him, then who?"

Martin said nothing to my question. A telling lack of response.

"You have a suspect," I said.

Still, he said nothing, neither confirming nor denying my assertion.

"Martin, if there's someone we should be wary of..."

"Proof, Fletch," he said. "When I have proof."

Twenty Eight

We had to do something. The illness was spreading. No one was on death's door yet, but those infected, now nearing half the town, were laid up, most in bed, not a one of them functioning at more than fifty percent ability. Maybe less. In a few days it could be the entire town, minus those who'd been granted some immunity from the virus.

Including me.

"There is an option," Mayor Allen said.

He'd stepped back into his old vocation, assisting Genesee at the town clinic. Taking five minutes away from his medical duties to talk to Schiavo, Martin, and me outside the front door of the town hall.

"Olin," the mayor said.

"This isn't what he told us about," I said. "He said it wiped out an Iraqi town in days."

"Do we know that?" Schiavo asked. "Does he?"

"He just described it as deadly," Mayor Allen said. "But he didn't specify the mechanism of death."

"This can't be Four Twelve," I said.

"He's a liar," Schiavo said. "He's trained to be."

"What if death doesn't come for weeks?" Martin suggested. "Or months? That would still give them time to introduce a vaccine and bring people back from the brink after any surrender."

I was beginning to get the gist of where they were going with this. My assumption was that the idea began with Mayor Allen, while he was pondering the spreading effects as Doc Allen. He'd likely run the idea by Schiavo next, who'd then sought Martin's counsel on the likelihood of me going along with what had been conceived.

"You want me to find Olin," I said.

"He said he'd be close by," Schiavo reminded me. "We know which way he headed when Sergeant Lorenzen dropped him at the checkpoint."

There were many factors to consider in what they were asking of me. I would have to head into and, possibly, through enemy controlled territory. I would be looking for something akin to a needle in a haystack. And, was there really a realistic chance that the man, if I was able to locate him, would be able to provide any assistance that would matter—if he was even open to doing so?

But, foremost in my concerns, and paramount in my thoughts, was something else entirely. Someone.

"Elaine is sick," I told the members of the Defense Council who'd been able to make the hastily called meeting. "Very sick."

Schiavo was getting worse by the day, but was pushing through. Martin was beginning to exhibit the first symptoms of the bug that had been airdropped upon us, congestion and body aches, but no fever as yet. Mayor Allen was still holding strong, with no symptoms—or none that he would admit to.

But Elaine...

"I can't leave her," I said. "I'm already doing patrols while she's home by herself."

"I will make sure she's taken care of," Mayor Allen said.

"She would tell you to go, Fletch," Martin predicted, accurately, I was certain.

Schiavo turned away and began coughing, planting her hands on the conference room table for support as the respiratory fit ran its course. After a full minute she looked back to me, Martin's hand rubbing slow circles upon her back.

"I can't order you to do this," Schiavo said. "But I can beg."

I shook my head at what she'd said.

"No," I said. "You won't do that. It's not in you."

She knew I was right. Even in desperation, Captain Angela Schiavo would not plead. Would not bow her head to another in submission. Would not fall to her knees.

But for her to suggest that she would in the face of all I knew about her, to me that spoke of the seriousness with which she saw our situation.

"I need to see Elaine first," I said, acquiescing to the request.

"Of course," Mayor Allen said. "Of course."

* * *

Elaine, my love, lay in bed, curled into a ball, the covers pulled tight as she shivered beneath them. I watched her from the doorway to our bedroom, a memory flashing back. A memory of Colonel Ben Michaels, his body wrecked by starvation and illness, wasting away, unable to take another step. But in that instant he had made a sacrifice unthinkable in the world as it was before the blight. He had given his life so that another might live.

So that Neil, my friend, might live.

Whether that offering now seemed worthy of the man who had squandered it, I did not care. Looking upon my wife as she suffered through the effects of the illness brought to our town, I knew that I would make any sacrifice, bear any burden, suffer any threat, if there was a chance that it would heal her.

"Hey," I said, entering the room and coming around the bed.

Her eyes opened and angled up to me, a smile building, bare and brief, but a smile nonetheless.

"Hey, yourself," Elaine said.

I crouched and then sat on the floor so that I was even with her face. The heat from her bled across the small space that separated us. Her fever was spiking, and she wasn't sweating. There would be no breaking of this sickness.

"Listen..."

I stopped there, trying to think of how to say what I had to say. How to tell her that, in this moment, when she needed me, truly needed me, I could not be there for her. I would not be there for her.

"You have to do it," she said before I could craft any explanation.

"How do you know? How could you know?"

She coughed and tried to lift her head off the pillow. I put my hand to her cheek and eased it back down.

"I don't know what, but I know that look."

"They want me to find Olin. They think he might know more about what's affecting us than he let on."

She thought on that for a moment, her gaze half swimming, half focused, some fitful, fevered sleep threatening to drag her down.

"What do you think?"

I shook my head and heard a quick knock at the front door.

"Fletch?" Mayor Allen called out from just inside our house.

"Back here," I directed him.

A moment later the old doctor appeared, old fashioned black medical satchel in hand. He approached the bed and sat on the edge, leaning so that Elaine could see him.

"How's our patient?"

"I'll beat it," Elaine told him.

"We're going to see that that happens," Mayor Allen said, his words sounding much like a promise.

Elaine nodded, her cheek sliding across the pillow. Once more she looked to me. The beauty about her, in her eyes, in every line and contour of her face, both warmed and pained me.

"What do you think?"

She repeated the question that she'd posed as the mayor's arrival interrupted us. I knew what she was asking—whether I thought the mission was worthwhile. The truth was, I didn't think so. But I also had to admit that, as Schiavo had said, Olin had been schooled in using the art of deception. Of inhabiting a lie so completely that what was real and what was manufactured for his own purposes might seem indistinguishable.

There was another truth, though, that made me wary of seeking the man again, and this was what I shared with Elaine as Mayor Allen slid a stethoscope over her back, listening to her rattling breathing sounds.

"I don't think he cares about us," I told my wife.

The mayor's gaze angled toward me as I spoke those words, some worry in it that I might still back out of what I'd agreed to do.

"He's here for his own reasons," I continued. "On his own mission."

"But he came to help Neil," Elaine said, her words wet and raspy. "If he's right about Neil sending the Ranger Signal for him. To tell him he was in danger."

"That's his story," I said, my internal emphasis on the word 'story'.

Elaine quieted for a moment as Mayor Allen slipped the stethoscope from her back to her chest and continued listening.

"Is there a one percent chance he might know something that will help?" Elaine asked me. "Five percent?"

"Somewhere north of zero," I told her.

My wife coughed, her body trembling beneath the thick blankets atop her. Mayor Allen eased the stethoscope away and put a hand on her shoulder to calm her through the hacking fit.

She could say no more, left gasping by the bug attacking every cell in her body. If something didn't change, if no progress was made, there was a very real chance that I could lose her. I could not let that happen.

"North of zero isn't zero," I said, leaning close and kissing her softly on the side of her forehead. "So I'm going to go make this happen."

Elaine closed her eyes, drifting off, some peace coming in sleep that eluded her while awake and battling the monster within.

"Take care of her," I told the old doctor sitting on the edge of the bed. "Please."

"Count on it."

I stepped away from the bed and crossed the room to the door, passing through without looking back. Without thinking of my love. My thoughts were focused now on one thing. On one man. He was out there, and I was off to find him.

Twenty Nine

Olin had left town on a slightly northeast course, as reported by Sergeant Lorenzen. That was the direction I headed as I began my search for the CIA man.

I left the northernmost checkpoint on our eastern border just after noon, a thick and welcome fog masking my movements as I blazed a slow, methodical trail through the dead woods. Every five minutes I would stop and take a knee next to the fattest tree I could find. From each spot I listened. Tuning my ears to the hush of the misty woods. Sampling the nothingness which used to be filled with the flutter of bird wings. The melodic chirp of jays. The quickened patter of prey scurrying toward burrows.

There was no more of that, but there was still prey. The prey that I sought, and myself, most certainly a target for the Unified Government forces somewhere in the damp haze.

My load was light, just the basics to survive a night or two in the elements, plus my AR, its slender suppressor affixed to the muzzle, and the Springfield on my hip. I wanted to use neither on this journey, which I had to complete quickly. Either Olin would be found by dawn the next day, or I would be making my way back to Bandon. To my home. To Elaine.

Two hours it took me to cover a mile. The air stank of wet death, the blighted trees soaking up the moisture and seeming to bleed some grey pus. It smeared on my coat as I brushed past stands of once mighty pines and firs, marking the stench upon me.

Once more I paused, just shy of a pair of fallen trees. The blight had taken them down, and, bit by bit, they were dissolving into the forest floor. Beyond them the fog swirled, pushed by a breeze that was funneled into a wide, low gulley, revealing more distant features in brief glimpses as the weather was momentarily parted.

Nothing. That was what I saw in the few seconds of clearing. Just a gentle slope rising toward the crest of a low hill, trees thinning out as the terrain angled upward. I thought I recognized this particular bit of the landscape, having patrolled, then simply hiked, the area around Bandon often since coming to the community. Before the top of the hill there was a shallow ravine that peeled off to the left, and a stream that drained to the north toward the Coquille River. Following that would give me excellent cover should the fog lift. It was also where I would have chosen to go had I needed a place to hole up—isolated, yet near enough to town that it could be reached in a few hours.

I decided to follow that route, hoping that, along the way, I would find some sign of Olin. Some marker of his presence. Tracks on the ground. A sound. A smell. Rising from where I'd stopped, I moved toward the fallen logs and stepped over the first, then the second, a thinner pine.

Immediately, I knew I was in trouble.

I felt no tripwire as my boot planted itself on the opposite side of the smaller log, but a sharp *twang* told me that I'd triggered something. Something that very well could obliterate me in the microseconds that followed.

But there was no explosion. No blast of shrapnel. Instead I heard a *snap* and then a whipping sound as something ripped fast through the air. I turned toward the sound and caught just a glimpse of the tensioned length of dead wood swinging toward me. There was no time to duck or roll clear. No chance at avoiding the trap I'd stepped

into. All I could do was draw a fast breath as the fat limb
struck me on my left side, just below my hip, the impact
launching me into the air, tumbling end over end until my
body slammed back to earth like a discarded ragdoll.

The wind had been knocked out of me. Worse, my AR
had been whipped out of my hands and jerked free of its
attachment to my chest sling. As I gasped for breath and
groped for my weapon, I heard something. Something
different than what had just cut through the silent forest.

I heard a man.

The Unified Government soldier stood over me, clad in
black, his face masked by a balaclava, only his eyes showing
through an oval hole in the garment. Just beyond him, lying
against the slope, was my AR, maybe five yards away. My
only other weapon, other than a knife sheathed on my belt,
was my Springfield, but the very capable .45 was pinned
beneath me as I lay on my right side.

"Keep those hands where I can see them," the soldier
ordered me.

I stayed fixed on him, my hands in front of my
crumpled body. His weapon, a familiar M4, workhorse of
the American military, was aimed just below my chin. If he
had any inclination to pull the trigger, he would not miss at
this distance.

"When I tell you to, you're going to roll slowly onto
your stomach and stretch your hands out above your head.
If you make any move I don't like, you're not going to see
another sunrise."

He didn't talk like a soldier. Not one trained as those
I'd come to know, anyway. His verbiage was almost cute, as
if he'd seen too many war movies when such things existed
in the old world. What this said to me was that this man,
this young man with his face hidden, was a recruit. A green
draftee into a force that needed warm bodies.

"Do you understand?"

I nodded. In the distance the fog rolled fast across the slope, washing the world with an opaque veil yet again. Out there, beyond the hilltop, would be his people. That was where he would take me once I'd been disarmed. Or from where his fellow soldiers would appear. That none had, as of yet, was more than a bit puzzling. Had this soldier been manning a post, watching a route of travel covered with traps? Was he by himself?

"Okay," the soldier prompted me. "Roll slowly."

A gust of wind rushed down the hillside, splitting the fog as I began to shift my body and extend my hand. I could make no move here. Not yet.

As it turned out, someone made the move for me.

The flat crack of a single rifle shot shattered the dead world's quiet. In my peripheral vision, I saw the side of the soldier's head erupt through his balaclava, neck snapping right, away from the origin of the shot. His body folded and fell to the ground at my feet, weapon dropping, its metallic clunk against the earth the last sound I heard before the footsteps.

I knew who had fired the shot. Knew without a doubt. I'd hunted deer in my native Montana, in Wyoming, and on trips to Michigan and Pennsylvania, to name a few. And universal amongst those places, in those hunting seasons, was the sound that the venerable .30-30 made.

Precisely the caliber of the lever gun that Olin had with him.

"Get your weapon and let's move," the spy said to me as he emerged from the wave of fog which had formed yet again. "They'll come to the sound of the shot."

I didn't have to be prompted again. Sore, but alive, I got to my feet and collected my AR, then fell in line behind Olin as he moved up the slope and turned north along the stream, traveling exactly the route I'd planned to.

"Keep moving," Olin instructed. "We've got a half mile to cover."

I stayed right on his six, glancing behind occasionally, though Olin seemed unconcerned with anyone following us. He was focused fully on the way ahead.

"How did you know I was there?"

"I didn't," Olin said quietly. "I knew he was there. They've been spreading sentries along their line, shifting them closer to town every day. He set that trap this morning. That's when I heard him. There's more of those backbreakers scattered through the woods."

The man stopped talking there and brought his arm up to cough into the crook of his elbow, muffling the sound. He was sick, it seemed, but still functioning. That was what I believed until we reached his hideout.

* * *

Twenty minutes later, Olin led me through a narrow space between two boulders and collapsed to his knees. He reached out and leaned his rifle against the granite wall to one side. Opposite it, another huge rock curved around, meeting the other to create a natural shelter, complete with overhang that reached almost to the only entrance.

Were it another person, I might have offered my hand to help them up. But it was not. It was a man who had brought news of a life my friend had kept from me. A life of deceit and darkness.

"I need information," I said, not wanting to prolong my interaction with him.

Olin put a hand to the rock face and levered himself up from the ground. He turned, facing me so that I had a good view of him after the quick hike to his hideout. My reaction must have been more overt than I'd thought.

"I look great, yeah?"

He didn't, and he knew it. Dark circles, looking almost like bruises, surrounded his eyes, giving the impression that he'd been beaten severely. Those markings contrasted hideously with the pale skin sagging over his cheeks. His lips, cracked and almost without any pinkish hue, were thin and stretched, leaving his mouth appearing as just a gash upon his face.

"What did they hit us with?" I asked. "Was it Four Twelve?"

Olin straightened himself and looked me over, unconcerned with what I'd just asked him.

"Dial the volume down," he said. "I'm not saving you twice today."

"Was it Four Twelve?" I asked again, hushing my voice to just above a whisper.

"But don't you look chipper? Almost like you're unaffected."

"Answer the question, Olin."

He smiled through a shallow, dry cough.

"They did something to you," he said. "Didn't they? When they took you."

I wasn't there to confirm his eerie read on my physical wellbeing, but that he was able to put the pieces of the situation, maybe any situation, together so quickly, and with such accuracy, it hurt to admit the realization that rose right then—Neil had always been able to do the same. I'd thought it part of his nature, but, beyond high school and college, I wondered if that nature had been honed like a blade's edge on a wet stone. Someone, somewhere, had taken my friend and made him into what he was—a near carbon copy of the spy before me.

"They're all running around, looking good, feeling strong," Olin said. "You're in as good a condition as the soldiers I see on their line."

"Do you want to help us, or not?"

"You don't look like you need any help," he said.

The man retrieved a steel cup and filled it with water from his canteen. He placed it over the narrow space between two small rocks, then slipped a fuel tablet in the hollow between, igniting it with a flick of a lighter. A blue and white flame took hold and licked upward to the bottom of the cup.

"If they'd dosed you with BA Four Twelve, we wouldn't be having this conversation right now. Because we'd both be dead. Eight hours tops after exposure. That's what the Agency brains estimated, anyway."

The chemical smoke from Olin's fuel tablet swirled about the hollow between the boulders, contained within the walls of his stone hideout. As the rain had done during my time at the shattered cabin, the fog here would dampen any scent before it drifted far from its point of origin.

"Estimated? You mean no one had first-hand experience with it? What about the Iraqi village?"

"Those were intelligence reports. Passed along. Third hand information."

"Third hand? That's your best intelligence?"

"Did you hear me? Anyone with first-hand knowledge ended up in a body bag. Trust me, they found something new and fun for all of us."

He dragged a sleeve across his mouth, coughing into it, stifling the sound as best he could. The bug meant for our town had gotten him, too, with a vengeance. When the spasm had passed he pulled his arm away and showed me the sleeve of his field coat.

"Pretty, huh?"

It wasn't. A spray of red mucus had stained the material, fresh blood over dried. He was bleeding internally, his lungs, most likely, or his esophagus.

"Four Twelve would be a measure of mercy right now," Olin said, then slid down onto his bottom, back against one of the boulders, a cold, makeshift chair.

"If it's not Four Twelve, then what is it?"

Olin looked at me. He managed a smile through the illness attacking his body from within.

"There was only one soldier on you," he said. "Just one. That should tell you all you need to know."

"They're not a big force," I said. "We already figured that."

"They're off in singles, setting traps to monitor a line that should take a thousand men to secure."

"So that's all it is?" I pressed. "Just some virus to weaken us? To even the odds?"

"No, making things even has nothing to do with it," Olin said. "What they hit you with, hit me with, it's going to leave everyone incapable of fighting until they bring you back to health. Then you'll be 'reeducated' to their way of doing things."

I leaned my AR against the boulder and slid to the ground, sitting against a rock face facing Olin. He reached out and tipped a pouch of drink powder into the cup of water just starting to boil.

"I'd offer you some, but not now," Olin said, lifting the cup and swirling the liquid to dissolve the contents. "I need my strength."

I wondered if a hardy constitution was the key to surviving this. Either the virus would run its course, over some period we didn't know as yet, or some underlying medical condition would combine with its effects to overwhelm the body's ability to sustain itself. Genesee had said people were going to die. Looking at Olin, and remembering how Elaine had been taken down by the bug, to imagine a weakened person not surviving this was not difficult.

"How does it feel to be a healthy island amongst a sea of suffering friends?" Olin asked, sipping the drink he'd made, a good portion dribbling down his chin as his hands trembled. "We can bet cash money that good old Neil isn't riding a fever, or hacking up a lung."

"You said he was in danger," I reminded Olin. "That's what the Ranger Signal was."

"People can be in danger in different ways," Olin said, setting the almost empty cup aside. "Sometimes they recognize a threat before it's actually upon them."

"So how do you help him? If he shows up. What do you do?"

Olin looked at me, just looked, then retrieved a thin sleeping bag from his pack and pulled it around him as he settled down to the dirty forest floor.

"You're not here to help us, you're here to help him. That's what you said, Olin, so how is it that you're going to help him?"

"You're welcome to stay the night," Olin told me. "You won't want to move in the dark back through their lines."

With that, the spy closed his eyes. The fog had lingered until almost sundown, just dissolving now as the day's last light trickled through the space between the boulders. He was right—moving at night, though it had its advantages, would, in this situation, put me in more jeopardy. I needed to see who and what was out there when I made my way back to Bandon. Back with nothing to show for my efforts.

With nothing to help save my town.

Thirty

Sometime in the night, as Olin slept, I heard two voices in the near distance.

I'd only dozed fitfully, knowing that the huge rock formation which protected us also trapped us. There was no escape or retreat from this position. One well thrown grenade would end us both.

And the voices I heard were nearly close enough to do just that.

I couldn't make out what they were saying, the tones hushed to avoid detection. It seemed plain to me that they had no idea how close they were to potential adversaries, which we certainly were. Though, at the moment, it appeared that I was the only viable combatant to face them.

Or so I thought.

As I rose slowly from where I'd bedded down, my AR in hand, I felt a hand grasp my leg just above the ankle. The fingers were strong, clamping tight, as if to hold me in place. To keep me from making any move.

Any foolish move.

I glanced behind and down, and in the weak slant of moonlight I could just make out Olin's face, free of the blanket covering the rest of his body. He gave a slight shake of his head, then released his hold on me, hand slipping back into his sleeping bag.

The voices drew closer. And closer. I held my position, weapon ready, finger just to the side of my AR's trigger. I began to be able to make out some of what the soldiers were saying. Something about movement. Plans. Big guns coming.

Then, the talking began to recede. The voices grew quieter. And quieter. Until they were lost in the whisper of the night's cool breeze.

* * *

I didn't sleep the rest of the night, and as dawn crept over the hills to the east I readied my pack and my weapons for departure.

"They walk at night," Olin said. "I hear them. They're untrained. They want a fight about as much as you."

"There was some discussion early on that we should just attack," I told him. "Maybe we should have."

Olin shook his head where he lay.

"What you heard, and what I shot, they're just cannon fodder. Just troops the Unified Government can lose. Probably drafted from some other town or city they rolled over. The real fighters are out beyond the hills."

"Big guns coming..."

I repeated what I'd heard in the night. Olin nodded.

"Things are about to get real," the spy said.

And we weren't ready. We were worse off. Our numbers were depleted by the virus. The thing that probably had some moniker like BA Five Five, but we would never know that. And those of us who lived through what was to come, a group I doubted I'd be part of, wouldn't care what name it went by.

"You didn't get what you came for," Olin said, his thin sleeping bag pulled tight around him. "If I had a miracle drug, yours truly wouldn't be coughing up blood."

He tipped his head toward a balled-up rag next to his canteen, splashes of dark red soaked into the once white material, stained like the sleeve of his jacket.

"I should say thank you," I said to the man as I picked up my AR and slipped into my pack.

"But you don't want to express gratitude to a guy like me," Olin said, reading me like an open book. "A dirty spy."

I clipped my rifle into the sling stretched across my chest and stepped toward the wide crack between the boulders.

"You can't go back empty handed," Olin said.

I stopped and looked to the man. He pushed himself up so that he was reclining against the rough granite face at the back of his shelter, his .30-30 leaning next to him. He didn't cough, just wheezed through several breaths, then he spoke. I listened, then left the man, expecting that we would never cross paths again.

I was wrong. Dead wrong.

Thirty One

I found my way back to our own lines as the day was fading and was taken quickly to the town hall. Schiavo and Martin met me as the Humvee pulled up.

"Don't get out," Schiavo said, climbing in next to me.

Martin took the shotgun seat next to Private Quincy, at the wheel.

"Take us to Fletch's house," Schiavo said.

I was instantly worried. Panicked, actually.

"Is Elaine all right? What happened?"

Schiavo half-turned in the seat to face me. Her face was flushed, but seemed not as weary as when I'd left.

"She's doing better," Schiavo told me. "Much better."

"Genesee had a small supply of anti-viral meds he'd been saving," Martin explained. "He broke them out for the sickest and those vital to the town's defense."

"Genesee," I said.

Martin nodded, noting my quiet surprise. The man I'd advanced as a suspect in Martin's mole hunt had, in this one act, removed his name from consideration as our traitor. There was no reason, even as subterfuge, that he would aid our ability to fight. Bringing some back to a semblance of health served only our purpose, not those the turncoat served.

"Elaine was vital and sick," Schiavo said.

"And you?"

The captain shook her head.

"She won't take anything," Martin said, his throat sounding like broken glass on sandpaper.

"And apparently you won't, either," I said to him.

"We're hydrating and medicating for the fever," he said.

How long those simple measures would allow both of the hard-chargers to keep ahead of the virus's worst effects was unknown. But that point of no return would be measured in days. Maybe hours.

"The Unified Government is moving up its best troops," I told them.

"Olin told you this?" Schiavo asked.

"No. Their troops on the perimeter aren't well disciplined. They talk too much."

Schiavo thought on this. The revelation didn't seem to worry her. Didn't seem to affect her in any way I could detect.

"More show?" Martin wondered.

Whether these forces would be used to up the pressure on us, to tighten the noose around Bandon, or to actually press an attack, all were conjecture. And we'd face any possibility as we were now, with our backs against the wall.

"Did you get anything from Olin?" Schiavo asked. "Anything useful."

There was only one piece of information I'd been able to pry from the man, and it was just a confirmation of a negative.

"It's not BA Four Twelve that they hit us with," I told them. "He said the intelligence on that would indicate everyone exposed would be dead within eight hours."

"And you believe him?" Martin asked.

"He has no reason to lie," I said. "He's as sick as either of you."

Martin shook his head, disappointed, it seemed.

"I actually thought he'd be able to provide something of use," the man said.

"He has," Schiavo said.

"What exactly is that?" Martin pressed his wife.

"He just confirmed that the Unified Government doesn't have it," Schiavo said. "If they did, they would have used it as a threat. There would have been none of this drama. No extended siege. They would have put Neil on camera to tell us about it."

"Neil didn't give it to them," Martin said, understanding, but only until more confusion rose. "Then why did they pull him out of here to go with them?"

"He could be using it as a bargaining chip," Schiavo suggested. "Forcing them to go easy on us or he won't hand it over to them."

"That would mean it's somewhere he can lead them," I said.

"Once Bandon is taken," Martin said.

Schiavo nodded and sat back in her seat, exhausted.

"It is here," the captain said. "He stashed it somewhere here."

"I don't believe that," I said, still holding to my gut feeling that Neil would never put his family near something so dangerous. "He wouldn't do that."

Martin, who'd shared the same doubt as me, did not echo my belief anymore. Did not back me up.

"Martin..."

He looked to his wife, then to me.

"I didn't think he was capable of such a thing," Martin said. "But we have to remember, if Olin is a liar, then so is Neil. They're cut from the same cloth."

Schiavo brought a hand up and coughed into it as Private Quincy turned the Humvee onto my street.

"I don't like spies," Schiavo said. "I can respect an enemy who takes up arms against me, an enemy in a uniform, but this..."

"It's necessary," Martin said. "It's part of warfare."

"That doesn't mean I have to like it," Schiavo said. "Not one bit."

The Humvee pulled to a stop in front of my house, but I did not immediately open the door.

"Olin did say something else," I told them.

Schiavo eyed me, with a hint of irritation, wondering, maybe, why I hadn't shared what I was about to earlier. His offhand remark as I was departing his camp had almost slipped my mind, as it seemed part wild prognostication, and part educated assumption.

"What did he say?" Martin asked.

"He told me the Ranger Signal would stop," I said. "Soon."

"How would he know this?" Schiavo asked.

"I don't know," I said. "Maybe it's because the virus is hitting us hard now. He said it's time."

"Time for what?" Martin asked.

"Time for them to make contact."

* * *

I came into our house expecting to still find Elaine in bed, despite what I'd just been told about her condition. Certainly the medicine she'd been given would not have a dramatic effect in the thirty hours I'd been gone.

Thankfully, I was wrong in my estimation.

"Hey..."

Elaine spoke to me from where she sat in the living room, resting easily in an overstuffed chair. I shed my gear and weapons and went to her.

"What is that smell?"

"A night in the woods," I told her.

She stood, surprisingly steady, and kissed me. When she eased back I took in the sight of her. There was still a bit of paleness to her complexion, and a hint of thinness about her jawline. But her eyes were bright, and her smile brighter.

"You look…"

I couldn't finish my thought, amazed at the transformation.

"Don't get used to it," Elaine said. "It's only temporary."

My heart sank, but nothing about her expression changed. She was letting the moment be the moment.

"How long?" I asked.

"A few days."

Others were still suffering through the virus. To be angry that we'd been granted some respite, however brief, while those afflicted could only claw their way through the fever, the pain, was to ignore this chance. Maybe our last at some normalcy.

But normal in our world, in this time, this place, was not what anyone wanted it to be. Reality would always intrude.

"We have assignments tomorrow," Elaine told me.

I nodded. No respite from the needs of our defense would come until we had won. Or lost.

"But that's tomorrow," Elaine said, reaching up to unbutton my soiled shirt. "Right now we need to get you into the shower."

She wasn't talking about simply cleaning the grit from my trek off of me. I knew that. There was suggestion in her voice, and in her gaze. In the way her fingers brushed my skin.

"Are you sure you should…"

She nodded, voiding any concern I was expressing.

"I'm tired, and sore, and I want you," she said, a seriousness now about her. "How many more nights will we have? We don't know. So I want this while we have this one. Okay?"

How could I deny this moment, with her, even if I wanted to. Which I didn't.

"Okay," I said.

She moved past me and flipped the light switch off. I followed her through the darkness as she walked down the hall.

Thirty Two

The radio went silent the next morning.

"Ten minutes ago," Schiavo said.

She stood on our porch, Elaine and I absorbing the news the captain had brought us personally.

"Just like Olin said would happen," I said.

The captain nodded, then looked to my wife and smiled.

"You look better," she said.

"Off death's doorstep," Elaine said. "For the moment."

Schiavo still hadn't accepted any medication from Genesee, insisting instead that it go to those sicker than she was. There was another reason, though, that she was passing on the potentially lifesaving drugs. She hadn't said so, but she didn't need to.

"The medicine is safe during pregnancy," I told the captain.

"You read the box Genesee left behind."

"I did," I said, confirming the captain's suspicion.

"I saw the term 'unlikely' in there," Schiavo said. "Effects on unborn children are 'unlikely'. That's not good enough for me."

"You laid flat by this thing won't be good for a child, either," I said.

"You could ask Genesee," Elaine said.

Schiavo rejected the idea with a weakened shake of her head. She reached out and planted a hand on the door jamb to support herself. I'd seen her like this, as had Elaine, when she'd refused to lighten her load after being shot on our way to Skagway so many months ago. She'd pushed through the pain there, and the weakness, driving forward and leading her troops, her men, to an ultimate victory against the Russian contingent which had invaded Alaska.

Here, though, the enemy was invisible to her. She could not battle it as she would her opposites in a firefight. But she was still charging forward, refusing to slow, making the fight itself what sustained her.

"My people all have the medicine," Schiavo said. "I'm just a desk riding bureaucrat with a sidearm."

"So you won't be on the line if the fight comes," I said, correcting myself quickly. "*When* the fight comes."

"We'll see," the captain said, allowing another smile. "Elaine, I need to change your assignment for today."

"Whatever you need."

She'd been scheduled to go with me to check our southern lines, but this sudden, if expected, quieting of the airwaves had necessitated some change in plans, I imagined. Along with an alteration of deployments.

"I need you at the com center to back up Private Westin," Schiavo said. "We need ears on our radios every second."

"The ultimatum's coming," Elaine said.

Schiavo didn't confirm what we all knew to be true. The demands from the Unified Government were imminent. Our response, and our reaction, would dictate what happened beyond that.

"Fletch, I want those checkpoints squared away," Schiavo said. "No weak links. No mistakes."

"Understood," I told the captain.

She stood there for a few seconds, just taking in the sight of us, two people, in love, facing their destiny together. Just as she and Martin were.

"Stay sharp," Schiavo said, then headed down the walkway to the Humvee she'd left at the curb.

"A fall baby," Elaine said as we watched Schiavo drive away.

"What?"

"They're going to have a baby in the fall."

I did the math in my head. Based upon what Martin ad Schiavo had shared, Elaine was right.

"October or November," I said.

"A long ways off," Elaine said. "A long, long ways."

So much could happen between now and then. Or between now and when the sun went down. We were promised this moment. That was it. Everything beyond that had to be earned.

"Let's get ready," I said.

"Yeah," Elaine agreed.

It was time to earn our tomorrow.

Thirty Three

I was heading toward the third stop of my assignment, inspecting the southern checkpoint nearest the shore, when Elaine came screaming up in an old pickup that had been used and abused hauling ammo to the new armory.

"Eric!"

She called out to me through the open driver's window and hung a fast one-eighty on the wide road, back tires slipping, the vehicle rattling as it threatened to fishtail before stopping, pointed back toward town.

"What is it?"

"They made contact," Elaine told me through a cough. She was more surprised than excited.

"The Unified Government?"

"Yeah," she confirmed.

"What did they say?"

"Get in," she told me. "You're not going to believe this."

* * *

Five minutes later I stood in the garrison's communication center with Schiavo and Elaine. The message, transcribed by Westin, had already been shared with Martin and Mayor Allen, both of whom the captain informed me were on their way to the very place I'd been quarantined.

"Why?" I asked.

"Read it," Schiavo said, handing me the slip of paper on which the message had been translated from dots and dashes to words that would carry some meaning.

I took the slip of paper and read aloud.

"Initiate ATV transmission and reception at thirteen hundred hours tomorrow. The Unified Government."

ATV. An Amateur Television transmission was what we were supposed to expect. A crude video broadcast sent over amateur radio frequencies, the same as Micah had received. Simple images of a thriving tomato plant which had sent us across the wastelands to retrieve the cure for the blight.

"Keep reading," Schiavo said.

"Request point of contact be Eric Fletcher," I read.

"You seem to be popular on all fronts," the captain said.

Elaine put a hand on my arm as I read the full message in silence again.

"You know what this means," my wife said.

"It means Neil will be speaking on their behalf."

I crumpled the slip of paper up and dropped it on the floor.

Part Three

Contact

Thirty Four

I sat at Micah's workstation, computers humming, the display before me a jumble of electronic noise alternating between fuzzy black and white static. The speaker connected to the system shifted between silence and hissing. It was an oddly rhythmic sound that seemed to match and mock my own quickened breathing.

Above it all, the red light of the camera aimed at me burned bright, like a brilliant speck of blood. My image was being transmitted without sound. We were sending video, but nothing, yet, was being received on our end.

"And what if they don't make contact?" I asked, glancing to my left where Schiavo, Elaine, and Mayor Allen stood just out of view of the camera.

"It's only a few minutes after one," Elaine said.

Watches with computerized brains kept precise time even in the world the blight had left us. But beyond that truth, she was simply trying to calm me. If I was right, I was about to see my friend, for the first time in months. The friend who'd abandoned us, presumably to throw in with a government which rivaled the one to which we still bore some allegiance.

"I'm afraid of what I'll say to him," I said.

"Be calm," Schiavo said. "You're our face and our voice for this."

"And don't give him anything," Mayor Allen added. "He doesn't need to know what we know. About his past, or anything else."

"Stay focused on our situation," Schiavo said.

I nodded and looked around the space. Micah's space. For a moment I had an overwhelming need to have Martin there. He'd guided his late son through so many discoveries in this very space. Now, he was off serving his town, serving all of us, still. Seeking the one who was betraying us on a nightly basis. But I wanted him here. Not as some father figure, but as a true friend as I faced the one who had deceived me.

Beeeeeeeep.

The singular alert sounded from the speaker. It was followed by a three note tone. High, low, high. Like one might play on an electronic keyboard.

Then, the display fuzzed to life, an image replacing the static, grainy and uneven, but beyond familiar.

"Hello, Fletch," my friend said to me across some unknown distance. "How are you?"

I was certain that my expression did not match his. Some degree of a smile lay across his face. I could manage nothing of the sort as I reached to the controls and turned on the audio portion of our transmission.

"I'm all right," I said.

To my side, Elaine coughed, a reminder that not everyone bore the immunity I'd been granted against the virus. The medicine Genesee had given her had blunted the effects of the virus for the moment. But that moment would not last.

"Not everyone is, though," I added.

On the monitor, Neil Moore nodded, seeming both determined and embarrassed at the same time.

"It wasn't my decision," my friend said. "But it was deemed necessary."

"By your Unified Government?" I challenged.

"Everything will be all right, Fletch."

"People are sick, Neil. People could die."

He shook his head.

"Not if you do what's inevitable. Just join us."

I didn't shake my head. Didn't react visibly at all. But inside I was raging.

"Force? Is that the way your people operate, Neil? By threats and violence and..."

I stopped myself there, not wanting to let my anger allow anything to slip. Anything about Olin, or the biological agents. Schiavo and Mayor Allen were right—we needed to maintain our secrets for the moment. We needed him, and those he'd allied himself with, to be as ignorant of our plans and actions as possible, a state that was difficult to create with a traitor in our presence.

"Do you think I'd send my family, my wife, my children, back to Bandon if I thought they'd be in danger?" Neil asked, his certitude plain even over the sketchy connection. "I'd never place them in harm's way. You know that."

I did. Or I wanted to believe that.

"They're a goodwill gesture, Fletch. To prove our intentions."

"Then why did you leave in the first place?" I asked my friend. "Why didn't your pals just reach out to the town? Send an emissary?"

He had an answer. I could see that in his expression. Still, he hesitated, just for a moment.

"Trust," Neil finally answered. "There've been incidents of resistance in other colonies. The government needed to regroup. Pull in its people."

"People like you," I said.

My friend nodded soberly at me. I glanced to my left. Elaine, Schiavo, and Mayor Allen eyed the screen from an angle with plain wariness.

"Fletch, I didn't want it to be this way."

I fixed on the display again.

"The Unified Government has a plan to bring all survivor communities back into the fold. To get the country moving forward again."

I tried to process the propaganda my friend was spewing like some coopted talking head. Some functionary insisting that indefensible actions were more than defensible—they were proper.

"Fletch, think about it. We can be together again. All of us. The world can start back up. Who knows, maybe in a few years you and me, we could be sitting courtside at a Hawk's game, drinking a beer."

"You're delusional," I said.

"No, I'm realistic," Neil countered. "We can get to that place, but we have to do it together. Not scattered everywhere with no central power structure."

I nodded at what he'd said, but not in agreement. In understanding of the motives he'd expressed, either inadvertently or by design.

"Power," I repeated. "Power."

My friend stopped there. Stopped attempting to convince me of the rightness of his actions. The purity of his motives. Instead, he looked to me, in ways that he had from our old times, our good times. He wanted to say something. Maybe say too much. In the end he defaulted to pleasant talk which could only mimic the closeness we'd once shared.

"How are Grace and our kids?"

I made myself smile at my friend.

"They're doing all right. You have a good looking boy there."

"He's a bruiser," Neil said, chuckling lightly. "Grace is a saint for pushing that kid out. A nine pounder."

We quieted there. Both of us. Searching for something to say. It was Neil who found the next point in our exchange.

"Krista made you a drawing while she was here," Neil said, the transmission chopping his voice into a staccato, almost faltering cadence. "She spent hours on this red rhinoceros thing. Did she show it to you?"

I shook my head at the screen, the camera mounted above relaying my reply. Relaying that I was now at a complete loss for words. Whatever this conversation's intent had been, it was not about us. It was pure prelude. This I saw plainly as the look on my friend's face shifted, from personal to professional.

"Fletch, the leader of the Unified Government forces wants to speak to Mayor Allen," Neil said. "Is he there?"

I looked to my left. Mayor Allen stepped into view. I stood and let him take the chair. Before I could move from in front of the camera, Neil called out to me.

"Fletch..."

"What is it?"

"Everything will be okay. Trust me."

Trust...

That was what my friend was asking for. A man who'd expressed an undying belief in hope had abandoned that and replaced it with plans for a future based on compliance and subjugation. How was this possible? I still, especially when watching and listening to my friend at this very moment, could not fathom what had driven him to this.

I said nothing to his promise and stepped clear of the camera, standing with Elaine and Schiavo as Neil, too, left his place on the other end of the transmission. For a moment the chair my friend had occupied sat empty, then a man came into view and sat down, his posture rigid and proper. He wore a uniform reminiscent of the old Army. Plain and crisp, green from head to toe. It was as if he'd stepped from central casting of some Vietnam War movie.

"I'm General Harris Weatherly," the man said. "And these are my terms."

Mayor Allen listened for several minutes, we all did, as the man outlined a future none of us could fathom, much less embrace. Centralized rule from a government headquartered on the opposite coast. Requirements to raise and transport supplies to Unified Government outposts. Civilian and military leaders of the town would be approved by Unified Government representatives. The current garrison would be disbanded and its members sent east for 'retraining'. And, finally, all arms must be surrendered to the occupying Unified Government forces.

"Your acceptance is required now," General Weatherly stated, waiting for the reply he expected.

He was going to be sorely disappointed.

"General Weatherly," Mayor Allen began, "I'm a doctor by trade, and I can give you some very clinical and anatomically correct directions on just where you can stick your terms."

The man on the monitor showed no visible reaction to the response he'd just received. He said not a word. He simply reached forward to some control box and killed the transmission, the screen flashing to static.

Mayor Allen leaned back in the chair and looked to us.

"Do you suppose that counts as a declaration of war?"

"I'd say so," I told the mayor.

The man looked to his military counterpart.

"It had to be done, Angela."

"Yes, it did," Schiavo agreed, drawing a breath. "I'd better talk to my sergeant. Things are liable to get busy."

She left us, Mayor Allen rising from the chair once she was gone.

"Interesting that Neil knew I was the town's leader," the mayor said. "He left before I took over for Martin."

"Our traitor has kept them well informed," I said.

"I believe I should probably take a few minutes and tell Carol what I've done."

"How is your wife?" Elaine asked.

The woman, elderly like her beloved husband, had been down with the virus almost since it had hit.

"She is..."

He tried, multiple times, to say more. To continue. In end, with emotion choking his words, he simply managed a hopeful smile that reeked of hopelessness and left us to fear the worst.

"This isn't right," Elaine said. "It's not right, and it's not fair. She's such a sweet woman."

Sweet. Devoted. Never complaining when her husband took on the mayor's role. It wasn't the way their life should have played out.

The blight, defeated now, even as its scars lay plain upon the planet, still rippled through every action, every happening, as the world spun on. Taking lives through events it had caused. By individuals and entities its appearance had created.

"I'm about ready to hate this world," Elaine said.

"No you're not," I told her.

She looked to me, bitterness in her gaze. Anticipating, maybe fearing what I was about to say.

"Don't," she warned me. "No lines about hope. Not now."

She'd misread me. I wasn't going to say any such thing. Wasn't going to appropriate the mantra my friend had ingrained in me. Because I could not bring myself to buy into anything he'd espoused, even if it was a universal truism. Mostly, though, it rang hollow at the moment.

We were entering a time where actions would matter. Not platitudes.

Thirty Five

At one in the morning, just hours after refusing the Unified Government's demand that Bandon submit to central rule, it was made clear that our resistance would come with consequences.

Elaine was asleep in our bed, but I was not. I sat in the living room with a single light burning, thinking about my friend. Trying to piece together the 'why' of his actions. But that act, which had infected nearly every waking moment I had, and many while I slumbered, was ended by a flash of light beyond the curtained windows and a sharp, thunderous crack that shook the house and knocked fragile glass knickknacks inherited from the previous owners from their shelves.

I bolted up and grabbed my rifle, slipping into my vest as Elaine came fast up the hallway from the bedroom, her gear in hand and eyes wide after being jolted from sleep.

"What was that?"

"I don't know," I said. "Sounded like it came from the north side of town."

In less than thirty seconds we were both geared up and heading out. We jogged up the block, others joining us, ready to respond. But respond to what?

BOOM!

Another explosion shook the very ground beneath us, a pulse of yellow light expanding to the north. A distant fire at the point of the blast illuminated a billowing black cloud rising into the dark sky.

"What's going on, Fletch?" Dave Arndt asked as he ran alongside, untied boots flopping on his feet and the pump action Remington shotty harnessed to his chest bouncing hard with every quickened step he took. "Is this the attack?"

"I don't think so," Elaine answered for us, keying in on something sounding off in the distance. "Those are secondaries."

Secondary explosions. Collateral damage of the initial blast. Ammunition was cooking off. That meant only one thing to all of us.

"The armory," I said.

* * *

We reached the area of the blazing building in five minutes, continuing explosions keeping those of us who'd responded back. Only the town's small fire department with its aging diesel pumper truck had closed in on the inferno, laying a stream of water on nearby buildings with the nozzle mounted atop its thousand gallon tank. Volunteers were dragging a feeder hose from the vehicle to a nearby pond to extend the supply of water that would be needed to keep the fires from spreading.

"I'm going to give the hose crew a hand," Dave said, and ran off toward the pond.

BOOM!

Another large blast ripped through the remnants of the old auto shop which had been appropriated as the town's central ammo dump, its already shattered walls toppling fully now as orange and white flames rolled outward from the origin of the explosion. The fire crew ducked behind their rig for cover, but kept the stream of water going.

"Stay sharp," Schiavo said as she ran past us in full battle gear.

So much for the desk riding bureaucrat, I thought.

Elaine and I followed as she moved past the cowering crowd to reach her sergeant near the pumper truck, Private Quincy at his side.

"Paul, what happened?"

Lorenzen stood tall, ignoring the secondary explosions popping off from the burning collection of ammunition for small and large arms.

"A missile," Lorenzen told her, pointing skyward into the night. "From up there."

"A drone strike," Quincy said.

Schiavo nodded at the private.

"I was just coming out of the town hall when I saw the streak of light," Lorenzen said.

"That's most of our ammunition," Elaine said.

Schiavo shook her head. Not at Elaine's comment, but at the decision she'd made to centralize the ability to distribute ammo in case of attacks.

"This one's on me," the captain said.

"It was the right move for our supply issues," I told her.

"That doesn't matter now," Schiavo fired back.

Another sharp explosion cracked, the few remaining windows in the storefront near us breaking, large shards of glass tumbling to the sidewalk.

"Any movement reports?" Elaine asked.

"None," Lorenzen said. "The lines are quiet."

"Weatherly's just putting us on notice," Schiavo said. "He knew exactly where the new armory was."

"Don't move."

The voice was Martin's. I turned with Schiavo and Lorenzen and saw him standing behind Private Quincy, a pistol in his hand, its barrel pressed to the back of her head.

"Martin," Schiavo said, calm and shocked all at once.

"Weatherly knew because his spy told him," Martin said. "Isn't that right, Private Quincy?"

"Ma'am," Quincy said, her voice trembling. "What's going on?"

"Keep playing the role," Martin said. "Feign ignorance. Pretend you have the sniffles. Keep the act up."

Quincy froze, fear seeming to fill her from her toes to her forehead. Then, without any hint that it was coming, she moved, swinging her M4 quickly up.

But not quickly enough. Martin's hand swung the butt of his old Colt .45 across the young woman's face, connecting with her temple. She fell backwards, and at the same instant both Elaine and I brought our weapons to bear, covering the downed soldier.

"Don't do it!" Elaine ordered.

Quincy stared up at us, recovering from the stunning blow.

"Keep your hands where we can see them," I said.

Schiavo looked to her husband, but did not speak a word. She didn't need to.

"I'm certain," Martin said.

Schiavo thought for a moment, eyeing the private, then nodded to her sergeant. Lorenzen hauled Sheryl Quincy up from where she'd fallen and stripped her of every weapon on her person, rifle, pistol, and knife, jerking her tactical vest off last so that she was clad only in her camouflage pants, long sleeve tee, and boots.

"This is crazy!" Quincy protested. "You have to be insane."

I kept my weapon trained on the private as Martin holstered his pistol and pulled a piece of paper from his pocket. He brought it up so that the nearby streetlight illuminated what was written on it. What he'd written on it.

"Leadership believes Four Twelve within town," he read. "Hidden by Moore."

Martin fixed his gaze on Quincy.

"That is decoded from a Morse message sent out the night Fletch returned from meeting Olin," he said. "There were four people who heard the conversation where we discussed that—me, the captain, Fletch, and you."

Schiavo took a step toward the newest and youngest member of her garrison. A young woman, capable and determined, who'd joined them as a replacement for Acosta, the burly soldier who'd given his life in Skagway as we battled hardened Russian troops. That the person she'd chosen to fill that void might now turn out to be the very one who'd turned against her brethren, who'd turned against us all, was an impossibility that the captain was facing through a veil of building rage.

"Captain, I wouldn't," Quincy said, her words half plea, and half proclamation of innocence. "I would not do this."

"This message was sent hours after we discussed its contents," Martin said. "From a transmitter hidden beneath the egg catcher in the chicken coops. The coops that Private Quincy here checks every day—your words, private."

For the briefest instant, Quincy's gaze broke, shifting among those staring at her. Searching for a sympathetic face. A believer.

"This isn't right!" Quincy shouted.

Martin looked to the sergeant.

"Paul, hold her," he said.

Before she could pull away, Lorenzen seized Quincy firmly from behind, pulling each of her wrists back, locking them in his hands that, at that moment, functioned as handcuffs made of flesh and muscle and fury.

"What are you doing?!"

Martin didn't bother answering the question Quincy shouted at him. He simply moved swiftly, reaching with his free hand to her right sleeve and tearing the material away, exposing the back of her bicep and a small, healing scar there.

"Look," Martin said, grabbing her arm almost violently and turning her so that Schiavo, Elaine, and I could see.

She'd received an implant. One whose entry point had scarred over. It appeared older than mine, and of those Grace and her children had been given.

"She's had this for at least a month," Martin said, fixing on the traitor he'd identified. "What did you do? Slip off into the woods and get your 'stay healthy' implant before all this started?"

Quincy gave no response to the question. She also stopped her protests, determination now replacing her faux surprise. Determination and a sly, pitying grin.

That was a mistake.

"Answer the question!" Schiavo ordered, bringing the back of her hand across Quincy's face.

The traitor's head snapped from the blow, and when she looked to the captain once again, still grinning, the slim smile was spotted with blood from a split lip.

"Go to hell," Quincy told her commander.

Schiavo let herself calm. It seemed to me she was working through some internal count to allow her anger and adrenalin to abate.

"Sergeant," she said.

"Yes, ma'am?"

"Get her out of here."

"With pleasure," Lorenzen said.

Martin reached into his pocket and retrieved a pair of handcuffs. Certain that he was right, that he had the proof he knew would be necessary, he'd come prepared. The sergeant took them and bound Quincy's wrists, then grabbed the short chain between them and lifted, levering her body forward as he walked her away from the scene of devastation.

"Find the mayor and have him meet us at the garrison headquarters," Schiavo said when the traitor was gone.

"Will do," I said.

"Stay with the fire crew," Schiavo told her husband. "Let me know if anything gets out of hand."

Martin nodded, his wife holding his gaze for a long moment.

"You did good," she said.

Schiavo headed off, trailing her sergeant and their prisoner. Martin put a hand to my shoulder, a gesture of thanks. For what, I wasn't certain. But there was plenty of gratitude to flow in all directions. There always had been in Bandon.

Martin left us and took a position closer to the pumper truck, grabbing a hose when a pressure spike caused it to buck and flail. He had been a leader, a great leader, and, through actions large and small, he continually proved himself to be a fine man.

"I'll find Mayor Allen," I told Elaine. "You go get Genesee and tell him what just happened. Tell him *everything*."

It only took a second for Elaine to understand why I was sending her off on a separate errand.

"Right," Elaine said.

We made our way away from the raging blaze, explosions still sounding. Our town had been hit. Hard. And more was almost certain to come. But we had finally blunted one of the Unified Government's most effective weapons. And, in doing so, it was possible that we might be able to improve our situation even more. Much more.

Thirty Six

Lorenzen shoved Quincy into a chair in the holding room at the garrison's headquarters and hooked a set of handcuffs to the pair that bound her wrists behind her back. The other end he pulled roughly downward and secured to one of the chair legs, leaving her body twisted at a painful, awkward angle as Schiavo and Mayor Allen came through the door.

For a moment nothing was said. Lorenzen and I looked to Schiavo as she glared in silence at the private who'd joined her unit before they'd come to Bandon.

"Do you want to tell us anything?" Mayor Allen asked.

"Yes," Quincy said. "Your time is running out."

The burst of almost childish insolence didn't rattle the four of us in the room with the traitor. She was caught, and she was resisting through some expression of bravado. That it might be fueled by a devotion to the Unified Government was beyond me to fully fathom.

"You've lived among us," I said. "You know us. We're good people. Not perfect, but good. We're decent. Why would you be party to something that seeks to destroy that?"

"Good?" Quincy challenged me. "You think 'good' is what matters?"

"I believe it matters more than anything," Mayor Allen backed me up.

Quincy, her eye swelling from Martin's blow and mouth bleeding from Schiavo's, shook her head, judgement and disdain in the gesture.

"Good equals weak," she said. "And this is not a world that will allow weakness to survive."

"We've made it this far," I reminded her.

"You think you can make this work?" Quincy asked us, her face twisted with a mix of pity and disbelief. "You really believe that everything is going to fall back into place without some sort of overall order?"

"There's nothing disorderly about what we've accomplished," Mayor Allen said.

Quincy smiled at the elderly leader. A man who'd devoted his life to helping, and healing, and community.

"This isn't order," she countered. "All you've done is evolve into some sort of commune with a few rules that anyone is free to disregard by leaving."

"We're not running a prison," I said.

The private shook her head slowly, now with open contempt toward me. Toward us.

"I can..."

Schiavo didn't complete her statement, a sudden coughing fit causing her to turn away and clear her throat as she faced the corner.

"You all right, captain?"

Schiavo composed herself and looked to her sergeant, nodding. Then she faced the traitor in our midst again and saw what we all did—a broad, almost knowing smile spread across her face.

"I can have you shot," Schiavo told Private Sheryl Quincy. "I have that authority."

"You have no authority," Quincy said. "Your government is finished. It's gone."

"You know nothing of the sort," Mayor Allen told the traitor.

"Is that so?" Quincy challenged him. "How's that Navy resupply you were promised working out? Where's the *Rushmore*? Where's any ship? And the airwaves are clear now, so where's the soothing call from *your* government?"

No one bothered to answer the questions she posed. Almost certainly because none of us could.

"If you help us, there will be consideration given toward you in any proceedings," Mayor Allen said.

"How many troops are we facing?" Schiavo asked, expanding her inquiry with rapid fire probing. "Where is your supply base? How many drone aircraft do you have? Has an attack day been decided?"

"Why would I help you?" Quincy asked, truly incredulous. "Why would I help perpetuate a failing, feel good system?"

We weren't getting anything from her. Nothing that we could use to better our position or prevent what we all knew to be coming now. That was what we all realized.

A knock on the door proved us wrong.

It opened and Commander Genesee stepped in, Specialist Hart with him. The latter man held a syringe, its needle shielded by a pale blue cover.

"Commander, what's going on?" Schiavo asked.

Elaine followed both men in as Genesee tipped his head toward Hart. The army medic stepped past Mayor Allen and popped the cap off the syringe as he brought the needle toward Quincy's exposed left arm.

"Hey!" Quincy protested, trying to wriggle away from Hart. "What are you doing?!"

"Specialist!" Schiavo shouted.

"Let him do it," Genesee said to the captain.

"Yes," I said. "Let him."

Schiavo considered both pleas, then relented with a look to her medic.

"NO!"

Hart jabbed the syringe into Quincy's arm as she screamed. He pressed the plunger down, injecting her, and before the shrieking sound of her protest was quieted, her head began to loll, eyes rolling back, mostly whites showing. When she was fully unconscious, Genesee crouched next to her and examined the back of her arm through the tear in her shirt Martin had made. After a quick check he looked up to Schiavo.

"Captain, your permission to remove her implant."

There was no hesitation from Schiavo, and no resistance.

"Granted. Make your vaccine, Commander Genesee. Just keep her alive."

We all knew what that last admonition was for. If we weren't certain, the captain left no ambiguity about it with her next words.

"I'm not done with her."

Thirty Seven

By morning the explosions were over and the fires had subsided to small licks of flame that danced upon the charred debris, smoke curling upward into the grey sky. Elaine and I returned to observe the scene of destruction after catching a few hours' sleep.

"Schiavo's going to kill her," Elaine said.

Private Sheryl Quincy, traitor, had been locked up in the town's small jail. Its only occupant.

"You mean execute," I said.

"Dead is dead," Elaine reminded me.

That was a universal truism. Once gone, you stayed gone. I feared that was also going to apply to Bandon. And to us.

"What if we lose?" I asked.

Elaine had no response to the possibility I was suggesting. That outcome had always seemed unfathomable. We'd overcome so much. Been victorious over long odds. But what we faced here...

"We're out gunned and outnumbered," I said. "They can take out our vital installations at will with strikes we can't anticipate, much less stop. Defeat is a possibility."

"What happened to 'there's always hope'?"

I was surprised that my wife had seized on that mantra, one which she, herself, had discounted so recently.

"It left on a helicopter and went to the other side," I shot back, almost angrily.

I didn't like losing. Or even the thought of such. Working hard, being successful, winning—all had been the way I'd lived my life since tearing up the field with Neil on our high school football team.

Team...

In that moment, with that thought, I remembered that there were other players. Others who might be impacted by the same entity we were facing.

"We have to let the others know," I said.

For an instant, Elaine didn't realize who I was talking about. Then the broadness that could apply to the term I'd chosen became clear.

"The other colonies," she said.

Yuma. San Diego. Edmonton. Those were the other bastions of humanity we knew of. There would clearly be more, and must have been. Neil had mentioned in the ATV broadcast that there had been trouble with other colonies. Whether that referred to those we knew of could not be determined. Not standing where we were sampling the smoky air.

"We need to find out who the Unified Government moved on before us," I said.

Elaine coughed lightly, the acrid haze working on her still compromised respiratory system. She was holding her own, but I found myself hoping, and praying, that Genesee's plan to manufacture a diluted vaccine would work. And work fast.

"Let's go," I said, wanting both to get Elaine clear of the smoldering site, but also to get to the one person who might be able to shed some light on the Unified Government's actions before it zeroed in on us.

"Where?" Elaine asked as I led her away from the shattered armory.

"To see Grace."

* * *

"Did Neil say anything about the other survivor colonies?"

Grace listened to my question and thought as she stood next to Brandon's crib, the piece of furniture brought to her house and tucked neatly next to the bed she'd shared with Neil.

"The other colonies?"

Since returning, as though she was in a state of low grade shock, the woman who'd been a sharp and determined individual, with a nursing degree to her name, had struggled to process even the simplest questions. It was as though each rattled around in her head, competing with raging thoughts, before any worthwhile response could be summoned.

"The people from Yuma, or San Diego," Elaine prompted her.

For a moment Grace thought on the question, then she looked to Elaine, some connection made to memories that should still be fresh.

"Edmonton," Grace said. "You forgot Edmonton."

"That's right," Elaine said, smiling as she reached out and put a hand on our friend's arm. "I did."

In his crib, Brandon slept, not even stirring as we talked quietly near him. Across the hall, through the open door to her room, I could see Krista on her floor, drawing in her notebook, a pile of colored markers and pencils next to her in-progress creation. Art seemed to be her companion at the moment. An almost therapeutic way to express thoughts and feelings.

"Do you remember him saying anything about the Unified Government going to those places?" I asked. "Or anyone there? Did anyone talk about those places?"

"I didn't spend much time with the others," she told us. "Neil was always with them, and he didn't want to talk about what went on."

She paused for a moment and looked down to their son.

"He never seemed happy once we were there," Grace added. "Never. I still don't understand why he made us go."

She was drifting off into a melancholy fugue. A state of simmering despair which we'd observed on several occasions since her return. We needed to pull her back from the edge of that mental abyss. For her own good, and for ours.

"Grace, we need to know about the other colonies," I told her. "We need to know if they've been threatened. We need to warn them about what's happening."

"Why don't you call them?"

The question, simple and innocent, came from the room across the hall. Krista's room. The girl was looking up from her book, the drawing she'd been working on stopped, a bright yellow marker in hand.

"They're a long ways away, sweetie," Elaine said.

"Micah said that didn't matter," Krista countered. "He said the radio signal can ride a skywave."

I stepped away from Grace and stood close to the bedroom door, Krista just a few feet away.

"Skywave?" I asked, the term vaguely familiar.

"It had a fancier name," the child said. "But Micah said that signals go up and follow something in the air."

"In the atmosphere," Elaine said.

"Right," Krista confirmed. "It was something in the atmosphere."

I looked to Elaine.

"We need to talk to Westin."

* * *

Fifteen minutes later, as we waited at Micah's workstation, Private Westin arrived with Captain Schiavo.

"Here he is," Schiavo said, personally delivering the man we'd wanted to see.

"You had a question about one of these radios?" Westin asked, eyeing the impressive setup which had been put together by Micah, for Micah.

"We do," I said. "Talk to us about skywave."

"Ionospheric skip," Westin said. "To put it simply, under certain conditions, radio signals can bounce off of charged layers in the ionosphere and reflect back to earth. Basically, it negates line of sight limitations to transmissions. You can send and receive signals over thousands of miles."

"So with the Ranger Signal gone, we could, potentially, reach out to one of the other colonies," I said.

"Sure," Westin said. "If you knew what frequency they'd be monitoring."

"And there are thousands of those," Elaine said.

The idea, though technologically possible, had this one inherent flaw.

"Scatter," Martin said.

I looked and saw the man standing at the end of the hall that spilled into the workstation area. He walked toward us and reached to the computer mouse, dragging it across the monitor to click on an icon labeled with the word he'd just spoken.

"Micah wrote this program to both scan all usable frequencies," he explained. "And to transmit on them. Record a hailing message and run the program. If someone is listening, they'll hear it."

"And if they transmit back, the program will know?" Elaine asked.

"The program will lock in that frequency," Martin said. "Then you initiate communication."

Martin stepped back from the workstation, staring at it for a moment. Staring and even smiling. As he'd stated before, this was where his son had lived. The cemetery was where he rested. I understood why this space soothed him—

it was where memories could seem real. If only for a moment.

"Let's record our message," Westin said.

* * *

We chose Elaine's voice to bear our message.

"Any survivors, this is Bandon calling. Please reply."

That transmission repeated thousands of times on thousands of frequencies through multiplexers Micah had constructed and wired into his array of computers and radios.

An hour after we began sending, the transmission stopped and the program locked in on a specific frequency where a response was detected.

"Put it on the speaker," Schiavo instructed her com expert.

Westin dialed the volume up and adjusted filters to clean up what was coming through. When the transmission became clear enough to recognize, our hearts sank.

The high, low, high tone repeating was identical to the alert tone which had preceded the ATV broadcast from the Unified Government.

"Maybe it's them," I said.

Westin, though, shook his head.

"This signal is not local. Not by a longshot."

A few seconds later we learned exactly where it was originating as the tones ended. And we learned this through a familiar voice.

"Bandon, this is Yuma, a colony of the Unified Government."

"Perkins," Martin said.

Earl Perkins, who'd been head of the Yuma survivors taken to Skagway with others from the lower forty-eight and Canada. He was an abrasive man, small in stature but big in bluster. An autocrat with few to lord over, I'd thought when meeting him after our trip north. Now, apparently, he'd found a like-minded entity which he could serve.

"Shall I respond?" Westin asked.

"Bandon, come in."

Schiavo looked to me.

"They've taken Yuma," she said.

"Or Perkins just invited them in," I suggested.

"Bandon, have you come aboard? Come in."

"No other responses?" Schiavo asked.

"Just Yuma," Westin confirmed.

"Bandon, are you there? Come in."

"Shut it off," Schiavo said.

Before Westin could, Elaine leaned in and killed the speaker.

"We may be the last," I said.

"Yeah," Schiavo said, disappointed, though that sentiment evaporated as quickly as it had come. "Or the seed from which many grow."

Thirty Eight

Commander Clay Genesee, malcontent doctor of the Bandon survivor colony, began administering a diluted vaccine to the population less than twenty-four hours after surgically removing the implant from Sheryl Quincy's arm and extracting its remaining contents.

It did not come in time for two residents.

"This morning," Mayor Allen said as Genesee prepared to give him his injection on the porch of his house. "She never woke up."

Genesee hesitated, the needle just above the old doctor's arm, glancing past the man to the open door, then to me. I'd been drafted to assist him in visiting those too ill to come to the clinic where Specialist Hart was handling injections for those still mobile. After he was finished there, the garrison's medic would begin a quick tour of the frontline checkpoints to administer the vaccine to our defenders who'd remained on the line through fevers, choking coughs, and debilitating aches.

Here, though, the Navy doctor and I stood with his predecessor, learning that his wife, sickened by the virus, had not made it through the night.

"Did we lose anyone else?" Mayor Allen asked as Genesee slipped the needle easily into his flesh on the outside of his bicep.

"The little Chester boy," Genesee said.

"Good Lord," the mayor said, his head shaking somberly.

The Chester household would have been our first stop once the vaccine was ready to distribute, but just before the process was complete word came that the child, not quite five years old, had succumbed. An asthma sufferer, he'd struggled from the beginning, growing sicker, and weaker, by the hour.

Until the hours ran out.

"If this works," Genesee said, "I think we'll be able to pull everyone else through."

Mayor Allen nodded, grateful for that assessment. Truly grateful. But the shadow of loss upon his face, in his eyes and his slack expression, made clear how deep a loss he was experiencing before our very eyes. He'd made the town his priority, at his wife's urging, I was certain. Even in her final hours, when she was still conscious and able to speak, I had no doubt that she'd pushed him to focus on the town, and to keep the residents foremost in his thoughts, and in his efforts.

"I'm sorry, Everett," I said.

The old doctor who'd accepted the mantle of leadership reached out and put a comforting hand upon my shoulder. Offering *me* support. This town I'd adopted, which had accepted and embraced me as one of their own, had its share of fine, fine people. To think that there was a time, not long after arriving, that I'd thought of leaving, of heading off to seek survival on my own, was almost folly now. I simply hadn't looked hard enough at the people around me to realize I was already in the best place, with the best people, that I could be.

Commander Genesee finished the injection and discarded the needle in a container we'd brought along.

"My condolences, doctor," Genesee said.

"Thank you."

"I'll have a burial detail sent out," I told the mayor.

He nodded and stepped back, settling into one of two rockers that sat side by side on the porch.

"I think I'll just sit until they get here," the mayor said.

"Of course," I said.

Genesee and I left the man to be alone with his wife in their home for the last time. There was going to be another funeral. Another burial. More than one, I knew. And still more beyond those. Because, even with the vaccine, and expecting that it would work, there were still two armies facing each other, waiting for the order to attack.

But we had a chance, now. A fighting chance. Thanks to the man I'd suspected of turning against us.

"You may have saved us," I told Genesee as we climbed in the Humvee in front of the mayor's house and headed for our next stop.

"Maybe," Genesee allowed as I drove us down the street.

Silence lingered between us for a half mile of town streets. I'd been waiting for the Navy doctor to speak, but I realized it was actually me who had something that needed to be said.

"I didn't really care too much for you," I said.

Genesee never looked away from the road ahead as he processed what I'd just admitted.

"And now?" he asked

That was a fair question. And the truth was, I didn't have a good answer.

"Get back to me in a couple weeks," I said.

"You planning on being my cellmate in a Unified Government prison camp?"

I glanced from the road to Genesee and saw that he was still staring straight ahead, his steely gaze over a very unexpected smile.

Thirty Nine

They came from every direction but the west, the Pacific our only secure flank. It was also the immovable bit of mother earth that our backs were up against. There was no retreat. We could not run. We either stood our ground, or surrendered. I knew what that meant. We all did.

People were going to die today.

"I'm deploying the bulk of our reserves to the south," Schiavo said, reacting to the volume of reports that put a sizeable force to the east. "I believe that's a diversion."

We stood together, the Defense Council, possibly for the final time. The events of the night to come would dictate whether we would all gather again in the town hall conference room where we now stood.

"And the north?" I asked.

Schiavo looked to both Elaine and me.

"That's where you two will be with Corporal Enderson," she said. "You'll be able to read whatever happens there and know if a full attack is coming."

"And if it does?' Elaine asked.

"Then I'll be responsible for the fall of Bandon," Schiavo said, with matter of fact honesty. "I'll be here. Sergeant Lorenzen and Specialist Hart will deploy with the eastern forces, and Private Westin with the southern forces on the front line. If we need the reserves, I'll join them."

"So will I," Martin added.

A map lay on the table where we stood. Schiavo had marked all the positions and her intended deployments prior to our arrival. Mayor Allen leaned forward, palms on the edge of the map, his aged eyes sweeping across the landscape reduced to two dimensional lines denoting streets and elevation contours. He'd had no time to mourn the loss of his wife. No time even to bury her. Her body, and those of Nathan Chester, remained in cold storage at the town's morgue. Victory would allow us to give them proper services. But that outcome was still far from certain.

"And what if it fails?" the mayor asked. "When do I step in?"

He didn't outright say it, but what he was thinking echoed the American principal of civilian control over the military. In essence, he was asking Schiavo at what point he would have to make the decision to surrender in order to save the lives of those who remained.

"You'll have to make that call, sir," Schiavo said.

"People won't follow any such order," Elaine told the town's leader. "I won't."

"If I have to cross that bridge, Elaine, I fully assume that everyone in this room will already be dead."

"Except you," I said.

Mayor Allen nodded soberly.

"And God help me."

Schiavo stepped away from the table and slipped into her battle gear, taking her M4 in hand but foregoing her Kevlar helmet.

"I'll be in communications," she said. "My guess is that radio reception will be interfered with, so use landlines if you can get to one to report anything important."

"All right," I said.

We shook hands. We hugged. We said our good lucks, which, we knew, might very well be goodbyes. Then Elaine and I left the town hall and drove north in the old pickup we'd been assigned.

Ten minutes after we arrived at our destination, all hell broke loose.

Forty

"On the left!" Enderson shouted, his M4 spitting rounds to the northwest from the narrow firing slit of the sandbagged bunker at the northern limits of the town.

"I've got movement on the right!" Elaine yelled back, firing controlled single shots from her MP5, trying to conserve ammo.

Between them, facing the bridge directly, I squeezed off double taps at what I was certain were groups of enemy across the span, maneuvering on the far bank of the Coquille River. Every volley we sent toward our enemy was returned in kind, with greater volume than ours, sometimes by a factor of four.

We were outnumbered.

"Where's the patrol?!" Elaine asked above the deafening ripple of incoming and outgoing fire.

"They pulled back!"

Elaine hadn't caught the report on our radio, just thirty seconds earlier, that one of three foot patrols, meant to plug the space between our location and the checkpoint three hundred yards to our southeast, had retreated to a more secure vantage point. With that repositioning, and the engagement to our own front, it seemed almost certain that the final assault on Bandon had begun.

Until, without warning, the guns pointed at us fell silent.

It took us half a minute to realize that we were the only ones still shooting. Once we ceased fire, we watched. And we listened.

"What the hell is going on?"

The corporal's question was well founded. Whatever tactics our enemy was employing, they weren't from any textbook he was familiar with, nor recognizable compared to any engagement we'd had in any conflict since the blight turned us all into warriors.

"They know we're low on ammunition," Elaine said.

"Just getting us to waste what we have," Enderson said, agreeing. "We need to hold our fire until the real thing comes."

"I thought this was the real thing," I said.

The enemy was out there. Moving. Positioning themselves. They hadn't yet come across the river, which was the natural barrier on our northern flank. For all we knew, the targets we'd been shooting at were just the fodder troops that Olin had spoken of. The real troops, the hardened soldiers, could be right behind them. Or in another area altogether.

"There's shooting to the south," Elaine said, listening through the sudden quiet in our area.

Sustained fire, I thought. Heavier weapons. Machine guns. They could be ours, but I was guessing theirs. As yet there had been no explosions, signaling mortar attacks. Or worse.

"You two take a break," Enderson said, his attention focused through the bunker's narrow opening.

"Thanks," Elaine said.

We shifted position to the back of the bunker and sat on the floor. The barrels of our weapons were still warm as we set them momentarily aside. Elaine reached to me and pulled an expended 5.56mm casing from where it had lodged against my collar.

"Glad it wasn't the other end of one of these that found you," she said, dropping the spent shell atop the others that had been ejected from our weapons during the firefight which had just ended.

The hint of gallows humor in her words was plain. But so was the truth that bullets would find people. Our people. Our friends.

As we were about to learn, that fact had already come to pass.

"We have two down."

The report came in over the radio, the voice calm and familiar. Schiavo.

"Jesus..." Elaine said.

There was no more information shared. Captain Schiavo, at the garrison's command center in town, was taking in reports from the fixed outposts via wired lines and field radios. Whatever was happening elsewhere in and around the town, it all flowed through her. And, when necessary, to us.

"Down doesn't mean hurt," Enderson observed.

I knew he was right. Elaine did, as well, I knew. Offering up a running tally of any wounded was meaningless. Deaths, where someone was taken completely out of the fight, was not.

"So much for your friend's word," Enderson said, never looking back as he scanned the battered span that traversed the dark waters.

"What do you mean?" I challenged the corporal.

He glanced to me, no apology in his gaze for what he had said, and what his words suggested.

"They don't want to hurt anyone," Enderson said. "Wasn't that his promise?"

"It was *their* promise," Elaine corrected him. "The Unified Government."

Enderson snickered lightly and looked back to the river.

"He's with them," Enderson said. "And that means he's against us. It means he now has blood on his hands."

What the corporal was stating couldn't be argued on the face of the facts that had become known. But in that moment, as he laid out what seemed obvious, another possibility rose. A possibility which, as I considered it, seemed, in almost every way, more likely that what Enderson was saying.

"We're going to check the old bunker," I said, taking my weapon in hand and rising.

Elaine looked up to me where I stood, puzzled. Possibly she was doubting my choice to leave the safety of the intact bunker for the rubbled remnants of what had once been known as Checkpoint Chuck. Or she might have thought it odd that I was retreating from any defense of my friend, however distant and strained our onetime inseparable bond had become.

I reached my hand down and she gripped it, standing with my help. She was weak, still, a combination of exertion from the firefight and the remnants of the bug almost everyone in town had been fighting. Genesee's magic was working, saving almost every resident who was old, young, or compromised through some chronic illness. The bit of medical magic had also lessened the effect of those who did contract the illness, like my love. That had allowed her, and others, to stay in the fight.

Whether they had another fight in them, I wasn't certain.

* * *

We moved through the darkness, bounding to cover each other until we reached the shattered remnants of the old bunker within sight of our checkpoint. I'd fought there alongside Elaine soon after arriving in Bandon, fending off an assault across the bridge by the drug-crazed hordes from Seattle. Then she'd been just a hardened survivor, wary of the newcomers. Now...now she was everything to me. I loved her. I trusted her.

And I needed to share something with her.

"What if we're wrong about Neil?"

I posed that question to Elaine as we stayed in cover, scanning the river snaking east. In the dim light of the quarter moon I could see doubt registering on her face, then curiosity.

"Wrong?" she asked. "How could we be wrong? You know what he did, and who he's aligned himself with."

"I know what we think he did," I countered. "There's one very glaring hole in this picture we've all painted of him being a traitor."

"What hole?"

"His family," I said. "Grace, Krista, Brandon. They're here."

"He said it was a goodwill gesture," Elaine reminded me. "That he wouldn't send them somewhere where—"

And then she saw it, too.

"Where they'd be in danger," I said, completing the thought. "Except they are in danger. And he had to know that this would happen. That we wouldn't surrender. Not after all we've gone through to keep this town going."

Elaine nodded and brought her arm up to cough into the crook of her elbow.

"Why would he send them to a place where they'd be in danger?" I asked her.

She thought for a moment, the revelation coming to her as it had come to me.

"He'd send them if the danger here was less than where they already were."

It was my turn to nod.

"There's more to what he did," I said, feeling, for the first time in many months, that the man I'd grown up with was not the turncoat we'd feared. "There has to be."

"But what?"

I didn't have an answer. Just a gut feeling. And as I let all that I'd learned since Neil left run through my head, bits and pieces began to stand out. Inconsequential snippets of facts and moments.

One in particular.

"The Hawks..."

Elaine puzzled at my statement. I looked to her, my heart rate quickening.

"He joked that when this was all over we could catch a Hawks game," I said, recalling the innocent slice of banter my friend had offered. "On the ATV transmission, he said that to me."

"So?"

"The Hawks were from Atlanta," I said, recalling the location of the NBA team in the world before the blight. "But we never were into them. Not into basketball much at all. Football was our sport. That's what we watched together. That's what we played together."

"Atlanta," she repeated, thinking along with me. "Why would say that?"

I didn't know. It was doubtful he was sending some covert indicator of where he was. I suspected he was far closer than the south. The activity in our area, and what Grace had been able to recall about where they'd traveled, pointed to somewhere between here and the Rockies.

"Atlanta," I said again.

"Could be what they are making their capital," Elaine suggested, almost immediately discounting the thought. "But how would telling us that help?"

"It wouldn't," I said.

Elaine eased her head toward the edge of the fallen bunker and peered around, scanning the riverbank to the east. As she took that moment, I focused on my friend. On what he'd said.

It was in those quiet few seconds that pieces began to tumble into some vague order.

"He didn't just send a message to me," I said, and Elaine looked back to me. "Olin thinks the Ranger broadcast was meant for him."

"Maybe it was."

If that was true, then my friend was using different methods to send messages to those beyond his physical reach. To those people who mattered to him.

To us.

"He's talking to us," I said. "There's more to that transmission than just the obvious."

I returned to considering why he might reference Atlanta. What could he be pointing us toward?

"Disease," Elaine said, offering an answer to a question I hadn't directly posed. "The Centers for Disease Control is in Atlanta."

"CDC," I said, using the government organization's acronym. "They deal with biological threats. Plagues. Anthrax."

"And viruses," Elaine added with ominous realization. "They would have samples of biological agents there. Things that could be used. Against us."

She was right. If money meant anything at the moment, I'd bet on the accuracy of what she'd just suggested.

"He was slipping in a warning," I said. "About what we would be facing."

Elaine nodded, puzzling at something after a moment.

"Why not just have Grace tell us?"

I shook my head.

"That would bring her into whatever he's doing," I said.

But what was he doing? What was he trying to tell us? To tell me?"

"If you're right," Elaine began, "then the person in the most danger may just be him."

I nodded, beginning to believe she was right. My friend's leaving was not the act of a traitor—it was a man taking on a mission. Just as he'd done with Olin in their old lives. Here, though, it appeared that Neil Moore might have gone into the belly of the beast to save the very people he'd abandoned.

But how?

"There's something else," I said. "There has to be more. He wouldn't have known about Atlanta or viruses before he left us. He had to discover that once he'd joined up with them."

"If what Olin said was right, they expected him to join the cause from the beginning."

Elaine was correct. But he'd grown disillusioned with what they might do, just as he'd grown disillusioned with the rightful government. Only he didn't tell them he'd changed his mind. He just took off.

To find me.

"What else could he have slipped into that transmission?" Elaine wondered aloud.

We could have mused on what my friend might be trying to say all night. But the rocket fired from across the river ended any speculation we might have undertaken.

Forty One

It was not an RPG. We'd been on the receiving end of that weapon on Mary Island, its screaming approach a distinctive calling card. This was not that.

The projective dragged a fast tail of fire across the flowing waters as it streaked toward the reconstructed bunker.

"Enderson!" I screamed, hoping my warning would reach the corporal in time and allow him to dive clear of the coming impact.

It did not.

The warhead exploded just below the narrow, sandbagged firing port facing the river, sending a shower of white hot sparks arcing outward, in every direction, bits of molten shrapnel raining down upon the position Elaine and I had moved to.

"Eric!"

She grabbed me. My wife. My love. Her strong hands dragged me back from the open ground I'd leapt into without even realizing it, pulling me down to a place of cover behind the jagged remnants of a reinforced concrete wall that had once been part of the old checkpoint. Fire drizzled down from the dark night like falling fireflies set ablaze. A tiny chunk of white hot metal landed on Elaine's leg, burning instantly through her pants and sizzling against her flesh.

"AHHH!"

I swung my gloved hand at the smoking patch of flesh, then unlidded my water bottle and drenched the spot, keeping a steady stream of liquid onto the wound through the squirt top.

"Are you okay?! Did you get hit anywhere else?!"

Elaine shook her head and planted a gloved hand over the burn.

"Check the river!" she told me, ignoring her own pain.

I grabbed my rifle and swung around the left edge of the rubble, checking the bridge beyond the smoldering bunker. It was clear. No sign of any movement. I shifted past Elaine as she took her own MP5 in hand and followed me as I crawled to the right side of the rubble, poking my head around to be greeted by a volley of rounds ricocheting off the shattered concrete slabs.

"Back!"

I pushed Elaine behind and swung my AR into a slice of the visual pie that was clear, squeezing off a series of bursts at a half dozen silhouettes charging along the bank, moving to flank us.

"We've gotta move!" she shouted.

I fired more bursts until my weapon ran dry. As I ducked back behind cover to reload, Elaine scrambled past and kept any movement on our right side at bay until a targeted volley of fire ripped into the rubble just inches from her head.

"Elaine!"

I grabbed her and pulled her body back, not sure if I was going to find in that instant that I'd been made a widower. But she rolled as I pulled, coming to her hands and feet.

"They're not trying to miss," she said, referencing the encounter with the enemy that Nick Withers and I had had in the eastern woods. "This is the real thing."

"We can't hold here," I said.

In the distance, due south of us, a heavy volume of fire began to roll across the terrain. A major attack was in progress, precisely where Schiavo had anticipated. What we were facing might be a diversion, but it was effective. And may have been deadly.

"We've got to get to Enderson."

Elaine nodded and fired a wild spray of fire over the top of the rubble.

"Go!" she shouted.

I didn't want to leave her. Despite any agreement I'd made to not favor her if danger should arise, I could not force down my desire, my need, to protect her.

But, I reminded myself, here we were protecting each other. Neither of us would make it out of here on our own. I had to let her do what was necessary to keep us alive as a partner, not a wife.

"Now!"

This time I did not delay at her direction. I brought my reloaded AR up and charged across the short distance to the smoldering remains of the bunker, the satisfying burp of Elaine's weapon firing behind me. I reached the cover of the back wall, a thin line of fire licking up what remained of its wooden structure, then brought my weapon to bear and fired controlled shots at the edge of the field where it began to slope down to the river. Elaine bolted across the same space I had just traversed seconds before, favoring one leg, but keeping her speed up until she rolled past me and took a position on the opposite end of the burning back wall.

"Mo!"

I shouted out to Enderson as fire peppered the wall, and the two sides of the bunker that were equally damaged. Splinters of wood erupted from each impact, and jets of sand popped upward with each hit on one of the sandbags that had been tossed about by the explosion.

"Mo!"

"Here..."

The reply was weak, and soft, and when I glanced behind toward where it had come from, I saw the upper half of Corporal Morris Enderson dragging the other half out, crawling low and slow, as if creeping beneath a barbed wire obstacle in training camp. But this was not training. It was all too real.

As were his wounds.

"Mo!"

I called to him as I backed away from the corner of the burning bunker and grabbed him by the jacket, pulling him clear of the rubble. He was stunned and bleeding, though I couldn't tell how much was from superficial shrapnel wounds and how much was from serious injury.

"They're across the river!" Elaine reported.

This was no feint by third rate troops. These were serious shooters moving on our position. And on us.

"We've gotta get him out of here," I told her.

"We've gotta get *us* out of here!"

She was right in her correction. Dead right, if we didn't hurry.

"Can you cover?" I asked her.

She reloaded and reached out. I knew what she wanted and handed her my AR.

"Where are we going?" she asked, incoming rounds ripping dangerously close.

We'd left the old pickup truck a hundred yards away from the checkpoint, on a side road due south of our position. That had to be our destination. There was no way we could carry the soldier to the next defensive line protecting the town, not with an enemy in pursuit.

"We try for the truck," I told her. "If we can't make it, we go west to the water."

The alternative was the worst option, trying to slog our way south toward town through sand and surf, totally exposed on the beach and the harbor's edge.

"We better make it to the truck," Elaine said.

"Agreed. Ready?"

With still more fire coming in, from the east and the north now, she nodded and popped up, firing with one weapon, the other ready for action. I heaved Enderson over my shoulders, arm around his leg and hand holding his wrist, locking him in position as I jogged south. I couldn't look back. Doing so would only slow us. The only way I knew that Elaine was alright, and still with us, with me, was hearing the constant bursts of fire covering our retreat.

A few minutes after beginning our withdrawal we saw the old workhorse vehicle on the shoulder of the narrow road.

"Are they following?" I asked as I eased Enderson into the back.

Elaine tossed me my AR as I climbed into the bed of the truck with our wounded man.

"I don't think so," she said, hobbling back to check on him with me. "They might be holding at the river."

If true, they were just drawing the noose tighter, slowly squeezing the amount of territory we had to call our own.

"Get us to town," I said.

Elaine got behind the wheel and pulled the truck through a tight turn over both rough shoulders of the road. Just minutes later we passed through our interior defensive line, which was now the front line of our town, and neared the center of Bandon, cows and goats and pigs scattered about the streets.

"They pulled the livestock in," Elaine said, shouting through the space where the truck's rear window had once been. "Damn!"

She swore as she jerked the steering wheel, swerving to miss a dairy cow trotting in fear down the center of the road.

"That means the pens were overrun," I said, knowing what that meant. "We lost the northeast checkpoints."

The enemy was less than half a mile from us.

Forty Two

We reached the clinic in the old pickup and pulled Enderson from the open bed of the vehicle with assistance from Genesee and two residents who'd volunteered as orderlies.

"Stay with us, Mo," Genesee said as he lowered the corporal onto a gurney and began wheeling it into the clinic through the open double doors.

Right past Grace.

"Are you two all right?" Grace asked, a set of too-big blue scrubs hanging on her frame.

I helped Elaine toward the entrance, keeping the weight off her injured leg.

"She has a nasty burn," I said.

"I'm all right," Elaine protested.

Grace hurried forward and helped me get Elaine into a wheelchair just outside. She crouched and slipped a pair of synthetic gloves on, tearing the singed fabric around the wound to probe the burn. Elaine winced and grabbed the tall rear wheels of the chair.

"You've got about a two-inch area of third degree burns," Grace said, looking up to Elaine, and then to me. "She'll be fine. You did good soaking it."

She could tell from the dampness of Elaine's pants below the knee that I'd dumped all the water I could on the wound.

"I'll take her in and get a dressing on it until the doctor can take a look," Grace said.

I was ready to follow her in, but Grace's glance past me signaled that someone else had arrived. The Humvee's screeching tires confirmed to me who it was even before I looked.

"How is he?" Schiavo asked, looking through the clinic doors as Grace wheeled Elaine inside.

"He's shaken up," I told her, having checked him more closely on the ride in. "Some minor shrapnel wounds. But I think he's just stunned."

Stunned could mask serious injury, I knew. A traumatic brain injury could present itself after experiencing what Enderson had. But for the moment, his prognosis seemed good. I hoped it would remain so.

"They crossed the river," I reported.

Schiavo nodded, not surprised.

"They pushed us back all along our lines," she said.

The noose analogy was seeming very appropriate.

"Did we lose any more people? We heard about the two."

"No," she answered, though that response didn't seem to assuage her any. "But we will when they come again."

I noticed that there was no doubt in her reply. No 'if', but 'when'.

"When do you think that attack will come?"

"They'll let us stew in defeat for a while," she said. "A day, maybe two."

For now, at least, it was quiet. But in silence, fears could multiply.

"We've got people pushing for a surrender," Schiavo said. "Mayor Allen and Martin are dealing with them right now."

"How many?"

"It only takes a few," Schiavo said. "And there are more than that."

The flyers had been seen by most residents, and those who hadn't been exposed to them first hand had heard, second hand, what the Unified Government was promising.

"If we lose more ground, he may have no choice," Schiavo said, referencing Mayor Allen's question about the right time to do the unthinkable. "We have no more buffer space. Their next stop is in the streets."

If there was any good news to be had, Schiavo didn't offer it.

"I'm going to go have a look at Mo," she said, then disappeared into the clinic.

I listened to the silence of the night, hoping it would last, then I, too, went inside.

* * *

"She won't be winning any dancing contests for a while," Grace said.

She stood next to the gurney that Elaine lay upon in one of the three treatment areas in the clinic. I held my wife's hand and sneered at the bandage showing where the lower leg of her pants had been cut away.

"Always in the leg," she said. "Why do I always get hit in the leg?"

In the battle we'd had aboard the *Groton Star* in the waters off of Bandon, she'd taken a ricochet just above the knee. Now she'd have a fresh scar. Another reminder of just how we'd fought to maintain this life in the face of daunting odds.

"Tomorrow will be better," Elaine said to me. "It will."

"You rest for a bit," I said, leaning in to kiss her.

I nodded toward the exit and stepped outside the treatment room with Grace. We stood in the hallway as Corporal Morris Enderson talked with Commander Genesee and Captain Schiavo two doors down.

"He's going to be okay," Grace said. "So is Elaine. She'll have some scarring."

"She hates her legs anyway," I said. "I'm kind of fond of them."

Grace smiled. A real smile. Something I might have seen on her face back at my Montana refuge, or when we first returned from Skagway. If I was being truly hopeful, I might say that she was turning some mental corner.

"And how are you?" I asked.

Grace smiled again and gave something that was part nod, part tip of her head.

"I had to do something," she said. "I had to help. Judy Newland said she'd sit with Krista and Brandon while I came down here."

Maybe it was the connection to who she was, to who she'd been. A nurse. I thought that getting back into familiar rhythms was doing her good. As she did good for others.

"Is it really that bad out there, Fletch?"

I couldn't lie to her. But I also couldn't say anything. I couldn't bring myself to utter any description of the deteriorating situation. All I could do was offer a small nod.

Grace's resurgent brightness dimmed a bit, but didn't crack.

"We'll get through this," she said to me, a skim of tears suddenly glistening in her eyes. "There's always hope."

Before either of us could react further to her words, to words borrowed from her husband, from my friend, she turned and went back into the treatment room with Elaine, leaving me in the bright hallway. Thinking on my friend's mantra. Wanting to believe them.

There's always hope...

He'd said that to me. Many times. Implied it in other ways.

What else had he said, without me knowing, without any of us knowing? As Elaine and I had discussed at the rubbled bunker, before the rocket attack took out the checkpoint, Neil was sending a message. By allowing Grace and the children to even be among us he was signaling that they were safer here. By referencing the Atlanta Hawks, he was hinting at the Unified Government's access to pathogens at the CDC.

That was what we believed. It was not what we knew, but what we felt was right.

There's always hope...

Yes, there was. And I thought back to the last time I'd seen my friend, on the static-filled ATV transmission. That was where he'd slipped in what I'd thought was an innocent reference to a sporting team. What other information might he have tried to covertly pass along in that exchange? From memory, I couldn't recall. But I wouldn't have to do that.

The transmission had been recorded.

Forty Three

Sitting at Micah's workstation, I queued up the recordings saved from every ATV transmission both received and sent from the Bandon station.

"Eagle One," I said softly, fondly, recalling the call sign the child had given himself.

There was much I could dwell on. Much nostalgia, both good and bad, in the recordings. The tomato plant growing before our eyes in a distant Wyoming greenhouse. The ultimatum delivered by General Weatherly. But I moved past those and found the precise snippet of digital data I needed to review.

Neil's freeze-framed face stared out at me from the monitor.

I brought the mouse cursor over the play button and clicked the button.

"*...we could be sitting courtside at a Hawk's game, drinking a beer.*"

I paused the playback there after my friend's words lived again. His meaningful meaningless inclusion of a Hawk's reference. I believed in my soul that he was trying to send me, send us, information that could help in our struggle against those threatening us. Against those he'd gone to not on a mission of treachery, but of sabotage.

"What else is there, Neil?"

I asked the question, wishing he would just answer me. That he would look out from the recording and speak to me, plainly, so that I would know what he was trying to do.

Again I let the recording play, stopping and listening to sections over and over. Waiting, searching, for something that would mean anything. For hours I pored over every second. Every image. Every word. The sun rose outside and bled through the lone window into the space.

"Help me, Neil..."

I played the recording again. And again. Exhaustion was numbing me. Dulling my senses. But I remained convinced that something more had to be here. In this exchange.

"Krista made you a drawing while she was here. She spent hours on this red rhinoceros thing. Did she show it to you?"

For some reason I stopped there. Maybe just to savor a simple thing. Something he'd said that was unrelated to...

"Anything."

Just like the Hawks comment was salient, without seeming to be, if what I believed to be true turned out to be so.

"Red rhinoceros," I said, repeated one part of the statement. "Red."

The Red Signal? Was he referencing that? But how could that play any role in what we were facing now? That repetitive beacon had begun as society crumbled at the outset of the blight. We were years past that.

"Rhinoceros," I repeated.

That, too, meant nothing. Or nothing obvious. A zoo? Africa? Horn? What could the meaning be? I listened and listened, over and over, struggling to understand. When I was about to give up on this snippet of the conversation, I saw it.

"Wait..."

I backed the recording up to the earlier Hawks reference, and I saw it there, too. I forwarded again to the red rhino section, and Neil, once again, did the same thing.

He let his thumb rise from where his hands were folded. He was giving a thumbs up on these specific parts of the broadcast.

From the beginning I watched the entire transmission, twice, and only at those two times did my friend signal with a thumbs up. But, as I watched closer, I realized that I was being too broad in my recognition of this gesture. He was not giving a thumbs up to sentences—he was doing so when particular words were spoken. And only then. Nowhere else as he spoke did his hands make any movement.

"Hawks," I said, watching as the thumb came up, and then receded, gone when my friend moved on to the next word.

I forwarded the recording once more and watched as I listened, pinpointing the very word he was speaking when his thumb flicked upward a final time.

"Drawing," Neil said on the recording.

"Drawing," I said in sync with my friend.

Krista's drawing.

I didn't bother shutting down the workstation. There was no time. I ran as fast I could from the house where Micah had lived and died.

Forty Four

Grace came to the entrance to their house and looked out at me through the screen door.

"Fletch. You look terrible."

I hadn't slept. The filth of the firefight and retreat from the northern checkpoint was still thick upon me. But I didn't care. Didn't feel weary or beaten. For the first time in days, maybe weeks, I was energized by possibilities. Possibilities that, oddly, were unknown to me.

I had come here to change that.

"Can I come in?"

There was no doubt I would be welcomed. My friend's wife simply stepped aside and let me in.

"I'm sorry if I'm dragging a bit," Grace said. "I only caught a few hours' sleep after my shift at the clinic."

I shook off her apology. For a woman with two children, who'd just tended to people wounded in battle, she looked remarkable. Strong. These were the things I knew Neil had seen in her.

"Grace, can I talk to Krista?"

The request drew only a quick flash of curiosity from her.

"Krista?"

"Yes."

"I'll get her."

I stopped the mother before she started down the hallway toward her daughter's bedroom.

"Can you ask her to bring her book of drawings?"

A minute later I sat next to Krista on the couch, the book I'd asked for on her lap, Grace just across from us in the comfortable easy chair.

"Krista, can I look at your drawings?"

"Sure," the child said, handing me the book.

"Fletch, what is this about?" Grace asked.

I held the book and looked to my friend's wife.

"In the transmission we received, Neil said that Krista had made a drawing for me."

"I did," Krista said proudly, reaching to the book I now held and flipping it to the page in question. "Right here."

The child beamed at the image of the red rhinoceros.

"I don't think I got the horn right," Krista said.

"I think it looks wonderful," I told her.

Down the hall, the baby began to fuss.

"And someone probably needs their diaper changed," Grace said. "I'll just be a few minutes."

I looked at the drawing as Grace left the room. Studied it. Searched for some bit of information that might have been hidden within the colors and lines and smudges. But I could see nothing but the playful and wonderful strokes of a child's artistry.

"Did Neil help you with this at all?"

"No," Krista said, both proud and perturbed at the suggestion. "These are all mine."

She flipped away from the red rhinoceros to show a selection of the other drawings she'd completed, all on her own.

"Krista, can I ask a big favor?"

"Sure."

I closed the book and held it, very carefully, as if it meant the world to me.

"Can I borrow this for a while? I promise I'll get it back to you."

Uncertainty flashed in the girl's expression.

"I promise."

"Why do you want to take it?"

There were ways to craft a simple white lie. I could tell her that I wanted to show Elaine, who'd been driven home from the clinic I'd been told on my sprint here from Micah's old house. Or any number of other falsehoods a child was sure to accept.

I chose another route altogether.

"Krista, I think there might be something in here that can help all of us. The whole town."

"The *whole* town?" she asked incredulously.

"Yes."

Krista eyed the book in my hand for a moment, then, with no more hesitation, she nodded her acceptance.

"Thank you, sweetie," I said, leaning over to plant a quick kiss atop her head.

When I did I saw Grace standing at the near end of the hallway. I stood, with the book in hand, the mother's gaze fixed on mine. Wondering and worried.

"I'll bring this back soon," I said.

Then, before Grace could press me on what I was doing, I left her house, their house, and made my way quickly home.

Forty Five

Elaine was limping across the living room of our house when I entered.

"What's that?" she asked, noticing the book in my hand. "Are those Krista's drawings?"

"Yeah."

"What are you doing with those?"

I explained to her what I believed I'd found in the ATV message.

"Let me see," she said.

But I held the book close and shook my head.

"I need to do this," I said. "He said that the drawing was for me."

"So?"

"What if he really meant that? That it was only for me to see? To know?"

"Eric..."

I stepped toward her. Behind us, through the open front door, a distant volley of gunfire erupted, then died out within a few seconds. No full scale battle had begun. Not yet.

"Let me do this," I said, gesturing with the book. "Let me find out what he was trying to say with this."

She didn't press the issue anymore. I kissed her on the cheek and headed through the kitchen, out into the back yard where a small table sat in the space where a lawn had once spread from fence to flowerbed, two chairs near it. I pulled one out and sat, resting the book upon the table and flipping to the drawing of the red rhinoceros.

Looking upon it I could still see nothing of note. Holding it close to my face, examining it with focused gaze, all that I could see was what was there—a child's drawing. I flipped the page to the opposite side and saw a trio of palm trees sketched out and colored in with earthy browns and vibrant greens. Nothing there, either, pointed to any meaning in the drawing that preceded it.

But some meaning I did find. Meaning that, itself, was preceded by mystery.

What is that?

The question rose silently as I turned the page back, feeling it, pinching both sides between thumb and index finger for the first time. There was something there. Some extra texture that felt out of place. I flattened both parts of the book to either side of the page and studied it from the edge. That was when I saw it.

Two pages were stuck together. Glued, it appeared, right at the edges, red rhinoceros on one side, palm trees on the other, creating a space between. A sealed space. A pouch of sorts.

And there was something in it.

I took the small folding knife clipped inside my pants pocket and extended the blade. Carefully I slipped the point into a small imperfection in the seal between the pages, working it in and very gingerly spreading the spot, sawing back and forth, separating first one edge, then the long side, until I could just slide two fingers in to probe the contents.

When they came out they held a folded slip of paper between them.

I set the book aside and closed my knife, returning it to my pocket as I stared at the paper, still folded over. Something was written within. I knew this. Something my friend intended for me. For my eyes only, I suspected.

When I opened it and read the first line of what was written, I knew that belief had been correct.

"The security of a secret increases exponentially as the number of people who know it approaches zero..."

I read the words aloud. Words that I'd heard before, verbatim, from Olin's mouth. It had to be some admonition each had learned in their clandestine careers. Here, now, Neil was prefacing what came next with that very warning.

As I read the remainder of what he'd written, I knew that I would have to take that warning to heart.

Part Four

BA 412

Forty Six

I did what I had to do. And I told no one.

Not even Elaine.

"What happened to your hand?"

The small adhesive bandage lay across the meaty flesh at the base of my thumb, a dark spot soaked through.

"I nicked it on the fence out back."

I'd been out in the back yard, and in the small garage which, until recent events, I'd been slowly converting into a small workshop. That I'd suffered some insignificant injury was not unusual. That I'd done so after retreating to the back yard to search Krista's book for some message from Neil was.

"Did you find anything?"

In my hand I held the book, closed tight, the pages I'd separated glued back together while in my workshop. I looked at the book, and not to my wife, even as she took a step closer.

"Eric..."

I handed her the book.

"Will you give this back to Krista?"

Elaine eyed the collection of drawings, then tossed it onto the kitchen table.

"Tell me what's going on," she said, more worried than annoyed, but enough of the latter that her displeasure with me was more than clear.

"I can't," I said.

She was ready to challenge me. To state some refusal to accept my reticence. But she didn't get a chance, as the ringing phone interrupted our exchange.

"I'll get it," she said, turning away, still agitated as she answered. "Hello."

She listened for a minute, glancing to me, whatever temper had risen gone as if never there, all about her now sober verging on grim.

"All right," Elaine said into the handset, then placed it back in its cradle.

"Who was that?"

"The mayor wants us down at the town hall," she said. "He's going to meet with Weatherly."

I absorbed the news. There would only be one reason Mayor Allen would choose to meet with the military leader of the Unified Government.

"I think he's going to surrender," Elaine said, guessing my very sentiment without knowing she was doing so.

* * *

A Humvee picked us up and dropped us at the town hall. A crowd had gathered outside, dozens in number. Angry residents, tired of fighting, demanding an end to the conflict. Elaine and I pushed through their raucous demonstration, aided by Private Westin, and made our way to the conference room.

Martin, Schiavo, and Mayor Allen were already there.

"Good morning," the mayor said.

It was anything but that. Still, I smiled at the genteel old man. A widower now. Yet here he stood, giving all he had for the town he'd agreed to lead.

"Our situation is untenable," the mayor said. "The group you see voicing their displeasure outside has doubled in the last hour."

"Some of them are supposed to be on the line," Schiavo said.

"We may lose our army before our enemy fires another shot," Mayor Allen said.

"Not everyone will desert," Elaine said.

"Enough might," Schiavo said.

Elaine walked unsteadily to the head of the table and stood close to the mayor.

"I will not lay down my arms," she said. "I will not. And there are a lot of people in this town who feel the same way. They will continue to fight."

Mayor Allen looked to her, as a grandfather might to a favored grandchild, smiling at her dedication. Her spark. Her idealism.

"I know," he said, then he looked to Schiavo. "Have the message sent that I'll meet with General Weatherly to discuss our situation."

"He'll only discuss surrender," Schiavo reminded the town's leader.

"Then tell him I'll discuss surrender with him," I said.

All eyes shifted quickly to me, but it was my wife's gaze that found mine first. Apart from my late mother, no other person, not even Neil, could read me as she could. From clues in my tone to the sometimes evasive choice of words, Elaine Morales Fletcher could tell, could sense, what motivation, what truth, lay beneath the words I chose to speak. Here, in her eyes, I could see that same understanding.

She knew that I had some plan in mind.

"This is not your responsibility, Fletch," Mayor Allen told me.

"No, it's not," I agreed. "But I'm volunteering. And I'm asking you to let me do this."

"Why?" Schiavo asked.

"Because Neil wants me to."

The captain's stare doubted me, some fire in it. Some anger that I was implying direction from one who'd abandoned us.

"Let him do it," Elaine said.

Before Schiavo could challenge her, another voice rose.

"Yes," Martin said. "Let him meet with Weatherly."

Mayor Allen absorbed the endorsements of my proposal, then turned to his military counterpart.

"Captain..."

He was asking for her opinion. Maybe her blessing. To her credit, Captain Angela Schiavo did not throw down any gauntlet of disapproval. She might be unsure of just what was happening, but I knew that, whatever doubt there was swirling about her thoughts, she trusted me. Even with her life.

Here, though, I was asking to be trusted with everyone's.

"I'll have Westin send the message," Schiavo told me. "I pray you know what you're doing."

"Me, too."

Forty Seven

The Blackhawk helicopter bearing General Harris Weatherly came in low from the east and settled into a hover over the clearing two miles from town. The dust of dead and disintegrating trees swirled in the woods that bordered the flat, barren meadow as the aircraft descended, its side doors sliding open. Hardly a second after its wheels touched down the military commander of the Unified Government stepped out, two armed troopers at his side.

I stood alone, fifty yards away. To my rear, in the sparse cover the wasting forest could provide, a dozen volunteers from Bandon waited along with Schiavo, providing security for me. As I'd expected, it was not to be needed. General Weatherly left his troopers behind and walked the short distance to meet me.

"You're Eric Fletcher."

"I am."

Weatherly looked past me, his gaze seeming to zero in on a particular spot at the edge of the woods. A spot where I knew Schiavo stood, not behind any tree, eschewing cover for some display of what defiance she could muster.

"Why isn't she here to receive our terms?"

"Because I am," I told the man.

In the slight shift of his head I could sense more than irritation. This man was not accustomed to insolence, much less defiance. In my words, and my mere presence in place of Bandon's ranking military officer, Weatherly saw both.

"Then you it is," he said. "My troops will enter town from the east on foot at seven tomorrow morning. Your garrison will be there to meet them and will surrender their arms. Another contingent will land on the beach via helicopter transport and will expect to see all civilian arms deposited there. At noon every resident will gather at your town hall to be informed of the town's new status as a protectorate of the Unified Government."

He stopped there, the directive I was certain he'd given more than once before to other survivor colonies complete.

"Is all of what I've told you clear?"

"Extremely," I said.

"Good."

"And we reject your terms," I told him. "We reject any terms, from anyone, and particularly from a government we did not participate in electing."

He didn't smile. I'd almost expected him to. A gesture of amused pity at a defiant streak he knew he could crush. Instead, his gaze and his manner hardened. I watched his posture straighten, as if he was coming to attention in slow motion, making himself taller, more formidable.

Invincible.

But he was none of that.

"My terms are not open to negotiation, modification, or choice. They will be enforced, with your cooperation, or without it."

He glanced over his shoulder to the helicopter which had brought him, and the troopers who'd accompanied him, as if to remind me, to remind us all, that what we saw was but a small part of the firepower he could bring to bear.

But he was not the only one wielding some unseen power.

"I'd like to show you something," I said.

"What would you like to show me?" General Weatherly asked with officious impatience.

I wore no arms. No pistol on my hip. No rifle slung across my back. I did not even carry a blade sheathed on my belt. What I did possess I carried in the shirt pocket beneath my coat. Slipping my finger and thumb into that pocket I retrieved a small, clear vial, and held it out in the space between General Weatherly and me.

His gaze fixed on the transparent container and the red-tinted liquid within, and for the briefest instant I sensed that he was about to take a backward step to put distance between us. Between him and what I held.

"You know what this is," I said.

Weatherly didn't respond. Not at first. He simply stared at the vial. At its contents. As if he was gazing at the face of the devil himself.

"BA Four Twelve," I said.

The military man looked up to me again, some controlled rage plain in his stare.

"You know what this can do," I said. "You know that all it will take is some in a mortar shell to wipe out your army. Or any of your protectorates."

"He said it didn't exist," Weatherly told me, his voice steady and strong. "Your friend said it was a phantom agent. Never even developed."

I smiled. A very, very real smile, one that I knew Neil Moore would appreciate.

"And you believed him?"

"No."

"Good on you," I said. "You were right not to. He's a spy, and spies lie."

The tip of Weatherly's tongue slipped from his mouth and moistened his lips. He was standing his ground. Maintaining control. But it was a struggle. Maybe for the first time since he'd initiated the siege of our small town.

"If you attack us, you kill yourself with the same weapon," the general said.

"Give us liberty, or give us death," I said to the general, his gaze coming off the vial I held to meet mine. "Sound familiar?"

He looked past me to Schiavo and the armed party arrayed near her.

"This won't just give you sniffles and a fever, Weatherly," I said. "Remember that as you make your choice."

The choice he made, quickly as it turned out, was the only option this new reality allowed him.

"We would have had to start from scratch with this pissant town anyway."

I ignored the insult and slipped the vial back into my pocket.

"By noon tomorrow your forces are gone," I told the general. "We'll send scouts out, and if we find you still in our area..."

"You won't," the man said, though he spoke the assurance with such restrained vitriol that it was hard to detect any hint of surrender in his voice. "Is that all?"

"It is."

The man wasted no time. He didn't linger for a long, telling, final look. He simply turned and walked back to his helicopter, its door sliding quickly shut after he climbed aboard. Within a minute it was airborne again, disappearing over the woods to the east.

I stood there, watching the emptiness where our enemy had stood just a moment before. Had it really worked? Was this really over?

"Fletch..."

It was Schiavo. She'd walked out to where I stood, alone, the remainder of the force we'd brought to the clearing hanging back.

"What happened?"

"We won't have any more trouble from Weatherly," I said. "For now. Or the Unified Government."

It was a belief that I stated, not a boast, and I could only hope that it came with no expiration date.

"I don't understand."

"They're leaving," I told her.

"Leaving? They're leaving?"

"Yes."

She studied me for a moment.

"I'm not following, Fletch. We were here to surrender."

"It didn't work out that way."

"And why not?"

I took the vial out again and showed her.

"Because of this."

I'd made no mention of what I held before her, but the things it could be, things capable of driving an army from the field, were frightening enough just in thought.

"What is that, Fletch?"

"It's water with a few drops of blood to make it look red," I explained. "But Weatherly thinks it's BA Four Twelve."

"You bluffed him? How..."

There were few I could trust with what Neil had orchestrated. Schiavo was one of those.

"Read," I said, taking the note from my pocket and handing it to Schiavo. "Neil hid that in Krista's drawing book."

She skimmed the admonition about the security of a secret, then the remainder of the note while I quickly explained how Neil had slipped covert messages into the ATV broadcast.

"Christ..."

I took the note back and read what I knew to be troubling her.

"Biological agent called BA Four Twelve exists. Color water light red to mimic it. Unified Government terrified of it. If Weatherly moves on Bandon threaten to use it. Real sample somewhere safe. Hope I can explain someday."

"He doesn't know we know," Schiavo said. "About Four Twelve or him."

"He has no idea Olin reached us."

"Somewhere safe," Schiavo repeated. "How can there possibly be somewhere safe for something like that?"

"I don't know," I said.

"Why didn't he just do this from here?" Schiavo wondered, confused. "He could have orchestrated this charade from our side. He didn't need to go over and fake a defection."

"I think he did," I said. "Or he thought he had to. It was the only way to know if Weatherly and the Unified Government believed that BA Four Twelve really existed. From the inside. He had to know if a bluff would work."

"Because using the real thing would be suicide," Schiavo said, understanding now.

"This was just another mission to him," I said. "His most important mission. One he had to conceive and carry out on his own."

Schiavo thought on that, then fixed on the note still in my hand.

"Burn that," she said. "As far as anyone knows, if the subject comes up, Neil left us a supply of Four Twelve before he left."

"Agreed."

I was no longer the sole bearer of the secret. If that should have eased some burden I felt, it didn't. Because I knew, as Schiavo did, that while we were now secure, now safe, the one who'd made that possible was not.

"He double crossed them," Schiavo said.

"He did," I confirmed, knowing what that meant, just as Schiavo did.

"Weatherly knows that, too, now," she said.

"Yes."

The result of that was a terrible reality neither of us could deny—my friend's life wasn't worth a damn.

Forty Eight

The alert of another broadcast had come over the open frequency, telling us to expect an ATV transmission at noon two days after General Weatherly pulled his troops from the area near Bandon. Elaine, Schiavo, Martin and I stood with Mayor Allen at Micah's workstation and watched the transmission resolve from static.

The first face we saw on the screen was Neil's.

"Dear God," Schiavo said.

The same sentiment, the same fear, rippled through me as I saw my friend, standing alone, a blue jumpsuit his attire, arms bound behind his back, his face swollen and bruised. Some bastardized version of the American flag was tacked to the dingy wall behind him, red and white stripes the same, but the field of fifty stars had been replaced by one large one. This, I knew, was what the Unified Government had adopted as their banner. As the emblem they would plant in conquered territory. In it I saw a symbol of what both Neil and I had always feared—a centralized government so powerful that the wishes of those across its lands were deemed secondary to maintaining its authority.

The blight had wiped out many things, but not some men's desire to hold dominion over others.

"Neil Moore has been sentenced to death," a voice said, its speaker just out of frame. "He has requested to make a statement."

"Should we get Grace over here," Elaine asked, any answer to the question bearing terrible consequences.

"And have her see this?" Martin challenged.

No. There was no way we could do that. No way that we would let Grace witness her husband's murder, even if it was the final chance she'd have to lay eyes upon him before he was gone.

Gone.

They were violating the prime rule of recovery that we'd come to embrace. Every life was precious. Every breathing member of our species, however reviled, had the capacity to contribute, even if not at the moment. It was the reason Sheryl Quincy was still alive. That simple chance, however unlikely, that she possessed some value. Some worth which might—

"Stop!"

I shouted the order, the plea, as I reached down and stabbed a finger onto the transmit button.

All eyes in the room shifted to me, but only until another face we knew stepped into view on the screen.

"What is it?" General Harris Weatherly asked, a mix of impatience and curiosity in his tone.

A few inches from the audio transmit button was the control to activate the camera. I did so, and saw my friend's expression change as our images became visible on whatever monitor they'd made available on his end of the transmission.

"Fletch..."

I wanted to return his greeting. To speak my friend's name. The name of a man I knew now hadn't betrayed us, but who had gone into the lion's den to save us. Risking everything. His wife. His children. His own life.

It was time to make that sacrifice right.

"All you do by executing him is lose one of your own," I said.

To my side, though I couldn't see it, I felt Schiavo's posture change as she shifted position, angling toward me. She sensed what I was doing. Or what I was about to do.

"He's not one of our own," Weatherly corrected me, errantly as it turned out.

"I'm not talking about Neil," I said.

The general glanced behind, eyeing the traitor in their midst for a second, then looked back to me, perhaps realizing, as his counterpart had, that there was another party to this dance of deceit.

"We have your spy," I said. "How much use to you will she be once she's been shot?"

I dared not even glance Schiavo's way. Chancing a look, a connection, might very well invite resistance to a proposal on which, for now, she was standing silent.

"One for one," I said. "An even trade. Neither of our populations decrease."

Weatherly did not reject what I'd offered. But he did not accept it, either.

"This is a numbers game, general. We both know that. Every person on our respective sides with a pulse matters."

I wondered if, standing next to his wife, Martin was allowing any smile as I appropriated the argument he'd made early on in the siege. Surrendering a town was defeat, but surrendering an individual was failure. I understood that now. We needed every single person, no matter their limitations or faults, who wanted to be part of our tiny, wonderful community on the Pacific.

"Sheryl Quincy for Neil Moore," I said. "It's your call."

Very purposely I laid the success or failure of my proposal at his feet. And, just as he'd avoided lingering in his decision to pull his troops from their siege of our town, General Harris Weatherly spoke his mind without hesitation.

"Agreed," Weatherly said.

I didn't smile. Neither did my friend. We looked at each other over the connection just before it ended, knowing that we would see each other once again.

* * *

Just outside, Schiavo asked Elaine if she could have a word with me. My wife obliged and let us peel off for a private moment.

"You have ice water in your veins," the captain said. "Or brass ones the size of coconuts."

"Excuse me..."

"You could have offered this trade when you were face to face with Weatherly the other day, except you couldn't."

"No, I couldn't."

I'd thought through that scenario, even before I'd been given the go ahead for my one on one with the general. What would the man have thought if I produced a vial of BA 412, then proceeded to demand he end the siege of Bandon and accept a prisoner swap involving my friend?

"Weatherly would have had doubts," Schiavo said. "I know I would have. Who is this really for, your town or your friend?"

"Maybe his doubts are enough that he calls my bluff," I confirmed.

Schiavo shook her head, in admiration, not doubt.

"Neil had no way of knowing we'd be able to swap for him," she said.

"No, he didn't."

My friend, I knew, had been ready to give his life for us.

"He couldn't run," Schiavo said, processing the realities of my friend's situation. "He had to stay. He had to play the double agent role right to the end."

"If he doesn't, then Weatherly realizes we don't have the real thing. He turns his retreat into an attack."

"Neil had to play up that he'd beaten Weatherly," Schiavo said. "To the man's face."

Neither of us wanted to imagine what my friend, what our friend, had been through once his treachery was discovered. But what mattered was that he was alive. And he was coming home.

Forty Nine

I waited in the same field where I'd met with General Weatherly and noted the hush of exotic rotors somewhere to the east. Almost instantly after the sound reached me the familiar black craft glided over the dead woods and banked right, coming to a hover for a few seconds before it descended, landing with a burst of dust but hardly a whisper. As the cloud of dried earth settled, I looked to my right. To the prisoner we were sending back to her own kind.

"I saved your life," I told Sheryl Quincy. "Not that it matters, but you should know."

"You're right," she said. "It doesn't matter."

The gritty billows of earth parted, and across the field I watched the black stealth helicopter, resting like some lounging predatory insect. I could just make out the silhouette of the flight crew past the angular cockpit windows, but nothing more within. The side door facing me remained closed.

"Do you think this is going to end anything?" Quincy challenged me. "Just handing me over and getting your own traitor back?"

"No," I said. "But we stopped you here. For now."

"You delayed the inevitable," she countered.

"The trend line of humanity should never favor more government control over the individual."

Sheryl Quincy snickered openly at what I'd just told her.

"What naïve philosopher spewed that pablum?"

"Him," I answered, nodding across the field toward the man stepping from the helicopter's side door as it opened. "Neil Moore. That's from a paper he wrote in high school. I always remembered that line. I think you should, too."

Neil walked a few yards from the aircraft and waited. Behind him, in the din of the passenger cabin, I could just make out three silhouettes, blacked out from head to toe, obvious weapons in hand. But not pointed in my direction, their barrels directed downward.

"Time for you to go."

I reached behind the traitor and slipped the key into the handcuffs that bound her. The bindings clicked open and fell into my hand. Quincy put her hands to her front and rubbed her reddened wrists.

"Walk halfway to the helicopter and stop," I instructed her. "Neil will walk out and meet you. You then continue to the helicopter and get aboard. If you deviate from those instructions you will be shot."

Quincy glanced behind. In the tree line behind us, Schiavo and Lorenzen stood with the remainder of the garrison, weapons also low but ready.

"If you shoot me, we shoot him," Quincy reminded me.

The process had been agreed upon in an ATV exchange following my discussion with General Weatherly. I imagined it might be similar to the trading of spies during the Cold War, with each crossing a bridge at the same instant to return to their handlers and countrymen. Here, though, what each side was giving fell lopsided in our favor, relative to any damage done. Neil had gone into the enemy camp on a mission of necessity. Of his own choosing. By his own design. And he had saved us.

Sheryl Quincy had been a simple spy. A mildly effective turncoat.

But, besides the ability to weigh one's worth against the other, what mattered to me was something more basic, yet more profound—I was getting my friend back, both physically and in esteem.

"Walk," I instructed Quincy.

Across the field, Neil waited as Quincy began to move. At the halfway point, as instructed, she halted, and my friend walked out to meet her. Once he reached where she was she continued on, tossing a sideways look at my friend as she passed. Hardly a minute later she reached the helicopter and climbed aboard.

The rotor spun up and the door closed. With a whining whisper the stealth aircraft leapt into the air, banking severely, nose dropping as it accelerated, skimming the dead trees as it flew east. Gone.

My friend, standing a hundred yards away, watched it go. Then he turned toward me and began to walk, and I began to walk toward him. I would not have been surprised to hear Schiavo and her troops rushing out to join me, but I didn't, and I understood why. She knew that this moment of reunion was for us. For Neil and me. There would be others, as he was reunited with Grace, with friends. The town, when they learned what he'd done, or the story of his exploits we allowed to be told, would be beyond grateful.

That, though, could wait.

We crossed the distance quickly until just a few feet separated us.

"Hey, Fletch."

"Neil."

He came forward and pulled me into a hug. I returned the gesture. For that instant we were back in high school, on the gridiron, celebrating after a stellar touchdown. The separation we'd endured for months melted away. We were together again.

My friend was back.

We eased back from our embrace and just looked at each other, smiling, in awe.

"I knew you'd get the message," Neil said. "You're such an anal nut job. Every wall has to be perfectly plumb. Use the right size nail. If something's not right, it gnaws at you."

"What if I'd been a closeted Hawks fan?" I challenged him. "This all would have fallen apart."

"Like I wouldn't know that."

The tone of the exchange shifted right there. Neil's mood quieted. Darkened by a degree. We'd come to that point in what had to be discussed, how one of us had never been the man the other thought he was.

"Fletch, I have to tell you some things."

"No," I said, shaking my head. "You don't."

"After all this, no, I do. I really do, Fletch."

"Neil..."

"Let me—"

"Olin reached us," I said.

Instantly, the mood I'd noticed darkening by a degree seemed to teeter on the edge of some abyss. It was as if the shadow of some hellish storm cloud had passed over him.

"Olin..."

"Yes," I confirmed, worried that my friend might think my opinion of him had lessened because of his colleague's revelations. "It's all right. He told us everything."

"Olin is here?"

I shook my head.

"He left. He said he'd be close by if you want to see him, but he was pretty sick. I don't know if—"

I could no longer ascribe my friend's expression and demeanor to mere surprise that I knew of his covert life. Something was troubling him. More deeply than anything I'd ever seen.

"Neil, what's wrong?"

"Ty Olin was here?" my friend asked, seeming to seek confirmation of an impossibility.

"Yeah. He heard your transmission. He said the Ranger Signal was meant for him."

What color there was in my friend's face drained completely. He turned quickly away from me, his gaze scanning the far edge of the woods, manically searching the dark spaces between the trees.

"Neil, what's wron—"

The sound from the far edge of the woods cut off my question. It was loud, and sharp. A rifle shot. Just one. One whose signature flat crack was unmistakable.

But even as my mind processed what the sound was, and from whom it had originated, my eyes were taking in a sight so horrible I was left frozen. Immobile. Just standing there as a single bullet tore into my friend's chest and blew a hole out his back, dead center, destroying his spine.

"Neil!"

A shower of my friend's blood sprayed over me as he dropped like a ragdoll. I dove to cover him as weapons behind me opened up, Schiavo and her troops laying suppressing fire on the shot's point of origin.

"Neil!"

I grabbed my friend and rolled him over, kneeling on the damp earth, a few wisps of new green beneath me as I cradled my friend's lifeless body.

"Neil, come on. Come on."

His eyes were rolled halfway back, head just dead weight at the end of his neck, blood trickling from his nose and mouth.

"Come on, Neil. You're okay. You're okay."

Lorenzen, Westin, and Enderson moved past, weapons up, not firing anymore as they pressed toward the woods. Schiavo stopped next to me as Hart knelt alongside and put his fingers to my friend's neck. What he felt, combined with the volume of blood he saw on the ground, and upon me, left no doubt as to what he'd determined.

"He's gone, Fletch."

I looked to the medic, then up to the captain, tears in her eyes. Then, I looked down to my friend, my best friend,

and I pulled him close, holding his body against mine as I
wept.

Fifty

Funerals filled the following days. Carol Everett's. Nathan Chester's. And Neil's.

My friend's services were a blur to me. Much of the days following his death were, as well. I remembered Grace absorbing the news without hysterics. With strength and some odd measure of understanding as to just what her husband had done for us all. I remembered Commander Genesee, in full uniform, saluting my friend's coffin as it was lowered into the ground at the cemetery. I remembered Schiavo reporting that a patrol led by Sergeant Lorenzen had located Olin's hideout, just where I'd described it, but there was no sign of the man.

And I remembered the meeting.

"We aren't what's left of the United States of America," Mayor Allen said as he opened the first Defense Council proceedings since my friend's death. "For all intents and purposes, we are the United States of America."

"What does that make everyone else?" Elaine asked.

"A threat," Lorenzen answered.

Schiavo didn't correct him. Didn't massage his words down to something less ominous.

"Which is exactly what we are to them," Schiavo said, adding emphasis to her sergeant's point.

"So what do we do?" Elaine asked.

"We do what we've been doing," Mayor Allen said. "Keep growing. Keep planting. Keep turning the world into something we remember."

"And while we do that," Schiavo said, "we stay ready to end anyone who tries to interfere."

It was the hopeful politician and the pragmatic warrior, each stating their case. Through it all, I said nothing. I simply listened. No one pressed me to offer any input. If they had, I wasn't certain what I would have said. Or could have said.

*   *   *

When the meeting concluded, Elaine and I left, walking together along the road's shoulder. To our right the sun was setting over crashing waves we could hear, but not see, long streaks of reddened clouds stretched across the sky. There was no talking head forecaster to tell us what the weather would be over the coming days, but you could feel it—a storm was on the horizon.

"Del said we'd lost the ability to sense things," I said to Elaine, for no reason other than sharing a bit of wisdom from the first friend I'd made after the blight. "That doesn't just apply to weather, I think."

I'd told her about Del Drake before. About our bond near my Montana refuge, and our fight against the dictatorial forces building near that once lovely slice of western territory. He'd sacrificed his life to save mine. That was a great gift, without question, but I often thought that the simple things he'd shared with me were more profound, and everlasting.

Now, another friend who'd sacrificed had been taken, but this time that event had unfolded without reason. Or without any reason I could fathom.

"Neil loved you."

I nodded.

"Grace will be all right," Elaine said.

Again, I nodded. She would be all right. And Krista. And Brandon. All of us would be. Every single person in Bandon, natives and those who'd come in search of survival, would have the chance for another day, and another, because of what Neil Moore had done. Because of what my friend had kept secret.

Another, though, had revealed secrets, though he'd wrapped them in deceit. He'd offered truths as lies, and lies as truths.

Black is white. White is black.

I doubted that my friend had anticipated what would ultimately happen when he'd offered that warning to me. And I was certain that, in no way, did he have any inkling that a man from his past would appear and be his executioner.

"Ranger meant nothing," I said, the statement offered to simply let it out. "All that mattered was Neil's voice. That was what brought Olin here."

"He meant to kill him all along," Elaine said, her hand tightening around mine.

She was right. The man, the spy, had been on a mission. How much was fact of what he'd told me, what he'd told us, was impossible to know. BA 412 was real. Neil had confirmed that. The rest of what Olin had shared could be treated as suspect.

"What about the sample?" Elaine asked.

With Schiavo's blessing, I'd shared that morsel of Neil's communication with my wife, just as the captain had with her husband, and with Mayor Allen. We were all bearers of that secret now. That some quantity of BA 412 existed, secreted by Neil Moore in a place whose precise location he'd taken with him to the grave.

"It's somewhere," I said. "But not here."

"We'll never find it," she said.

"Good," I told her.

But that response was simplistic, I knew in my gut. It mattered more that *no one* would ever find it.

Fifty One

Ten days after Neil's death, as Elaine and I slept, the phone rang.

"What time is it?" Elaine asked groggily.

My watch on the nightstand gave me the answer.

"Two forty."

"Will you get it?"

I planted a quick kiss on the back of her head and swung my legs over the edge of the bed, soles of my feet slapping cool hardwood as I moved from our bedroom to the hallway, and from there to the living room where the offending device continued to blare. There was no urgency about me. The town had settled back into a state of near normalcy. Most of the checkpoints had been deactivated, and only a few patrols journeyed beyond Bandon's borders each day. We were wary, but not worried.

"Hello," I said as I lifted the handset.

I expected to hear Corporal Enderson's voice, or one of the other members of the garrison who were on night watch. Possibly a fence at the livestock pens had fallen, and cows had slipped out. A fire might have erupted. Or a leak might have sprung at one of the oil wells outside of town. There were any number of reports that I, as a member of the Defense Council, might be receiving.

But it was none of those things. It wasn't even a resident of our town on the other end.

"Hello, Fletch," Tyler Olin said.

For a moment I could not respond as my brain worked through the possibilities of how the man who'd killed my friend was speaking to me. The most likely scenario involved him accessing one of the deactivated checkpoints whose hardwired phone was still connected. At each such device was a listing of town numbers so that, should a particular need arise, those occupying the facility could reach any person in town. Olin had simply exploited this oversight.

"What do you want?"

"Well, first, I want to say that I'm sorry."

"Sorry..."

"It doesn't mean much, I know," Olin admitted. "But it needs to be said. Just as what I did needed to be done."

"Killing my friend was a necessity?"

"He was my friend, too, Fletch."

My fingers drew tight around the plastic handset.

"You didn't call to apologize," I told the man, the murderer.

"Where is it?"

"Where is what?"

Olin chuckled softly at my resistance.

"Please, you drive off a superior force with, what, empty threats?"

"Actually, yes," I told the man, just a morsel of the reply a falsehood.

"No," Olin said. "No, it doesn't work that way. Besides, I saw his face."

"What are you talking about?"

"Our friend, through my rifle scope. He looked surprised. Maybe even frightened. What was it, did you tell him about me? That I'd stopped by?"

I had, and Neil had reacted just as Olin was surmising. But how could the man read the situation so clearly? Was it simply that his training, and the life he'd led, gave him the ability to lay bare the truth of almost any observable event?

"I'm going to hang up, Olin. But first I'd like to give you some advice."

"Advice? There's something you can tell me I don't already know?"

"Yes," I said. "You should probably run. You should run far. And keep running. Because if I ever see you again, or if I find out you're somewhere close, I will come for you. And I will kill you."

There was silence on the other end. I thought that the man was just absorbing what I'd told him. The warning I'd given. The promise I'd made. But the quiet continued. No response came. Not even the sound of breathing.

"Olin?"

But he was gone. I didn't even know if he'd stayed on the line long enough to hear what I'd said.

"Olin?"

I eased the phone away from my face and stared at it, fingers bearing down harder, tighter, until the handset cracked in my grip.

"Eric..."

I turned to see Elaine at the end of the hallway. She stared at me in the din of the living room.

"Who was it?"

"No one," I said. "No one at all."

Thank You

I hope you enjoyed *Ranger*. Please look for other books in *The Bugging Out Series*.

About The Author

Noah Mann lives in the West and has been involved in personal survival and disaster preparedness for more than two decades. He has extensive training in firearms, as well as urban and wilderness Search & Rescue operations, including tracking and the application of technology in victim searches.

Made in the USA
San Bernardino, CA
22 June 2016